THE GOOD NEWS AND THE BAD

Lorna could congratulate herself that she had saved her innocent younger sister Melanie from the insidious charm and seductive strength of the infamous Earl of Norwell.

That was Lorna's only consolation for the fact that she had pledged herself to become this same infuriating gentleman's bride.

Still, Lorna had the satisfaction of forcing the Earl to agree to let her be his wife in name only as they went their separate ways. But even that one bright spot clouded over when Lorna discovered in the arms of another suitor that her heart belonged to the nobleman she had done so much to enrage and had no idea of how to woo back. . . .

The Calico Countess

More Regency Romances from SIGNET

THE CALICO COUNTESS

by
Barbara Hazard

A SIGNET BOOK

NEW AMERICAN LIBRARY

The author acknowledges with gratitude the information found in Philip Howard's book *London's River*, published by Hamish Hamilton Ltd., Great Britain, 1975, which was used in the preparation of this novel.

SIGNET TRADEMARK REG. U.S. PAT. OFF. AND FOREIGN COUNTRIES
REGISTERED TRADEMARK—MARCA REGISTRADA
HECHO EN CHICAGO, U.S.A.

SIGNET, SIGNET CLASSIC, MENTOR, PLUME, MERIDAN and NAL BOOKS are published by New American Library
1633 Broadway, New York, New York 10019

First Printing, May, 1984

1 2 3 4 5 6 7 8 9

PRINTED IN THE UNITED STATES OF AMERICA

The Duel

The gingham dog and the calico cat
    Side by side on the table sat;
'Twas half-past twelve, and (what do you think!)
Nor one nor t'other had slept a wink!
      The old Dutch clock and the Chinese plate
      Appeared to know as sure as fate.
There was going to be a terrible spat.
      (I wasn't there; I simply state
      What was told to me by the Chinese plate!)

The gingham dog went "bow-wow-wow!"
And the calico cat replied "mee-ow!"
The air was littered, an hour or so,
With bits of gingham and calico,
      While the old Dutch clock in the chimney-place
      Up with its hands before its face,
For it always dreaded a family row!
      (Now mind: I'm only telling you
      What the old Dutch clock declares is true!)

The Chinese plate looked very blue,
And wailed, "Oh dear! what shall we do!"
But the gingham dog and the calico cat
Wallowed this way and tumbled that,
Employing every tooth and claw
In the awfullest way you ever say—
And, oh! how the gingham and calico flew!
      (Don't fancy I exaggerate—
      I got my news from the Chinese plate!)

Next morning where the two had sat
They found no trace of dog or cat;
And some folks think unto this day
That burglars stole the pair away!
      But the truth about the cat and pup
Is this; they ate each other up!
Now what do you really think of that!
      (The old Dutch clock it told me so,
      And that is how I came to know.)

—Eugene Field, *Poems of Childhood*

Prologue

The Dowager Duchess of Wynne, who even at the advanced age of sixty and some years, the exact total of which had never been disclosed, kept her finger firmly on Society's pulse, and nothing of even minimal importance was allowed to escape her attention. There was not a person in the Ton who did not at least know of her. In general she was apt to be described as "a holy terror," especially by those members of her own extensive family who had come under her scrutiny and domination.

It had not always been so, however. Born Agatha Margaret Truesdale in the year 1749, she had married Reginald Allendon, the Duke of Wynne, when she was nineteen, thereby gratifying her parents and astonishing her contemporaries.

She had been a tall girl—much too tall by anyone's standards— and along with her height she had a large-boned frame and a patrician rather than a beautiful face surmounted by a mass of fine brown hair that was apt to escape its bonds and float in tendrils that she impatiently and continually pushed out of her way. Being so tall called attention to her lack of grace, due in part to her poor eyesight, which caused her to stumble into furniture and upset carelessly placed bric-a-brac. In addition, she was given to blurting out whatever came into her mind at the most inappropriate times, and no amount of lecturing could cure her of her disastrous frankness. In spite of these numerous faults, she had captivated the Duke by a method she had never chosen to divulge, and up until his death in 1803 after thirty-five happy years of marriage and four sons and a pair of twin daughters, had been content to remain very much in the background of the social scene.

But after a year of mourning her dear Reggie, the Dowager Duchess changed her milieu for London and proceeded to dominate Society in short order, thereby astounding both the Ton and her family, all of whom expected the

7

old lady to do no more than putter around the dower house, ceasing to be a factor in any matters of importance at all.

Her Grace had no such intention. Looking about her, she could see there there were several pressing situations that should be attended to among her descendants, and since no one else seemed to be making the least push to solve these weighty problems, and she had never been one to shirk what she considered her duty, she proceeded with zest into the fray.

Since that time, she had married off two granddaughters who had hitherto been resigned to spinsterhood; had separated a great-nephew from a scandalous liaison with a married lady some years his senior and procured for him an appointment in the Life Guards to his doting mama's distress; had brought one of her brother's estates into solvency again; and had reunited another granddaughter with her estranged husband.

These accomplishments, although admirable, were not universally admired. Her methods often upset everyone's peace, and her instructions were blunt to the point of rudeness. Since she had taken to traveling about the countryside visiting her relatives when she was not in residence in her smart town house in Berkeley Square, there had been many a shudder and cry of distress at the breakfast tables of those relatives who received the announcement of her imminent arrival, "to see what you have all been up to now," as she was wont to put it.

She was still tall and large-boned, but age and a straight spine had given her a dignity she had not possessed as a girl. This and the proud, distant expression she had adopted because of her poor eyesight—for she was never sure in a crowded room if she were smiling at her dearest friend or at a complete stranger—caused some of her more impressionable relatives to fear her and her methods. Then, too, not all of them took kindly to being saved from folly of their own making. Still, it was a curious fact that the younger members of the family were inclined to think her "a great gun," "a knowin' one," and "an old dear," while their parents seemed more apt to endure her interference with tight lips and a distrustful civility. They were helpless to stop her, however, for it did not do to offend such a wealthy, august matriarch as the Dowager Duchess of Wynne, nor had anyone ever had the temerity to try.

The Dowager lived with two middle-aged sisters who were believed to be distant cousins of hers. Such was the force of her personality that their presence was rarely remarked, and although she had often been heard to say that she did not know what she would do without the council of her dear Eliza and Jane, no one was at all sure what these ladies did that was of such value to her. They seldom spoke unless directly addressed, and neither had ever been heard to offer any opinion that differed from her Grace's in even the most infinitesimal way.

Now, in late November in the year 1813, the Dowager Duchess looked about her for some new dilemma that required her services and decided that the time had come, and indeed was long overdue, for her great-nephew, Lord Peter Truesdale, Earl Norwell of Kent, to take himself a wife. Accordingly, a week later a message was sent around to his rooms on Albany Street asking him to attend her at his earliest convenience in Berkeley Square.

No one in London would have been at all surprised to learn that he arrived on the Dowager's doorstep that very same afternoon.

1

Lord Peter Truesdale stood at one of the long windows of the drawing room in Jarrett Hall staring out at the blustery December day as he wondered for perhaps the twentieth time in the last hour why he had allowed himself to be maneuvered into making this visit. It was sure to be uncomfortable at best, and might lead to a life sentence at worst. He raised his chin and with one big hand tugged at his cravat, which had suddenly become too tight by half, and then he frowned. Since Lord Peter did not possess conventional good looks, this frown made him appear even more forbidding and glowering than did his usual demeanor. Set under dark hair brushed à la Brutus and cropped shorter than even the fashion of the day demanded, his broad forehead and strong nose were balanced by a powerful jaw, a jaw that seemed to serve notice that he was not a man to suffer fools gladly, nor would he stand for any nonsense from members of either sex. His mouth was well formed, but above that rugged chin, its pleasant lines faded into insignificance as did his surprisingly handsome gray eyes. When he had occasion to smile, there was a great deal of warmth to his expression, but now his eyes were narrowed and his mouth grim.

He was here in Dorset at the express command of his Great-aunt Agatha, and now, as he waited alone in the Jarretts' drawing room, he reviewed again the extraordinary interview he had had with this lady only a few days ago.

After her butler had served them both a glass of excellent sherry and bowed himself out, her Grace had wasted no time in coming to the reason for her imperious summons.

"I have been observing you for a number of years, Peter, and it is apparent to me that you are unable to form a lasting attachment for any one of the myriad number of girls who have come your way," she had begun abruptly. "I am speaking of young ladies of good family, of course, not one of your opera dancers or any of the other members of the *demimonde* you have had under your protection."

Lord Peter had raised an eyebrow at this blunt speaking, but his great-aunt had pressed on before he could make any comment. "You are now thirty-five, and as the only male descendant of my nephew, it is time you began looking in earnest for the next Truesdale wife. You will, of course, correct me if I am wrong, but I believe there is no one in your eye at the present time for that post?"

The old lady had paused for a moment until m'lord shook his head, and then she had said dryly, "Just so. Since that is the case, I have begun to arrange the matter for you."

At this, Lord Peter had leaned forward in his seat, but her Grace had raised a deterring hand. "You may thank me later, Peter, but for now I would appreciate it if you would listen to me without interruption. There is no great mystery to these affairs, you know. It is only a matter of finding a suitable girl from a suitable family, and heaven knows England is littered with 'em! But left to your own devices, it would take you much too long to accomplish, if indeed you could be brought to persevere to a successful conclusion. After all, in all the years of your majority, and even though your name has been coupled with this girl and that for many a Season, no one has ever been able to bring you to the sticking point."

"Perhaps that was because I was not interested in—er, sticking, ma'am?" her great-nephew had interjected in a deep voice he tried hard in his annoyance to keep noncommittal.

His great-aunt had nodded her head, completely unperturbed by his sarcasm. "I daresay. But since that is the case, why should you have any objection to an arranged marriage? Think of the trouble it will save you! Besides, you have an obligation to the continuance of the name; I expect you to do your duty. Now, I have been in communication with an old friend of mine, Lady Morthman. Her daughter married John Jarrett—the Dorset Jarretts—you know the family, of course. There was only one child of the union, a girl named Melanie. These silly modern names—tchh! But never mind that. As her father's sole heiress she brings with her great wealth as well as impeccable bloodliness, and since Lady Morthman assures me she is perfectly presentable, I see no reason why you should not ride into Dorset, make her acquaintance, and ask for her hand. It is all arranged; the Jarretts expect you within the week."

"You don't feel it might be embarrassing for the young lady to be approached this way by a complete stranger?" Lord Peter had asked, settling back on the brocade sofa and crossing his legs in their well-tailored breeches and polished boots. There was a decided look of anger in his gray eyes now, which his great-aunt, being so nearsighted, failed to notice.

"Why should it be? The gel is only eighteen; she cannot know her own mind, which should certainly please you, since I have noticed you dislike being crossed in any way. You will be able to mold her to your will without any trouble at all, and if she can find a husband without leaving her home, so much the better for everyone. I understand her mother is sickly, which is just what one might expect from a woman who could produce only one offspring, and a female one at that."

"You are harsh, ma'am," Lord Peter had remarked. "Has it occurred to you that perhaps 'the gel,' as you call her, might take after her mother? I only mention the possibility since I assume the purpose of my marriage is to sire a great number of descendants for your illustrious line?"

Far from looking shocked at this frank speaking, the Dowager had only nodded again. "But of course. I have always admired your quick grasp of any situation, Peter, and I rely on you to ascertain the state of her health before you commit yourself. We want no weaklings, no delicate fainting flowers in our family! But on that head you must be the judge. If Miss Jarrett does not come up to our standards, you are to feel in no way pressured. There are several other suitable young ladies whom I have in mind."

"Your reliance on my good judgment almost unmans me, ma'am," Lord Peter had snapped, trying to overcome the feelings of anger that were rising in his breast at his great-aunt's managing ways. He would have denied her, but he knew from past experience that if she said that all was in train for his visit, then it was already a *fait accompli* and there was no way for him to escape the journey without being insufferably rude. Very well, he had decided as he took his leave of her Grace a short time later, I will ride down to Dorset, I will meet the young lady and do the pretty, and as soon as it can possibly be contrived, I shall excuse myself and return to Town. Great-aunt Agatha may think I dance to her piping; she shall learn otherwise.

Now he stood in the drawing room of Jarrett Hall and tried to control his chagrin at being placed in such an impossible situation. And to add insult to injury, he thought to himself, I have been here for some time now and no one has come in to welcome me or offer me refreshments. He frowned and decided country manners in the West of England left a lot to be desired.

Suddenly the drawing-room doors were thrown open and a low, musical voice cried out, "My dear, the most diverting thing, just wait till I . . ."

Lord Peter turned from the window, and the dark frown on his face was replaced by an unbelieving look of complete shock. Whatever he had expected, it was not this tall young woman in a russet habit, running toward him impetuously, her crop and riding hat still in her hands and her auburn curls wildly disarranged from what must have been a bruising morning ride. He felt a sudden constriction in his throat and a feeling a more cowardly man would have called foreboding. It was as if he suddenly saw into a future in which he would not be at all comfortable, or content, or in command, a future full of alarums and arguments and agitation. He shuddered.

The young woman skidded to a stop and tilted her head to one side, the better to observe him. Lord Peter felt his anger returning. How dare she look at me as if I were some tradesman, he thought, unaware that he himself was staring at the lady intently. She raised her eyebrows in question and he was recalled to his manners.

"I beg pardon for startling you, Miss . . . er, it *is* Miss Jarrett is it not?"

The lady inclined her head, but she did not lower her eyes, which remained locked with his own. He noticed they were a particularly brilliant shade of blue as he continued, "I am Lord Peter Truesdale. I believe I was expected?"

His voice was so tart it recalled Miss Jarrett to her duties as hostess. She moved forward again with her quick stride, stripping off her riding gloves as she did so before she extended her hand.

"Your pardon, m'lord. Of course you have been expected, but since we had no word of the *exact* day of your arrival, you have caught us unawares. Won't you be seated?"

Lord Peter stared at the face now near his own. As a man of above-average height, he was used to looking down at members of the feminine sex from a far greater distance than he now found necessary to employ, and he was so bemused that for a moment he did not move. There was something about Miss Jarrett that was quite out of the common way. It was more than the fact that she was tall. He studied her face—yes, she was undoubtedly a handsome young lady, and he had already noted her excellent figure.

So what was there about her that had caused him to feel that first vague stirring of fear? Was it because there was too *much* of the lady in every way? She was almost too handsome, too deep-bosomed and long-legged. Her voice was too deep and too strong, and her manner too assured. His great-aunt would certainly approve the lady's physical condition. Why, she was positively blooming with good health. And, he noticed, not once had she lowered her eyes from his, and he somehow knew the brilliant color of her complexion was the result of her ride in the brisk December air and owed nothing at all to his unexpected presence. He thought her much too coming. If this meeting did not make her tremble and blush, at least she should be looking a little conscious to be here alone with him, knowing as she did the reason for his visit.

The lady rang the bell to summon the butler, and Lord Peter bowed as she seated herself and indicated a sofa on the other side of the fireplace. How rude the man is to keep staring at me, she thought as she arranged the skirts of her habit. He is so sure of himself and his welcome as Melly's dazzlingly eligible suitor that he does not accord me even common courtesy. She felt her quick temper rising at such arrogance and determined that this dark, harsh-featured Earl would not get the better of her in the encounter.

Even as she chatted of the weather and inquired after his

journey and instructed the butler to pour him a glass of wine, she continued to observe him and come to her own conclusions. It would not do: the man would eat Melly alive in a minute! Whatever could Aunt Mary be thinking of even to contemplate such a union? But then, she added, trying to be fair, she has never met the man and so has no idea of his fierce airs and domineering nature. He was obviously used to having his own way; the jut of his jaw told her that, as well as the imperious way he held his black head, and the firm set of his mouth. She put his age in the middle thirties—much too old for her cousin. At eighteen Melly was barely mature, and although she appeared demure and well mannered, she was still the complete romp she had been as a little girl.

Poor, poor Melanie! She had looked forward eagerly to her first Season, and she had been so disappointed to discover she was as good as promised before she even left Dorset that she wept for two whole days. Miss Jarrett shook her head a little. We shall see, she thought as the butler left the drawing room, for there is nothing decided as yet. Now, if it were I, I know I would be able to handle him, but then I am five and twenty and have been about the world a bit.

M'lord's deep voice interrupted her musings. "I am delighted to see that you feel no awkwardness, Miss Jarrett, even though the situation we find ourselves in cannot be said to be a common occurrence for you." His tone was mocking and he raised a derisive eyebrow as he added, "My compliments!"

As he raised his wineglass in a sarcastic toast, Lorna's blue eyes widened. Of course! He thought *she* was Melanie! She had nodded when he called her Miss Jarrett, for, as Melanie's cousin, that was also her name; and he had assumed she was his intended.

When her parents had died suddenly in a boating accident three years before, Lorna Jarrett had agreed to come and live with her uncle and his family. In her grief and loss, it had seemed the simplest thing to do, and although she kept her old governess with her so she might travel and be independent whenever she wished, she had succeeded in fitting herself into the household until it seemed she had always lived there. Her Aunt Mary, being lazy as well as inclined to ill health, relied on Lorna to serve as chaperone to her cousin, and her Uncle John loved her for her good sense and the way her lively personality brightened his home. Melanie had been a little in awe of her at first, but had soon come to think of her as an older sister. In fact, Mr. Jarrett sometimes wondered how they all got on before Lorna came to run the household and order the servants, see to his wife's care and Melanie's education and amusements, and assist him about the estate as well.

Now this accomplished lady inclined her head at m'lord's sarcastic compliment and came to a sudden decision. Perhaps she was taking too much on herself, but she saw no reason why little Melanie should not have her Season, no reason why she should be forced to accept this most unsuitable suitor just to spare her mother the trouble of taking her up to Town.

Lorna knew Melly could never love a man like Peter Truesdale, even with all his wealth and title, for she had listened to too many enthusiastic confidences about Mr. Robertson and Sir Gregory Bell, Melly's most persistent admirers. Both these gentlemen were in their early twenties, slight in build, and gentle and courtly in manner. To compare them to Lord Peter would be like comparing two well-bred colts to a wild stallion. Besides, Mr. Jarrett had a soft spot for his only daughter and had been most reluctant to agree to his wife's and mother-in-law's plan to give Melanie's hand to the first man to ask for it. Lorna knew he and Melly both would approve of her decision.

Praying that her cousin would not come in to find her, or her aunt and uncle return from their morning call too soon, and trying to quiet the little qualm she still felt at what she proposed to do, she said, "I am glad that you feel no awkwardness either, sir, for there is something that I must tell you and I would not cause you any embarrassment." She paused and observed m'lord's intent look before she drew a deep breath and continued, "You see, there has been a change of plans. When your visit was agreed to, Mrs. Jarrett was not well. Since that time she has decided that she would prefer her daughter to have at least one Season in London before settling down to the married state."

"And do you agree with her, Miss Jarrett?" Lord Peter

asked. "Forgive me for pressing you, but I would know your mind."

"Yes, I do agree," Lorna said with a decisive nod of her head. "After all, you appear to have had any number of years to make up your mind to this decision. Why should a girl have any less opportunity when it comes to deciding her fate?"

Lord Peter was not used to having his will crossed, and even less used to discussing women's rights, and his temper rose until he completely forgot his own reluctant dread of this marriage.

"Perhaps it is that you feel we should not suit, Miss Jarrett?" he prompted her, his face as dark as a thundercloud and his voice taut with rage. "Although how you can tell on such short acquaintance I am hard put to discover!"

Suddenly Miss Jarrett smiled, a dazzling smile of complete amusement, and even in his anger he thought, Of course! I knew she would have a dimple just there in her cheek. Now how did I know that?

"I agree I do not know you, m'lord, but if I were forced to make a quick judgment, I would have to say that no, I do not think that we would suit at all."

And then, as he glared at her ferociously, she added in defiance, "Do you remember the old epigram, sir? 'I do not love you, Dr. Fell, But why I cannot tell; But this I know full well, I do not love you, Dr. Fell'? Perhaps it is something like that—an instantaneous antipathy over which I have no control at all."

Lord Peter felt a pang of mortification to be dismissed so quickly, but that passed in an instant as his anger returned, deeper and stronger than before. Dr. Fell indeed! "I see you do not hesitate to speak your mind, Miss Jarrett. Somehow you seem much older than the eighteen years I was informed you have in your dish."

"Oh, I have never been missish," Lorna agreed with complete cordiality, "and surely that must be a relief to you, sir, for why should you waste your time with coyness and dissembling? Now that you have made up your mind to marriage at last, you will be able to approach some other young lady that much sooner. I am sure you will find someone willing who will be admirable for your purpose. You do not appear to be *too* selective if you would be content with an unknown bride. Why, I might have had a squint or a bad stutter," she added with a kind smile, the dimple flashing again. "You must not take *my* refusal too much to heart, you know. There is bound to be someone . . ."

She waved her hand vaguely in the general direction of the heart of England and rose from her chair. "I would ask you to remain for luncheon, Lord Peter, for I am sure all the Jarretts would be delighted to make your acquaintance, but perhaps, under the circumstances, it would be disconcerting for you to remain. May I therefore wish you a pleasant journey back to Town and bid you good-bye?"

Lord Peter stood up, clenching his fists, and the dark anger of his face forced Lorna to take a tiny step backward before she checked herself. She knew it would be a mistake to show this man even the smallest bit of fear. Instead, she tilted her chin in an almost exact copy of his defiant jaw as he said through gritted teeth, "My apologies, Miss Jarrett, for disturbing you, and my sincere sympathy to your mother and father. I foresee that your stay with them as a daughter is bound to be a prolonged affair."

Suddenly he stopped speaking and came toward her to grasp her arms in his powerful hands and stare down into her face. Lorna stared back at him, her heart pounding with fright, until he lowered his head and kissed her full on the mouth. It was not a gentle kiss, and it was such an unexpected move that for a moment she felt frozen in disbelief. As his lips grew even more demanding, she tried to pull away, but there was no fighting the power of the man. She realized that until he chose the moment to release her, she was helpless in those compelling hands that held her so closely against his hard body while his kiss deepened in insistence. Lorna was no green girl; she had been kissed before, but she had never experienced anything remotely like Lord Peter's embrace.

When at last he raised his head, she glared at him, but before she could catch her breath and speak, he bowed and moved away. "Perhaps you *have* been too hasty, Miss Jarrett?" he asked in his deep voice, now ragged with some emotion she did not care to question too closely. "It seems to me that not only would we suit, but that we would suit very well indeed!"

"How dare you?" Lorna demanded, coming toward him in a rush, her hand raised to strike him.

Lord Peter caught them up in one large fist and easily held her away from him. "No, no, my dear Miss Jarrett, it is too late to beg me to take you in my arms again. You have had your chance and you have refused it, and it is useless to change your mind now, for the offer is no longer open." Suddenly he grinned down at her, his gray eyes alight with hidden meaning as he said, "I just wanted you to see what you will be missing."

As she gasped at his temerity, he added, "My compliments to your parents, Miss Jarrett. Perhaps we shall meet when you come to Town. I shall be very interested in the identity of the man you finally select as a suitable husband — very interested indeed. I can almost picture him now: tall, of course, but weak and retiring; a 'parfit gentil knight' whom you will dominate in a week. Poor, poor man, I wish him joy of you! I only hope he is not a friend of mine, for then I would be forced to warn him. It would be my duty as a Christian gentleman. For now, my dear, I bid you good-bye."

He barked a laugh and flicked her chin with one careless finger, and then he left the room. She remained standing there, her knees quivering and her blue eyes dark with anger and shock.

Nor did she move until she heard the front door close behind him and the butler's measured tread returning to the back of the house. Only then did she drop into the nearest chair and put her hands to her flushed, hot face. Perhaps she had asked for his sarcasm by behaving in such a flippant, insulting manner herself, but she had never expected a member of the peerage to forget himself so far as to actually force her to kiss him. Lord Peter Truesdale was no gentleman! She was glad she had at least saved Melanie from his hateful embraces and arrogant manners, even though she suspected that she had not won the encounter and was even stretching the truth if she called their meeting a draw.

By the time her aunt and uncle returned and Lorna joined the rest of the family for luncheon, she had herself well in hand again. She had changed from her habit to a morning gown of leaf green and she was able to participate in the conversation around the table with her usual calm and good humor.

She waited until the servants had left the room after the last course had been served before she remarked, "I almost forgot to tell you. Lord Peter Truesdale called this morning; he was so sorry to have missed you, Aunt Mary, Uncle John."

Melanie dropped her fork with a clatter and gasped, and Lorna smiled at her in encouragement.

"Lord Peter was here, and we were not on hand to welcome him? Oh dear," Mrs. Jarrett mourned. "But why did you not ask him to remain for luncheon, Lorna? Now he will be forced to call another day."

"Lord Peter will not be calling at Jarrett Hall again, Aunt," Lorna informed her.

Her aunt stared at her, her faded green eyes perplexed and her thin hands fluttering to her breast. "I . . . I do not understand. Did you see him, Melanie, and make his acquaintance? What was he like?"

Her daughter shook her head, her face as white now as the fichu she wore on her shoulders. Lorna could see that she was too frightened to speak, so she added quickly, "There is no need to fear him any longer, Melly. I spoke to Lord Peter myself, Aunt, and I took the liberty of telling him that Melanie felt she was much too young and inexperienced to enter matrimony for some time. That was after I took his measure as a gentleman and a man, of course."

Mrs. Jarrett moaned and slid quietly from her chair to the floor, but since Lorna had been expecting her to faint, her usual reaction to any unpleasantness, she was at her side in an instant. "Some water and a napkin, Melly! I will tell you both all about it later, but for the moment we must take care of Aunt Mary."

It was several minutes before Mrs. Jarrett was restored to consciousness and had been helped from the dining room by a footman and her maid, to recover in her own rooms, and the others could take their places again at the table.

"It appears to me that you have been very busy this morning, my dear Lorna," Mr. Jarrett remarked in what he tried to make a stern, disapproving tone, although his niece could see a twinkle in his eye.

Lorna smiled at him. "In this instance you would applaud me for what I would generally shun as pushing, encroaching ways, Uncle. I knew it was not *my* place to repulse his offer, but the man is clearly impossible! He is in his thirties, and he is arrogant and rude and domineering, with a ferocious expression and the manners of an ape. It is plain that he must always have his own way, that he will tolerate no interference, and that his wishes must always prevail. Can you imagine such a brute as Melly's husband?"

Her uncle looked at his daughter, who seemed as likely to faint now as her mother had a few minutes before. Melanie Jarrett was a very lovely girl, with the same auburn curls as her cousin, but there all resemblance ended. She was only an inch over five feet and as slim and straight as the stem of a flower, with narrow hands and feet. Her fair complexion had only the hint of roses coming and going in her pale cheeks, and although she was eighteen, she seemed much younger in her innocence and physical immaturity.

"Well, well, if what you say is right, my dear, I am glad you turned the man away," Mr. Jarrett said heartily. "I trust your judgment, Lorna. If Lord Peter did not please you for Melly, then we shall say no more about it. Of course, Mary and Grandmother Morthman are going to be disappointed. It appeared to be such a good match in the eyes of the world —his title and family connections, and his wealth—but my pretty little Melanie is not to be forced into a distasteful marriage merely to satisfy the wordly ambitions of her mother and her grandmother."

He nodded and smiled at his daughter. "There, Melly, that should make you feel better. Now you can look forward to a stay in the metropolis, thanks to your cousin's decisiveness and good sense. But I do not envy you the task of soothing your Aunt Mary, m'dear," he added to Lorna as he wiped his mouth with his napkin and prepared to leave the table. "I am afraid this will cause a spell of illness that will keep her in her bed for some time."

Lorna rose and kissed him. "Dear Uncle John, do not be concerned. Between us, Melly and I can bring her back to a happy frame of mind, can't we, my dear?"

"Oh, yes, indeed!" her cousin agreed, her eyes sparkling with relief at her narrow escape. "How good you are to me, dear Lorna, and how glad I am that you will be with us in London. It will make it all so much more comfortable."

Mr. Jarrett went off to his estate office and Melanie took her cousin's hand and drew her into the drawing room, shutting the door behind them. "Now," she demanded, "tell me everything that happened. Was he really such an ogre? A brute? What exactly did he say? Did he scowl at *you*, Lorna, or shout? Weren't you afraid?"

Lorna took up her needlepoint. She could see that the mysterious and wicked Lord Peter would be the primary topic of conversation not only for this afternoon, but for several days to come.

Mrs. Jarrett's prolonged illness and a particularly upsetting visit from Lady Morthman, as well as preparations for Christmas and several parties to plan for, more than kept Lorna busy in the days that followed. And yet, there were times when Lord Peter's dark scowling face swam before her eyes and his harsh words came to her mind unbidden. And sometimes, just before she dropped off to sleep at night, she would remember the strength of his hands and his insistent kiss, and shiver a little, even as she was thankful that she had been able to send him out of all the Jarretts' lives forever.

2

Lord Peter rode back to London as fast as his horse could take him, his anger increasing with every mile that passed under the gelding's pounding hooves. Impossible jade! Opinionated shrew! He had had a narrow escape, he told himself. He might have found himself tied to that horrid virago for the rest of his life.

He had every intention of calling on the Dowager Duchess immediately, to tell her in great and comprehensive detail of the so-called paragon she had arranged for him to wed, but somehow, when he gained his rooms in Albany Street after two exhausting days in the saddle, that inclination left him.

He threw himself back into his usual pursuits, and if his friends wondered at the sudden deadly aim of his hard right in Gentleman Jackson's boxing saloon, his abstraction in the middle of a convivial evening at cards, or his reason for leading them all on a race to Richmond in the brutally cold air that was covering England that December, he did not enlighten them.

His mood seemed to swing from a black rage at her airy dismissal of him as a desirable husband to somber musing when he remembered her beauty and the way she had felt clasped in his arms, her lips joined with his in the passionate kiss he had exacted from her as revenge. He knew his great-aunt would hear of his return to Town in short order, and not wanting to be summoned by her again, he wrote her a brusque note, explaining in the most restrained words he could find in his vocabulary exactly what had happened up to that kiss. This letter took him an entire morning to compose, and as he affixed his seal and summoned his footman to deliver it, he told himself that it put paid to any obligation he had to either lady. Miss Jarrett did not want him: good! He most certainly did not want Miss Jarrett. As for Great-aunt Agatha, it was none of her business, and the unsuitability of the alliance she had chosen for him only showed clearly that the poor old dear was beginning to fail.

Her Grace read his letter with raised eyebrows. She was taking tea with her two companions, who were whispering together over the teacups, but when she exclaimed, "My word! How very extraordinary," Eliza stopped in mid-sentence and both sisters put down their cups and leaned forward expectantly.

"Just listen to this, m'dears," the Dowager said. "I have here a most unusual missive from Lord Peters. You remember we sent him into Dorset to get himself a wife?" The ladies nodded in unison as the Dowager, not waiting for them to speak, continued, "Well, it appears that the gel wouldn't have 'im. Ha! Quite a set-down for my great-nephy, wouldn't you say?"

"Not *have* him?" Miss Jane asked in incredulous tones.

"Not have him at *all?*" Miss Eliza echoed.

"She was most positive in her refusal, according to Peter," the Dowager said. "There is a great deal here I do not understand. If the alliance had the blessing of her parents and grandmother, how could the young lady refuse? A miss of eighteen! It was not so in my day, or in yours either. To think that a green girl barely out of the egg would dare go against the wishes of her elders. Tchh! But I can tell from the tone of this letter that my dear great-nephew is in a towering rage. He does so hate to be crossed, as you have pointed out to me so many times, Eliza; and I have not forgotten, Jane, that you told me our scheme for his marriage would not meet with his approval. See here where he says, 'I count myself the most fortunate of men to have escaped a liaison with such a bold, saucy miss. Her bad manners are equaled only by her overabundant charms.' Well, well, how promising! I can hardly wait to meet the young lady; I am sure we will deal extremely together. We shall have to look into this further, m'dears. I think, however, that for the present time we will not summon Peter again. I would like to find out a little more about this independent and particular Miss Melanie Jarrett before I confront Lord Peter. How unfortunate that I am going into the country for the Christmas Season. As soon as I return, I shall call on Lady Morthman. She has been in Dorset, supposedly to drink the happy couple's health, and she will be able to tell us more. It is so important to have all the facts before dealing with a gentleman of Lord Peter's stamp."

"Most important," agreed Miss Eliza.

"Without a doubt," chimed in her sister, Jane.

The Dowager pointed a bony finger in their direction. "You, my friends, will be busy in my absence. Go out and about and cover as much ground as you can. I want to find out in the minutest detail all the particulars of the Jarrett family. You know the drill: some quiet questions over the teapot, a little prodding here, a few reminiscences there. I rely on you."

As her companions smiled and nodded, her Grace rose and left the room to rest before dinner, managing to knock over only one small vase that fortunately she had never cared for in her progress down the room. Miss Eliza poured out another cup of tea for her sister before they began to make their plans.

"Perhaps Lady Tranwell, Sister?" Miss Eliza suggested. "And her aunt Mrs. Burns? They are always such fonts of information, being quite the most inquisitive ladies in London."

"Perfect! And do you think perhaps Mrs. Winston-Fenwick? She is from Blandford Forum in Dorset, if you recall," Jane replied, taking a small notebook and pencil from her tatting bag and marking down the names. By the time the first dressing bell sounded, the two sisters had drawn up a plan of investigation that would have done Wellington himself proud.

"The only thing that bothers me, Jane," Miss Eliza said as they climbed the stairs arm in arm, "is that description of Miss Jarrett as possessing 'overabundant charms.' Surely Lady Morthman said her granddaughter was small of stature and slight of build?"

Plump little Miss Jane tittered. "My dear, remember the West Country teas! All that clotted cream, the crumpets and scones and honey, and I must remind you, remember Lady Morthman. A dear old lady, of course, but one cannot deny she is exceeding stout! To her, anyone of normal weight would present a slim appearance. Besides, dear Lord Peter was in a pet; he was bound to find fault with the girl after she repulsed him, no matter what she looked like. It was probably just his way of speaking, but I shall remember to inquire."

Her sister smiled as they prepared to part. "I cannot tell you how delighted I am that the dear Dowager has set us this task, Jane. It will be sadly flat without her here in London, and it has been such a long time since we were able to add our mite to the successful conclusion of the problem of Miss Warfield and the curate and the missing church plate."

The Dowager left for Wynne in two days' time, but until the carriage carrying her and her maid and the modest amount of baggage that was all she ever took with her regardless of the length of her stay had disappeared around a corner of the square, the sisters were too busy to begin any of the proposed inquiries.

That very afternoon, however, at an afternoon reception given by one of their old friends, they opened their campaign without delay. They knew they must make haste, for the Dowager would not remain at Wynne for very long, even though she had been invited to visit there until the end of January. She always intended to stay and she always left early. It was not that she did not love her son, the current Duke, and dote on her four grandchildren, or that she held the present Duchess in dislike. In fact, the Dowager was a great admirer of Lady Marjorie, although why this should be so was a puzzle to the rest of the family.

"I am sure I do not understand why she captivates the Duchess so," a timid niece had once remarked. "It is obvious that she pays no attention at all to Aunt Agatha's advice and admonitions, and although she is courteous in her casual, offhand way and thanks her mother-in-law for her concern, she always does exactly what she herself had planned to do originally. I should never dare to cross my aunt so, never!"

All the Dowager's children, their spouses, and their offspring came to Wynne at Christmas, as well as sundry other aunts, uncles, and cousins. Thus, the huge stone palace was noisy and overrun, but it was not for that reason the Dowager could generally be found taking coach for London no later than January 4. Marjorie had taken to breeding English sheepdogs as soon as her children were out of the nursery, and the Dowager considered her daughter-in-law much too lenient in allowing her animals the run of the place instead of keeping them penned up in kennels. The Dowager enjoyed all the children; what she could not abide was the fact that she was constantly in danger of being upset by large, woolly, gamboling sheepdogs, all excessively loud and vocal, and all seemingly determined to show this revered guest their devotion by kissing her with large wet tongues whenever she was careless enough to sit down in their presence. When the Duchess was apprised of this problem, she merely stared and then said vaguely, "I daresay the darlings *are* a bit overexcited with all the crowd here. They will soon grow accustomed."

"But will I?" asked the Dowager tartly as she pushed away an eager canine admirer bent on trying to eat the bows on her slippers. It suddenly occurred to her that the problem of

Lord Peter and his reluctant bride awaited her in London, and she made up her mind to leave Wynne as soon as it was decently possible to do so.

In the meantime, Miss Eliza and Miss Jane were steeping themselves in the lore of Dorset and the condition and number of the present members of the family Jarrett. Mrs. Burns related several stories of Mr. Jarrett, for whom she had cherished a *tendresse* in her youth, and she was not at all loathe to remark on his wife. From her comments, the sisters were able to piece together a mental picture of a fading, ineffectual middle-aged lady who was prone to fainting spells and lingering illnesses and was in no way worthy of her paragon of a husband.

Mrs. Winston-Fenwick cried a little when she told how Mr. Jarrett's older brother and his wife had been lost in a storm at sea, leaving behind them one daughter.

"Poor, poor child, orphaned like that, so sad," she said, wiping her eyes with her handkerchief. "Although perhaps that is not entirely accurate, for I remember Miss Jarrett was even then in her twenties and, as such, could hardly be called a child. Although she is a considerable heiress, she makes her home with her aunt and uncle now; I hear she is quite a comfort to her aunt and a most competent woman as well. Since she is well past any girlish starts, I am sure it must make Mary easier to know Melanie is so well chaperoned."

Miss Jane nodded and pressed another macaroon on her guest. She could hardly be blamed for thinking from this description that Miss Lorna Jarrett was a faded spinster, long past her last prayers.

"What does Miss Melanie look like, Mrs. Winston-Fenwick?" she asked, abandoning this unpromising old maid. "I heard somewhere that she is very plump for a young girl."

Her guest dropped her macaroon in her surprise. "Never say so, dear Miss Jane! The merest child, so slim and slight and lovely. Whoever could have told you such a falsehood?"

Miss Jane murmured that the name of her informant seemed to have escaped her mind. "And do the Jarretts plan to spend the Season in Town?" she inquired next. "We shall be a considerable throng, if everyone from the country descends on us. I have heard of no less than ten families who have already leased houses this year."

Mrs. Winston-Fenwick added the names of four more. "As for the Jarretts, I cannot say. It seems to me there was some scheme afoot—Miss Melanie is eighteen now, you know—but that, of course, would depend on Mrs. Jarrett's precarious health. If they do come, be sure they will stay with Lady Morthman in St. James's Place."

From Lady Tranwell, the sisters heard much the same information, although this lady had at her fingertips the size of Mr. Jarrett's fortune to within a few pounds, the exact acreage of his estate and what stock was raised there, and the amount of Miss Melanie's dowry as well as her middle name, which turned out, not surprisingly, to be Morthman. Of Miss Lorna Jarrett there was no mention beyond the statement that she had been a gift from heaven to her ailing aunt and was dearly loved by her cousin Melanie and her Uncle John as well.

Loved by Melanie and Uncle John she might have been, but it was obvious to Lorna in the days that passed that she was not at all loved by Lady Morthman. The woman lost no opportunity to chastise her for her impetuous boldness in sending Lord Peter on his way, and she soon brought Aunt Mary around to her way of thinking as well. Lorna began to long for the old lady's departure, but since Mrs. Jarrett had succumbed to an infectious sore throat, her mother would not consider abandoning her side.

Dinnertime became a trial, for Mr. Jarrett could not silence his mama-in-law's complaints, Melanie could not redirect the conversation no matter how she tried, and Lorna was forced out of courtesy to endure all the old lady's constant criticism and disappointed sighs.

A few days after Christmas, when Mrs. Jarrett was lying on a chaise before the fire in her bedroom, well wrapped against any drafts, Lady Morthman went to sit with her, and it was not long before the entire household was disrupted by her screams for help. Mrs. Jarrett's heart was beating irregularly, although whether that was from a heart attack or just dismay at her mama's piercing cries was hard to tell.

The local doctor was summoned, and he shook his head dourly after examining his frightened patient. Lady Morthman barely waited until his gig started down the drive before she began to campaign to get Mr. Jarrett to move his wife to London, where she could have the care of the finest physicians.

"I shall not rest until I have my dear Mary safe in Town," Lady Morthman declared, her voice still trembling and all her chins shaking in her agitation. "What can this Doctor Ewen know of her condition? If he were more competent, surely he would have a practice in the metropolis himself. I have never trusted country doctors. He is no doubt able to deal with rheumatism and broken bones, but in a delicate case like this—for Mary has always been frail, and even as a child there were times I despaired of ever raising her—well! And you heard what he prescribed—the very idea. Exercise! Fresh air! Bah!"

Since Mr. Jarrett agreed with Dr. Ewen's diagnosis that lying on her couch coddling herself was the worst thing his wife could do, he did not know what to reply, especially since he suspected that Mary, aided and abetted by her mother, was dramatizing the situation. But he also knew that between the two of them, he would have no peace until he gave in to their demands.

A week later, three coaches started a slow and stately journey to town, and if Lorna and Melanie could not approve the funereal pace, at least they were both delighted at this unexpected opportunity for a change of scene. They were riding alone in Mr. Jarrett's carriage, followed by a coach carrying servants and all the baggage, for Lady Morthman had insisted her daughter ride with her, their maids in attendance and with a large valise of medicine, potions, pills and smelling salts, extra shawls, a fur rug, and such other items as might be needed on their journey. Not surprisingly, Mr. Jarrett chose to ride.

Melanie, in her excitement, had kept up a gay chatter most of the time, but when at last the first villages that formed the outskirts of London appeared ahead of them four days later, Lorna noticed that her cousin had fallen silent. When she looked at her, she saw a tiny frown between those delicate eyebrows. Questioned, Melanie confessed she had been worrying about Lord Peter Truesdale.

"Whatever shall I do if I am presented to him, Lorna? I

shall die of embarrassment, I know, for even if it was you who turned him away, is he not apt to be angry with me as well?"

Lorna suddenly recalled that in her explanation to the family of Lord Peter's visit, she had at no time thought it necessary to mention that she had allowed milord to think that he was speaking to Melanie. A small pang of disquiet stirred in her breast. It was much too late to explain such singular behavior now. Why, how Uncle John would stare at her and Aunt Mary might be shocked into a real heart attack. Lady Morthman's reaction she refused even to contemplate. No, she thought as she stared at her tightly clasped hands in their neat tan gloves, I must keep my own counsel and pretend that all is well.

Taking a deep breath, she said to her apprehensive cousin, "Remember, my dear, we are not here to go to balls and parties, and we will no doubt remain very secluded until your mother recovers her health. In all likelihood you will not have to meet Lord Peter. Besides, most of the fashionable world does not come to Town until the Season properly begins some months ahead. I daresay Lord Peter himself is away, either on his estate or visiting friends."

Melanie's face brightened, and even Lorna felt better at this comforting thought. Of course, she should have realized there was little danger of an encounter this early in January. She put firmly from her mind the question of what she was going to do when she came face to face with the gentleman, as she was sure she must eventually. No need to borrow trouble, she reminded herself as the carriages clattered ever closer to London.

But it was only a few days later, as Lorna stepped down from Lady Morthman's barouche in front of the apothecary's, where she had gone to purchase some new medicine for her aunt, that she saw the tall, broad-shouldered figure of Lord Peter striding toward her across the cobblestones. Praying he had not seen her, she tried to hurry into the shop, but she felt her arm grasped in a firm hand before she could even reach the first shallow step.

"Miss Jarrett, we meet again. What a pleasant surprise," Lord Peter said in his deep voice, removing his beaver and bowing, although his face was dark and set and there was no sign of any pleasure writ there for her to see, in spite of his polite words.

"Lord Peter," Lorna replied. She curtsied before waving her maid to precede her into the shop, absurdly glad she was wearing her new royal-blue velvet cloak lined in soft brown fur, with a matching hood that framed her face and called attention to her brilliant blue eyes.

"You are in a hurry this morning, Miss Jarrett, are you not? Or can it be that you do not care to exchange amenities, or even that you wish you might have avoided me? How distressing that would be!"

Lorna wished that his gray eyes were not so intense, the hand on her arm so compelling and relentless, and the twisted smile on his lips so sardonic, and that her heart were not beating as erratically as her Aunt Mary's. "My sole purpose here is to purchase some medicines, sir," she replied. "You must excuse me, for the errand *is* urgent."

"I am sorry to hear it, Miss Jarrett. Since you yourself are in full and healthy bloom, just as I remembered you, it must be some other member of the family?"

Lorna nodded and freed her arm. "I must bid you good day, sir, for I am awaited in St. James's Place."

"Ah, staying with Lady Morthman, of course; I thought I recognized her carriage. I shall look forward to seeing you again, Miss Jarrett, when this, er, illness passes and we have more time to talk. London is so thin of company, we are sure to meet over and over again.

"Oh, you need not refine on our previous meeting," he said knowingly, seeing her start at his words. "I myself have quite forgotten it, I assure you. It was, after all, of no great moment, certainly not enough to cause you embarrassment or distress. I came almost immediately to thank the fates that you felt as you did, and to consider myself the luckiest of men. A narrow escape, to be sure, for both of us, but all's well that ends well, eh?"

Lorna's blue eyes flashed fire. Rude man! How dare he take her refusal so lightly and in such a careless manner? She nodded her head coldly before she picked up her skirt to climb the steps to the shop, refusing to rise to his baiting and lose her temper. As she opened the door, he remarked, "By the way, have you met your 'parfit gentil knight' yet? If not, may I recommend Sir Digby Fortescue? Tall and handsome, yet amenable and easily led, and just what you are looking for, no doubt. I am sure you will have him under the cat's foot in a week. Your most obedient servant, ma'am!"

Lorna whirled and glared down at him, and his gray eyes lit up with laughter before he bowed again and replaced his beaver at a jaunty angle to stroll away down the street, obviously pleased at the success of this ploy.

Completing her purchase, she stepped back into the barouche, thankful that Lord Peter was nowhere in sight. She found the drive home much too short to give her time to contemplate this new, disturbing development, and she was glad to send her maid to deliver the medicine while she escaped to her room to think until the luncheon bell sounded.

So, Lord Peter was in London after all. She agreed with him that they were sure to meet again. Lady Morthman had already begun to talk about receptions and tea parties and drives in the park, adding in a gloomy tone that since Miss Lorna Jarrett had seen fit to discourage the most eligible man in town, she supposed it was her duty to take her granddaughter out and about in the hope she might attract another *parti*. Not, she said, that he would be anything like the paragon who had been sent about his business by Melanie's older and interfering cousin, but one must try. To this end she was busy outfitting her granddaughter at all the best *modistes* and mantua makers, and even Mrs. Jarrett seemed much improved in spirits whenever Melanie came to her room to show her a new evening gown or a handsome walking dress with all the requisite accessories.

Lorna herself had gone shopping with her cousin and had purchased almost as many outfits for herself, for she had not been in London for some time. When she also visited her aunt to model a new bonnet or riding habit, she could tell Mrs. Jarrett was feeling much more the thing and would have no qualms about allowing either her mama or her niece to serve as chaperone for Melanie at any party they were invited to attend. Melanie seemed to have forgotten her fears of the rejected suitor in her anticipation of the delights ahead, for she never mentioned Lord Peter's name again.

And yet, it appeared that it was only a matter of time before the real Melanie Jarrett came face to face with Lord Peter Truesdale. Lorna shuddered. She did not have to wonder how he would take the deception; she knew he would be furious to be gulled in such a way. She wondered what course his revenge might take, knowing he would be sure to exact recompense. He might call himself a Christian gentleman, but he was not the kind of man to take such trickery lightly, especially since he had been bested by a woman. No, he was sure to make her life a misery, one way or the other.

The bell for luncheon sounded just as she reached that unappealing conclusion, and she went downstairs no wiser than before about how she was to handle this contretemps. If only the man would be called out of town, she thought. If only he would decide to take a long sea voyage, or an extensive trip abroad—or perhaps she herself would be wise to do so as soon as it could possibly be arranged.

As she reached the dining-room door, she realized that, short of absenting herself for the next year, her best protection would be for Lord Peter to fall in love with some other girl, and from the depths of his happiness in that marvelous state, be able to laugh with her at her machinations. As she nodded to the butler and went to join the others, she wondered why this solution had so little appeal. In fact, if she were to be honest with herself, it held absolutely none at all.

But it was not Lord Peter who discovered the deception first. The Dowager Duchess, attending an afternoon reception with Miss Eliza and Miss Jane, was pleased to see Lady Morthman there as well, for she had not known that the lady had returned from her visit to Dorset.

Of course the Duchess did not really *see* Lady Morthman. Miss Eliza pointed her out, for the Dowager could not distinguish the guests from any distance and had long depended on her companions to act as what she herself called "my opera glasses."

At Miss Eliza's whisper, she raised an imperious hand, and Lady Morthman waddled to her side at once. After a short, almost brusque exchange of greetings, Lady Morthman plunged straight to the heart of the matter foremost in both ladies' minds. She began by bemoaning the lost match, but since her conversation was disjointed in her anguish and she was still panting from her rush across the room, the Dowager did not understand her.

"Too coming . . . such pushing, encroaching ways," Lady Morthman declared, shaking her head so violently it threatened the feathers that waved above her turban.

"Your granddaughter?" the Dowager asked, eyebrows raised, but Lady Morthman rushed on, unhearing.

"I have never liked her . . . no, not at all! And to take it on herself . . . I ask you, Agatha, what is the world coming to? And Mr. Jarrett all compliance about accepting *her* opinion . . . hmpph! You may be sure I have done my best to try to bring the family to a real sense of their loss, but outside of my dear Mary, I have no allies there. Oh, no, quite the contrary! And so, I am forced to take my granddaughter about, hoping that she will catch someone's eye—someone suitable, of course, although no one could compare to dear Lord Peter. I can only be thankful that what has occurred is not common knowledge in the Ton, for if it should get out, I would never be able to hold up my head again. Turning down Lord Peter, and in *such* a way. The shame of it! I never!"

As she buried her face in her handkerchief to wipe the tears from her eyes, the Dowager had a chance to express an interest in at last meeting Lady Morthman's granddaughter, and Lady Morthman sighed heavily as she waved to a girl in pale-green muslin who was standing some little distance away, conversing with another lady in a fashionable gown of deep blue. From her position behind the Dowager's chair, Miss Jane's eyes widened and her little mouth fell open in amazement. Excusing herself, she bustled over to waylay her hostess and engage her in what appeared to be a most serious conversation.

As her grandmother presented her to the Dowager Duchess of Wynne, Melanie blushed scarlet and her curtsy was not performed with her usual grace. The Dowager peered at her and then shook her head.

"Why, the child's as thin as a reed! Whatever was the man thinking of, Eliza?" she asked the middle-aged lady at her side. Miss Eliza looked puzzled, but she was not required to give an answer, for the Dowager continued, "Sit here beside me, child, and do not look so distressed. If you could not like Peter, then that's the end of it, but I am interested in knowing what there is about him that offended you so on such short acquaintance."

Melanie caught the eye of a tall lady in deep blue, who, at the desperate look of appeal on her face, came toward them at once.

"B-b-but I . . . I . . ." she began, and the Dowager snorted.

"Stutters, by all that's holy! I wonder how she got her refusal out at all?"

"Melanie," her grandmother exclaimed, "whatever is the matter with you, child? Tell Lord Peter's great-aunt at once that you had nothing to do with it, that it was all the interference of that bold chit of a cousin of yours, Miss—"

"Miss Lorna Jarrett!" A triumphant Miss Jane broke in as she rejoined the group. "She is the lady who is approaching even now, Your Grace."

"Aha!" the Dowager said as the deep-blue gown came close enough for her to make out that its owner was a tall, handsome, well-built woman in her twenties, with high color and a head of auburn curls. "Present me, Lady Morthman, and then you may take Miss—Miss Melanie, was it?—away. I wish to converse with the other Miss Jarrett alone."

Melanie rose with alacrity and helped her grandmother to her feet.

Lady Morthman performed the introduction, mentioning the Dowager's relationship to Lord Peter in a stiff, sullen way that did not appear to discompose the lady in blue at all.

"Your Grace." She smiled, her dimple flashing as she sank into a graceful deep curtsy.

"Excellent! Wish I'd had your aplomb years ago, Miss Jarrett," the Dowager chuckled. "First time I met Reggie's mother—*she* was the Dowager Duchess then, of course—I misjudged the depth of my curtsy in an effort to show my respect for the lady, and proceeded to tip over at her feet." She chuckled again. "Not the best way to impress your future mama-in-law, lying in an untidy heap on the floor, eh? But perhaps that was what did the trick. Reggie picked me up and proposed the very same evening." She shook her head at her memories and then added, "Sit here beside me, young woman. I cannot tell you how anxious I am to hear all about everything that happened at Jarrett Hall. There is little sense to be got from Lady Morthman and none at all from Miss Melanie. By the way, does the gel have all her wits? Pretty as a picture of course, but sad . . . very sad!"

Lorna was arranging her skirts, but at this assessment of her cousin she said in her low, firm voice, "Of course she does, your Grace, except when she is discomforted by the awkwardness of meeting a relation of a suitor whom she denied. Or that, I should say rather, I denied for her. Then, too, your personality is overwhelming to someone just eighteen and not really out as yet. Melanie is a dear girl—a love."

"I'll accept your more intimate knowledge of her," the Dowager said more mildly. "But what I want to know is, why *did* you deny him? And why did Peter accept *your* dismissal? Surely that was your uncle's prerogative?"

"I was the only one at home when Lord Peter called," Lorna explained, not taking her eyes from the Dowager's haughty gaze and hoping she could get through the next few minutes with a whole skin. "It did not take me long to get his measure as a man, and when he assumed I was Melanie, I could not resist seizing the opportunity to send him about his business before my cousin had to meet him. You see, I had no confidence that she would be able to deny him, and she might very well have found herself engaged to be married even though she dreaded it. Melanie is only a child, and Lord Peter, besides being much too old for her, has a very, er, *forceful* personality." She sounded more than a little tart and her blue eyes darkened with memory.

The Dowager prompted, "Go on, go on! Why did you take him in such dislike? Was he rude? Knowing Peter, I'd wager my best diamond pendant he insulted you in some way, did he not, my girl?" She chuckled again.

Lorna sat up even straighter and clasped her hands together in her lap. She did not think the Dowager seemed disturbed by what she had done, nor at all shocked or dismayed as other older ladies might have been, and this gave her the confidence to say, "It would certainly be fair to say that his manner was insulting in the extreme, ma'am, but it was not for that reason I refused his offer. You know your great-nephew and you have met Melanie. Can you see them together as man and wife? I could not. He would run rough-shod over her in minutes. Furthermore, I do not believe there is an ounce of kindness or charity in his makeup. Melanie deserves better than a life of being browbeaten by such a brute."

She paused, afraid she had gone too far, but the Dowager only nodded as she clapped her hands. "I see that Lord Peter has inspired a dislike in you of the highest order, Miss Jarrett. You will not be surprised, I am sure, when I tell you that it appears to be mutual. You see, I was the one who sent Peter into Dorset to get himself a wife. Left to his own devices, he would never have made the journey. The note he sent to me on his return, although couched in conventional language, made it quite clear what he thought of you."

"Oh?" Lorna inquired with raised eyebrows. I will *not* ask what he dared to say, she told herself even as she opened her mouth and asked, "And what was that, your Grace?"

"If I remember correctly, he said you were a bold and saucy miss."

"And bad mannered," Miss Jane said brightly.

Lorna stiffened as Miss Eliza added, "Don't forget that he claimed she had 'overabundant charms,' your Grace."

Lorna glanced down at her gown of deep blue, which fit her figure so admirably, and felt the anger that rose in her breast, causing it to swell and threaten the tiny buttons that fastened her bodice. How dare he call her fat? She was *not* overabundant; why, everyone admired her figure.

The Dowager was close enough to see her frown as Lorna looked down at herself, and she patted her hands. "Now, my dear, one must not take too much to heart what a gentleman says when he is angry. I am sure he said much worse when he found out you were not the Miss Jarrett he had been sent to captivate, did he not?"

"But, Your Grace, he doesn't know yet," Lorna admitted, bringing her troubled eyes back to the Dowager's face.

"He doesn't know? You mean to tell me that he still thinks you are Miss Melanie Jarrett?" the Dowager asked, pushing some gray hair back from her face, the better to peer at her companion.

"Somehow the chance to tell him never arose. Then, too,

I did not think we would ever meet again. I certainly never imagined Aunt Mary's illness would bring us all to London at this time, nor did I expect to find Lord Peter here. It is all such bad luck, and the most frightful mess!"

Lorna looked so distraught for a moment that the Dowager patted her hand again. "There, my dear Miss Jarrett. Yes, it is a frightful, er, mess, as you so succinctly put it. Whatever do you plan to do when the horrid truth comes out, as come out it must?"

"The only sensible thing that has occurred to me is to take a long sea voyage immediately," Lorna admitted, causing the Dowager to cackle with mirth.

"No, no, not such cowardice from one who appears to be the type of woman who throws her heart first over every fence. Besides, you do owe my great-nephy an apology, don't you think? One must hope he will not find it necessary to strangle you, though. He has a frightful temper. Jane, when is Lady Grant's ball?"

Bewildered by the sudden change of conversation, Lorna stared as the three older ladies put their heads together. A moment later the Dowager said, "Excellent, next Thursday! I know Peter has been invited, and I myself would not miss this confrontation for the world. You *have* been invited, have you not, Miss Jarrett?"

Lorna nodded. "Yes, it is to be Melanie's first real excursion into Society, and she will be escorted not only by her father and grandmother, but by myself as well, if I am not so fortunate as to be run down by a hansom cab before that."

"Nonsense! You will face Lord Peter with what I am sure is your usual aplomb. He cannot murder you in a crowded ballroom, after all, although I cannot advise you strongly enough not to go apart with him after he learns your true identity, not for that evening nor even for some time to come."

Lorna was fervent in her agreement that this would be a foolhardy thing to do and that she had no intention of ever being alone with milord if she could help it, and the Dowager patted her hand once more before dismissing her.

As Lorna moved gracefully away and Miss Jane came forward to take the seat she had vacated, the Dowager said,

"Now this is something like. She is perfect for him, just perfect, don't you agree, my dears?"

"So handsome and healthy," Miss Eliza enthused.

"So spirited," Miss Jane added.

The Dowager chuckled. "Yes, it is her spirit that quite decides the issue for me. Peter will not ride roughshod over that young lady—oh, no! He is more in danger of finding himself manipulated, maddened, and mastered, as well as married. All we have to do is get the two of them to admit their mutual attraction. A formidable task, my dear friends, probably the most formidable task we have been set in many a year, but I am hopeful of the outcome—most hopeful."

"If only they do not behave like the gingham dog and the calico cat," Miss Jane remarked a little doubtfully.

The Dowager thought for a moment and then laughed right out loud. "We shall be on our guards to prevent them from tearing each other to pieces like that old nursery rhyme. I feel *so* much better, why, even this frigid January weather cannot dampen my spirits now."

3

The following Thursday dawned bitter cold but clear. There was no sudden blizzard, no torrential downpour that would cause a cancellation of the evening's festivities. As Lorna lay in bed sipping her morning chocolate, she realized she had not even been fortunate enough to contract a bad head cold to prevent her from spending what she was sure was going to be the most unpleasant evening of her entire life.

She sighed. It had been impossible to discuss with Melanie what was going to happen, for to do so would ruin all her innocent enjoyment in the evening before it even began. Besides, she had yet to devise a way she could admit, even to little Melanie, that she had pretended to be her cousin when Lord Peter came to Dorset.

For Melanie, the hours dragged with a tedious slowness, but for Lorna it seemed no time at all before she was being dressed for the ball. She had decided to wear one of her new gowns, the prettiest one she had, to give her courage, and she was so particular about her hairstyle and jewels that her maid scented a romance in the offing.

Melanie was wearing a lace-trimmed white gown as befitted a debutante. Lorna thought she looked very young and lovely when she went with her to Mrs. Jarrett's room so that their toilettes could be admired before they left. Melanie had already exclaimed over Lorna's gown of navy-blue silk with its deep round neckline and tiny sleeves. The gown was confined under her breasts with an empire sash of blue velvet, and with it she wore sapphires that glittered in her hair and on her wrists and throat. Lorna accepted the compliments, but wished that her décolleté were not quite so revealing, for it displayed what Lord Peter would undoubtedly describe as her "overabundant charms." As she remembered that remark of his, her back stiffened and she marched down the stairs behind her cousin with an almost militant expression on her face.

Very well, so it had been wrong of her to impersonate Melanie, but she would do it again in a moment to save the girl from the likes of Lord Peter Truesdale. She was determined to stand up to him, and if he made even one derogatory remark, she would know how to answer him, she told herself. Lorna barely heard Mr. Jarrett's compliments or Lady Morthman's sniffs as she took her seat in the carriage, and she was glad Melanie chatted so gaily with the others so she could be alone with her thoughts.

Lady Grant's town house was one of the grandest in Park Lane, and the ballroom, which had been decorated in a winter theme of silver and pale blue, was rapidly being filled with all the members of the Ton who were presently in town. After greeting her hostess and introducing the two girls, Lady Morthman went to some seats along the ballroom wall, and Mr. Jarrett excused himself to speak to an old friend he had not seen for some time. Melanie's eyes were sparkling with delight as she whispered to her cousin, "How wonderful and exciting it all is, Lorna! I am so glad to be here. Oh, do look at that handsome young man over there. I swear he is staring at us."

Lorna barely spared the gentleman a cursory glance, for her eyes were searching for the tall powerful figure of Lord Peter. He was nowhere in sight, and for a moment the apprehension in her heart lightened. Perhaps he had been unable to attend? Perhaps he had been the one to contract a bad cold? How wonderful that would be! And then she realized that if he failed to put in an appearance tonight, she would have to go through this fearful anticipation at another time. She almost prayed he would come through the large double doors immediately so she might get the unpleasantness over with at once.

But Lord Peter was not there. He was not there when the opening set formed and she took her place with Lord Haven, nor had he appeared when the musicians struck up the first waltz. Lorna relaxed and decided she might as well enjoy herself. Melanie had met any number of young men anxious to talk and dance with her, and Lorna's own card was just as quickly filled.

She smiled a little to herself when Sir Digby Fortescue was presented to her by Mr. Jarrett, for the gentleman was just as tall and handsome, just as mild and pleasant as Lord Peter had claimed. Sir Digby was intrigued by the beautiful Miss Jarrett, that was plain to see, and did not leave her side until he had secured her promise for the supper dance. He was a well-dressed gentleman in his late twenties, with well-formed features, a warm smile, and carefully brushed blond hair. Lorna thought him an uninspired conversationalist, but untaxing to be with, and she did not demur at his request.

And then, coming off the floor after a vigorous schottische with Lord Landford and laughing at her partner as she came, she found herself face to face once again with Lord Peter. He took the time to look her up and down through his quizzing glass before he bowed.

"Miss Jarrett," he said in a noncommittal voice.

"Lord Peter," she replied, hoping her breathlessness would be atribulated to the dance she had just performed.

"So you two have met, have you?" Lord Landford inquired. "Might have known that you would be before us all in making Miss Jarrett's acquaintance, Peter, although it was too bad of you to nip in before the rest of us had a chance, old boy."

"Miss Jarrett and I met in the country, Percy," Lord Peter explained. "And I do not think that you will find my, er, nipping in, as you put it, will be any detriment at all to your interest in the lady."

"Indeed no, m'lord," Lorna said with a warm smile for her partner. "It was only a short, formal meeting."

"Short but one could hardly say sweet, don't you agree, Miss Jarrett?"

"My sentiments exactly, m'lord," Lorna replied, trying to slow the pounding of her heart as Lord Landford looked from one to the other, a little frown coming to his face at this incomprehensible repartee.

Lord Peter swung his quizzing glass in a lazy circle, his gray eyes teasing. "And yet," he added pensively, "there was one sweet moment that I cherish to this day."

"Indeed? I cannot recall a single second that could be classified that way," Lorna said as she clenched her hands in the folds of her gown, and then the moment she had been dreading arrived in a whirl of white skirts and a light, girlish voice.

"Lorna, my dear, Grandmother wants you—Papa is nowhere to be found. I beg your pardon, sirs," she added, "I hope you will excuse my cousin for a moment."

"I will come at once," Lorna said, turning to lead the girl away, but as she had expected, that strong hand that she remembered so well from previous encounters grasped her arm and detained her.

"I do not believe I have had the pleasure of meeting your *cousin*, Miss Jarrett," Lord Peter said in quite a different tone.

Lorna took a deep breath. "No, she was not at home when you called in Dorset, sir. My cousin, Miss Jarrett. Miss *Melanie* Jarrett. My dear, this is Lord Peter Truesdale."

Melanie turned as white as her gown and took a little step backward at the dangerous expression of sudden fury on that dark face so far above hers.

"M-m'lord?" she whispered, looking as if she wished she

were anywhere else on earth but standing before him.

He nodded to her impatiently, even as his eyes went back to Lorna's face. "So, this is Miss *Melanie* Jarrett? And you, Miss Jarrett, I believe she addressed as *Lorna?*" The Earl's voice was quiet now and the fury that had transformed his face had disappeared. In its place was a still, icy demeanor that seemed even more dangerous.

"Yes, I am Lorna Jarrett," Lorna said as evenly as she could.

"Percy, dear friend, take Miss Melanie to her grand-mother," Lord Peter ordered, and after one quick look at his face, Lord Landford was quick to offer his arm to the young lady, who appeared only too anxious to disappear.

Lorna tried to pull away from the hand that was still grip-ping her arm, but of course it was impossible to free herself. Her own temper overcame her fear as she demanded, "Release me at once, m'lord! How dare you detain me when Lady Morthman awaits me?"

"Lady Morthman can wait. I have something to say to you, my girl, and I will not be denied," Lord Peter informed her as he bowed to Princess Lieven and her escort, then he tucked her hand in his arm and led her to a small alcove in which was placed a conveniently empty sofa.

Lorna knew that, short of making a scene that would put paid to any of the Jarretts' hopes of acceptance by the Ton, she had no choice, and the sight of the Dowager Duchess of Wynne and her two cronies watching with great interest some little distance away did little to comfort her.

Lord Peter turned his back on the throng of dancers and onlookers, effectively blocking anyone's view of the scene, and forced Lorna to sit down on the sofa, taking the seat beside her and once again grasping her arm so she could not escape.

"I think you owe me an explanation, Miss Jarrett," he said in that quiet but no less deadly voice. "I am waiting to hear it."

Lorna tilted her chin. "I will not apologize for the mis-understanding, sir, for if you remember, I never claimed to be Melanie, in so many words. I never claimed to by anyone but Miss Jarrett and it *is* my name too. The error was all yours; if you cared to think me the young lady you had come to inspect, that was your privilege. I certainly saw no need to correct you."

The Earl bent his dark, harsh-featured face closer, and Lorna had all she could do not to draw back from the curious light in those gray eyes set under frowning brows, from the stern line of his mouth and the rigid set of his jaw. "So, it was my fault, was it? And was it my fault that I was led to believe, by your rejection of my suit, that you were the young lady in question?" He paused and Lorna lowered her eyes. In that same unemotional voice he added, "You are even more bold and saucy than I thought, Miss Lorna Jarrett. In fact, you are a strumpet and a jade."

Lorna looked up, her face flushing as he continued, "A *lady* would have corrected me at once, a *lady* would never have interfered in an affair that was none of her concern, a *lady* would have waited for her aunt and uncle to receive me, a *lady*—"

"Do you think I care what you believe of me?" Lorna snapped, her temper exploding at his insults. "I will accept your assessment of my character without further elucidation. I am no lady."

"For the first and probably the last time, we find ourselves in complete accord," he replied. "Good evening, m'lord, madam," he added, smiling to a couple passing the alcove. "Allow me to add that I have never in my entire life encountered such conceit as you have displayed. To set yourself up as the sole judge of what your cousin's future should be is so arrogant it boggles the mind. But stay! Perhaps it was jealousy?"

He paused and Lorna's indrawn breath told him he had scored a hit.

"Of course! At your age it must have been particularly galling to have to watch your younger relative make such an excellent match. Now I understand," he continued. "Unsuccessful spinsters very often become old-cattish in their disappointment."

"You terrible man, how I hate you!" Lorna exclaimed, leaning toward him in her anger. "I was *not* jealous! How could I be when I pitied Melly so sincerely? It was only the thought of her misery, married to such a brute as yourself, that made me determined to do everything I could to help her escape that fate."

"And you were very sure she would be miserable, were you not?" Lord Peter asked. "You are not as wise and all-knowing as you think, Miss Jarrett. I can give you any number of references from some very satisfied ladies as to my expertise as a lover. You yourself were not entirely indifferent to me when I had you in my arms, if you recall."

Lorna gasped. "You go too far, sir. I deny any attraction and I do not care to hear about your amatory adventures with what I am sure could only have been women of the lower classes."

His sharp intake of breath told her she had scored a hit in return by implying that such an unattractive man would have to pay for his mistresses, and she hurried on, "Besides, you may be sure Melanie thanked me for my 'interference' in a most heartfelt manner — she did not care to marry you, and has not regretted your loss."

Lord Peter controlled his fury and asked in a deceptively calm voice, "But how could Miss Melanie object to a man she had never met? Surely it was just the thought of marriage to anyone at this time that distressed her, was it not?"

Lord Peter noticed the tiny doubt that crossed her face and added, "But now, thanks to your autocratic ways, that question will never be resolved. You have been a great deal too busy, Miss Jarrett, and you should be whipped." He released her arm and rose.

Lorna sprang to her feet. Speaking through the tears that clogged her throat and quivered behind her eyelids, she said passionately, "It would give me a great deal of pleasure if I never had to see you or speak to you again, Lord Peter. I may have overstepped the bounds of propriety in my concern for my cousin, I may be no lady, but you are certainly no gentleman. You are rude and coarse and overbearing, and I am glad I saved Melanie from your hateful proposal. I would do it again in an instant."

Lord Peter stepped closer for a moment, and Lorna saw how he clenched his fists before he said, "What a shame that you are not a man. I would know how to deal with such impertinence then. But perhaps there may still be a way to punish you as you deserve—"

"Miss Jarrett, Lord Peter, servant, sir," Sir Digby's gentle baritone came from behind them. "This is my dance, I believe?"

Lord Peter turned and smiled, a smile that did not reach his icy gray eyes. "Digby, of course. I knew somehow I could expect to find you in this lady's train, dear fellow. Miss Jarrett, until we meet again. And we *will* meet again, you may wager on it."

He bowed and strode away, and Lorna took Sir Digby's hand, wishing with all her heart that she might have a few moments alone to compose herself. Fortunately, her partner seemed to realize that she was struggling under a cloud of some distress, and with exquisite manners, he chatted lightly of the ball and the other guests until her breathing slowed and she was able to join in the conversation.

Lorna was not surprised after the supper dance to find the Dowager Duchess of Wynne beckoning to her. She had noticed that Lord Peter took his leave within minutes of quitting her side, but she was still so heartsick at the things he had said, still so tremulous in her anger and dismay, that even his hurried retreat could not give her any sense of conquest.

"Rolled up, foot and guns, m'dear?" the Dowager inquired as Lorna rose from her curtsy. "Perhaps I should have warned you that in addition to a terrible temper, Peter has a devastating way with words. They cut like a rapier, or so I've been told, for, of course, he has never gotten up to his tricks with me."

"I am sorry if it pains you, Your Grace, but I must say that your great-nephew is a horrible man. Never in my worst imaginings did I ever think I would have to listen to such insults, be abused in such disgusting terms, or treated to such a tirade. But I cannot speak of it now. I am too angry and upset, and I feel I might explode—or scream and rave, if I try. You must excuse me."

The Dowager smiled at her flashing blue eyes and heightened color, thinking she had seldom seen such a handsome young woman even as she said, "I understand. Do me the kindness to call on me tomorrow morning at eleven. I shall see that we are quite alone—not even Jane or Eliza will be present. Run along now and try not to be too distressed. I promise this will all pass, my dear, and someday, after the happy ending I have in mind, we will laugh about it together."

Lorna's incredulous stare said she very much doubted it. She took her leave of the Dowager and very shortly thereafter the Jarrett party left the ball. The Dowager asked Miss Eliza to have their carriage called.

"We might as well go home, my friends. The excitement is over for this evening. At least he did not kill her—not yet, at any rate."

Miss Jane chuckled as she collected the Dowager's stole, reticule, and fan. "Neither did Miss Jarrett kill him. A promising beginning, your Grace."

If Lorna found it difficult to sleep in her big bed in St. James's Place that night, she was joined in her wakefulness by Lord Peter a few streets away in his rooms on Albany Street. He had dismissed his man after he had made up the bedroom fire, and then he sat before it until very late, staring into the flames and going over the events of the evening.

The woman was maddening! Never in his entire life had he felt such an urge to strangle someone as he had this evening, and not even in his encounters with his worst enemies had his rage threatened to overpower him this way. She must have been sent to punish me for my past sins, he thought as he poured himself a snifter of brandy from the decanter beside him. Be that as it may, we shall see who wins in the end, Miss *Lorna* Jarrett, for I am not about to be bested by an arrogant, opinionated termagant, oh, no! When I am finished with you, you will be begging for mercy, and I shall laugh and walk away.

Rolling the mellow liquor over his tongue, he bent all his thoughts to the form his revenge would take. The first solution that came to mind was quickly discarded. It would be easy for a man in his social position to ruin the lady's reputation with the Ton; a few well-placed words here and there, a raised brow, a slight sneer, and Miss Lorna would find herself shunned by Society. But that was too simple, Lord Peter told himself, not wanting to admit that he instinctively shied away from such underhanded action. He might want revenge, but he was a fair fighter, and besides, he told himself, there was no subtlety in such a course. His retaliation must be not only sweet but discreetly satisfying as well.

He considered several other possibilities, till at last, when he went to bed, he had decided on a course of action that would be such a masterstroke it would shake Miss Lorna Jarrett to the core! An unholy smile of genuine amusement softened his well-formed mouth and harsh-featured face as he closed his eyes and slipped immediately into slumber.

Lorna herself fell asleep in the gray dawn, exhausted from emotion and the turmoil of her thoughts, and she did not wake and call for her maid until almost ten. Recalling her engagement with the Dowager, she hurried to dress and run down the stairs to her waiting carriage, completely missing an enormous and exquisite bouquet of roses that lay on the hall table.

Melanie, dancing down the stairs on her way to breakfast a few minutes later, blushed when she saw the bouquets that had come for her, especially the beautiful roses. Although a novice flirt, she knew she had made conquests last evening. Were the roses from Mr. Wilton? Lord Landford? Perhaps —and here her heart took a little leap—perhaps even from Sir Digby? She had been much taken with him. He was old enough to give her consequence, and a marked contrast to the very young and green cavaliers her other admirers had been.

She tore open the card, and her mouth formed a perfect O of astonishment. They were from Lord Peter, and his note was so complimentary that it would have turned the head of even a less impressionable young lady.

A poser for you, Miss Jarrett . . .

Could a young lady forgive the behavior of one who was so overcome by her beauty and grace last evening that the thought that he had been denied the chance to meet her caused him to lose his temper and frown? If you should smile at me when next we meet, I shall have your answer.

Do not be cruel, I beg you! Forgive me.

Yours, etc,

Peter Truesdale

There was a postscript in French that Melanie could not translate. She thought of asking her cousin, but somehow she did not like to bother her, especially with this note. Then she remembered that her mama spoke French, and she carried her letter away after instructing the butler to have the roses brought to her room. Somehow Lord Landford's nosegay of pink rosebuds and the message that accompanied them—"Lovely flowers for a lovely lady"—paled in comparison, for although she had been terrified of Lord Peter last evening, surely this note and flowers showed that she had nothing to fear from him. And how satisfying it was to know that she had made such a conquest, for as Grandmother Morthman was continually pointing out, Lord Peter could have any woman he wanted.

Not, she told herself as she poured out a cup of coffee and reached for the muffins, that I have any intention of forming a lasting attachment, for loverlike or not, he is a frightening man, but what a feather in my cap to have such a leader of the Ton under my spell. She resolved to give him her warmest smile at next meeting.

The leader of the Ton was at that moment engaged in conversation with several friends at Brooks Club, where he had looked in after visiting the florist. Lord Landford joined the group and in a few minutes beckoned him to one side for a few private words.

"Now, Peter, what was that all about last night? Since I took Miss Melanie away at your request, I think I am entitled to hear the reason for your rage. Out with it, man! If looks could kill, the lady in blue would never have seen the dawn."

Peter laughed and expertly took a pinch of snuff. "Dear boy, would you know all my secrets? I had a score to settle with the lady—in fact, I still do. I beg you to keep mum about it, but it may afford you some amusement if you keep an eye on the situation."

"She is a beautiful woman, isn't she? Of course, knowing you, there would be no score to settle if she were not," Lord Landford replied.

"If you care for that kind of overpowering charm," Lord Peter said in a careless way. "Now I myself found her cousin much more appealing. Such a delicate beauty, and so young and fresh! I intend to spend a geat deal more time with Miss Melanie than Miss Lorna in the future."

"Here, I say, Peter! It is too bad of you to admire the girl I have in my eyes. I beg you to reconsider! Miss Lorna is much more your style, assure you, dear fellow. . . ." Lord Landford stared at milord's sudden ferocious frown and was quick to take his leave.

The Dowager Duchess of Wynne was delighted to meet her great-nephew that evening at Mrs. Beresford's reception. Her visit with Lorna had been most illuminating, but to be fair, she felt she must hear the opposite side of the story, or as much of it as Lord Peter was willing to divulge.

He was not adverse to taking the chair beside her and grinned at Miss Eliza and Miss Jane when she waved them away.

"I saw you last evening with Miss Jarrett, Peter," she began with no preamble. "Whatever did you say to the girl to make her color up and look so angry? I was not aware that you even knew the lady."

"You must mean Miss Lorna Jarrett, ma'am. I met her in Dorset when I went at your request to court Miss Melanie. For some reason, the lady does not care for me. I assure you her feelings are reciprocated." He seemed about to say more, but then his lips closed in a tight line and he folded his arms before him.

The Dowager sighed. Men can be so mulish, she thought as she prepared to drag the truth from him. "I met the misses Jarrett last evening too," she remarked. "I must say I was astounded Miss Melanie ever found the courage to tell you she did not care for you, for in my presence she stuttered and acted about two and ten. Are you by any chance slipping, Peter? I should have thought with all your address and experience, you would have had her all complaisance in a trice. Now if it had been the other one, I could well believe she might send you packing."

She chortled and Lord Peter frowned and looked uncomfortable.

"I see there is nothing for it but to admit the truth," he muttered. "You may find this hard to believe, ma'am, but it was Lorna Jarrett who denied me. I never even met the right young lady. Can you believe such sauce? Why, she even pretended to be Miss Melanie! And that, of course, was why I was so very angry last evening, for it was there that I learned of the deception."

"How very unusual," the Dowager said blandly, shooing away a smiling Lady Morthman, who was waddling toward them. "I can believe it of her, though, for she did impress me as a strong-minded gel. Why didn't she like you?"

This blunt question seemed to confuse Lord Peter, and he threw out his hands in defeat. "I have no idea, Aunt. True, I was not particularly conciliatory, for I found the situation uncomfortable in the extreme. Miss Lorna's behavior was so free for a girl left alone with a strange man come to seek her hand that perhaps I was overly sarcastic. That far I will go in admitting a fault; the rest of the debacle is on her head."

"Is it possible she liked you too well, my dear?" his great-aunt asked next.

Lord Peter stared, unable to follow this line of reasoning. "A fine way she had of showing it, then, ma'am. No, it is plain she took me in aversion at first sight, and without a bit of maidenly modesty proceeded to tell me so. Such impertinence!

The Dowager chuckled. "And how lowering for you, dear boy. If what you have told me is true, it is obvious that Miss Lorna seized the moment and your ignorance to save her cousin from what she considered would be a distasteful marriage. One almost has to admire her courage and ingenuity."

"How dare she find me distasteful?" Lord Peter demanded in a voice full of loathing. "There is nothing I can find admirable about such a woman, Aunt. She is a witch."

He collected himself and rose, adding, "However, she does not matter now that I have finally met Melanie. Do you know, I find I completely agree with your original plan? The child is lovely and I intend to pursue her with, er, all my address and experience. How happy it should make you, Aunt Agatha, to know that your scheme for my marriage has my heartfelt approval. Trust me to bend all my skill to a successful conclusion."

He grinned at the Dowager, who in her astonishment looked more haughty and forbidding than ever.

"Marry that insipid little girl? It is out of the question! Having met her myself, I find I have changed my mind as to her suitability. Why, she would bore you in a week."

"But I never expected marriage to be exciting, ma'am. I hope you will be the first to wish me happy, in not too many more weeks to come."

As he bowed and moved away, the Dowager sat dumbstruck before she muttered to his retreating back, "Be sure I shall wish you happy, dear boy, but not on the occasion of your marriage to Miss Melanie Jarrett. Oh, there you are, Eliza, Jane. You will never guess what has just happened, and I fear when I tell you, you will be downcast. It appears we must work even harder than I thought in the matter of Lord Peter."

But the Dowager did not have the chance to tell her eager companions what had occurred, for Lady Morthman arrived to talk to her, all smiles and breathless exclamations, and she would not be denied. For the next half-hour, the Dowager was forced to listen to the lady's raptures about Lord Peter's roses; the card he had written, which had quite turned the child's head; and the cunning postscript in French that, when translated, compared Melanie to an opening rosebud.

The Dowager bore this monologue stoically, but as soon as possible, she broke in to say she had the headache and must take her leave. Lady Morthman promised to call when there were further developments, and the Dowager and her entourage made their way home to spend a comfortable hour planning their strategy.

Miss Eliza was set the task of cultivating a friendship with Mrs. Jarrett in order to keep abreast of the doings of the family; Miss Jane volunteered to watch Lord Peter and the young lady he was determined to pursue; and the Dowager took on the task of persuading Miss Lorna Jarrett that she was a worthy confidante and adviser.

As they prepared to go up to bed at last, Miss Eliza said, "At least, your Grace, if Lord Peter is determined to court Miss Melanie, he will be in constant contact with Miss Lorna, for they must meet all the time."

"And surely when they are so much together, he will come to recognize her good qualities," Miss Jane chimed in.

"True, very true," the Dowager agreed, sweeping some wisps of hair from her eyes. "If only he can keep his hands from her throat until that time, and Miss Lorna will refrain from shooting him in a fit of rage. But we must not despair, my dears. I have every confidence that we will win through in the end."

The Dowager would not have been so complacent if she had seen the sweet, tremulous smile Miss Melanie bestowed on Lord Peter at the theater the next evening, or the grateful grin her great-nephew returned as he tenderly pressed her hand. Mr. Jarrett, who had accompanied his daughter and niece to the play, received a warm handshake and some genial talk, but Miss Lorna Jarrett had to make do with a cold stare and the most infinitesimal bow.

4

It seemed to Lorna in the days that followed that she was constantly in the company of the despised Lord Peter Truesdale, for no matter where the Jarretts went, he was sure to turn up beside them at some point during the evening. Not only that, he began to call in St. James's Place, and when he was not there, his footman was at the door with flowers or notes for Melanie. It was all very uncomfortable, especially since her aunt expected her to act as Melanie's chaperone. There was no way she could avoid the man, not when she was forced to join him and her cousin for drives in the park, expeditions to Richmond, the Royal Enclosure, and Astley's Amphitheater, and in short, everywhere it pleased Melanie to go.

M'lord did not seem to be bored by these childish amusements, and he derived a great deal of pleasure from Melanie's enjoyment of the various spectacles that London had to offer.

The coldness with which he had treated Lorna after the Grant ball gradually abated as they were forced more and more into each other's company, and although he was always stiff and formal in his manner to her and never favored her with a smile, at least he did begin to include her in the conversation. Lorna did not consider this an improvement. He treated her as if she were some sort of retired governess who had been pressed into service as a duenna. Sometimes she longed to hit him, and more than once she almost screamed in frustration, but she swallowed her anger. She had decided that nothing the man said would cause her to lose her temper and lash out at him, no matter how provocative his remarks.

Melanie's attitude toward the Earl was difficult for her to understand. From an abject terror of the man, in a short time she seemed to have grown to depend on him as her primary flirt, and it was evident that she enjoyed the way he took care of her, gently inquiring if there was anything she required, shielding her from crowds, or fastening her cloak for her against the cold. Lorna could have shaken her for the coquettish smiles she bestowed on Lord Peter, and lowered lashes and girlish blushes with which he was honored. She could see that the Earl was being extremely careful not to frighten Melanie with any loverlike gestures or too direct expressions of his growing regard. Indeed, he behaved in an exemplary manner that she would not have believed possible of him, always kind and considerate and much more apt to tease Melanie as a child than make love to her as a grown woman.

He was also careful not to expose her to the gossip that was sure to result from too much time spent at her side in public, and although he always came to her sooner or later at any party and signed her card twice at a dance, he did not single her out in such a way as to damage her reputation. In fact, he often asked another gentleman or two to join them on their expeditions, and to Lorna's fury he often chose Sir Digby Fortescue as her particular escort.

Besides Lord Peter, Melanie began to assemble a little court of admirers, not the least of whom was Lord Landford. He pursued her with an almost desperate devotion, as if he were only too aware that Lord Peter could easily cut

im off. Lord Landford was much the better-looking of the
two men, with his handsome, open face and curly brown
hair, but he was only twenty-five and slight of stature, and
no match for the older, more debonair Lord Peter, with his
powerful build and teasing gray eyes.

Lorna knew her cousin was proud of having conquered
such a man of the world, even though Melanie never sought
her out to discuss it. Between them there remained some
little uneasiness that Lorna knew was the result of the way
she had sent Lord Peter away after her first assessment of his
character. And so, while Melanie might chat of what Lord
Landford had written to her, or how Mr. Wilton had whispered the most delightful compliments in her ear, Lorna
was never allowed to hear anything Lord Peter had said or
how Melanie had replied.

It hurt Lorna to see her cousin grow secretive and aloof,
and sometimes she longed to go to her and put her arms
around her and tell her that she only wanted her to be
happy, and if her happiness depended on having the Earl as
a husband, she would try to be glad for her. But when she
considered doing this, she realized that deep inside she still
thought him an unfit husband for her cousin. Any man who
could speak to a woman the way he had spoken to Lorna,
any man who would force her to accept an embrace so
brutally, was not the man for innocent, fragile little Melanie
Barrett. Lord Peter did not fool her, not for a moment, she
told herself, and sometimes when he rose from bending
attentively over her cousin, she could not help but give him a
direct stare, as if she were asking him what he thought
he was about.

Lord Peter himself was deriving a great deal of satisfaction from Lorna's discomfort and suspicions. He knew she
hated to be in his company, hated to see him making so
much of her cousin, and was wary of his motives, but there
was nothing she could do about it.

He had no intention of proposing to Melanie, of course,
which was the primary reason he guarded her reputation so
carefully. After only a single meeting he knew that they did
not share a single thought in common, and she was just as
boring as his great-aunt had claimed. Marriage might be a
dull affair, he told himself, but there was no need to allow it

to drive him insane. He had worried a bit that his attentions might be unfair to the girl and raise expectations that he had no intention of gratifying, but from certain things she let fall in her conversation he realized that although flirt with him she might, she did not propose to marry anyone for a long time. Miss Melanie was thoroughly enjoying her new popularity and was not about to abandon it, for the rosebud was opening to bask in Society's sunshine with a vengeance. Reassured that she was gaining as much consequence from his attendance as he was gaining revenge by courting her, he continued on his course.

Where this situation was likely to lead he never considered, but he waited patiently, sure that sooner or later Lorna would betray herself and take him to task for his attentions to her cousin. He could hardly wait for her to do so, for he had stored up several unanswerable phrases that were sure to vanquish her in short order.

Her only ally that he could see was Mr. Jarrett, who was still so formal in his manner it was obvious that he had not made up his mind whether to approve Lord Peter or not. Lady Morthman, needless to say, was delighted and had even stopped sniffing whenever Lorna appeared; and Mrs. Jarrett, who was finally beginning to come down to the drawing room for short periods each day, was all complaisance and smiles. Left to those two ladies, he might take Miss Melanie and welcome, anytime he wished.

After a week of even lower temperatures than London had already been enduring—the weather this winter was the coldest in recent memory—Lord Peter arranged to escort both girls on an inspection of the Thames. People were already discussing the possibility of another Frost Fair, for the Thames was almost solid ice from one bank to the other.

He arrived promptly at two on the afternoon that had been appointed for the outing, and after making Melanie have her maid bring her a warmer pair of mitts and a woolen muffler, he led the way to his Town carriage. Melanie was always delighted to ride in this smart equipage, and today she smiled her thanks to the Earl when she saw he had provided hot bricks and fur rugs to ensure their comfort.

Lorna was not too surprised to see Sir Digby Fortescue

there to help her to her seat, and after a short discussion of which pair preferred to sit with their backs to the horses, Lorna and Sir Digby winning through easily, the Earl announced they would go to Westminster Bridge, where they would have the best view of the river, and the carriage set off.

During the short drive, Lorna conversed with Sir Digby, who took his duties as escort very seriously indeed. After inquiring about her health and asking her if she had enjoyed Mrs. Booth's musicale the previous evening, he complimented her on her fur-lined cloak and told her she was as pretty as a picture.

Lorna could have wagered a fortune on his opening conversational gambits, for he always began their meetings exactly the same way. Since she was out on this icy day, it must be obvious to anyone of the meanest intelligence that her health was excellent, and since Sir Digby had sat beside her in Mrs. Booth's drawing room last evening and heard her enthusiastic applause, and since he had complimented her on her blue cloak at least four times previously and always admired her looks, Lorna was hard put to control her expression and appear gratified. She stole a glance at Lord Peter and turned away quickly when she saw the gleam of amusement in his gray eyes at her predicament.

They left the carriage on the northern side of the bridge and walked halfway across the span, Melanie holding tight to Lord Peter's arm and already beginning to complain of the cold. Lorna took Sr. Digby's arm and walked quickly, as was her habit, soon passing their companions in her enjoyment of the fresh air and tangy breeze.

Sir Digby had grown use to Miss Lorna's stride, although he secretly considered it too mannish. He was used to ladies who took tiny steps and dawdled rather than stepped out so briskly. As they walked, Lorna breathed deeply and watched the gulls wheeling and crying overhead. When they reached the middle of the bridge, they leaned against the parapet. Only here was there any break in the ice and some small floes moving swiftly downstream with the tide, the dark cold river speeding them on their way.

Lorna was fascinated, and when Lord Peter and Melanie reached them, she said, "It is hard to imagine the river will ever completely freeze over, the current is so very strong."

"The floes that you see, Miss Jarrett, will return on the next tide," Lord Peter said. "I was by this way only a few days ago, and already the ice is thicker, the open water narrower."

"I should never dare to go out on it, never," Melanie exclaimed, her eyes wide.

"Not even if I am with you to protect you, Miss Melanie?" Lord Peter asked. "You cannot fear I would ever allow *you* to go where it is not safe."

Melanie laughed and said of course she knew she could trust him, and Lorna gritted her teeth.

"I have heard that the river froze twice before, and that great fairs were held on the ice," Sir Digby announced in his pleasant baritone. "There were booths built from one shore to the other, and bullbaiting and all manner of games and amusements, and people drove their carriages and teams right onto the ice past the ships that had not sailed in time and were held fast till spring."

Lorna, looking back at the north shore below the massive walls of Westminster Hall, noticed a small schooner and several fishing dories heeled over in the grip of the ice, and could well believe it.

"Yes, the first fair lasted from December 1683 to February '84, and the river froze again in 1740. Perhaps we will see the same sight in 1814 — a once-in-a-century opportunity," Lord Peter informed them.

Studying the frozen river which was glittering in the weak winter sunlight, Lorna murmured, "The Silver Thames — how true the name is today."

Lord Peter looked interested in spite of himself. "That was Dryden's name for it, was it not, Miss Jarrett?"

She brushed back an auburn curl that had escaped her hood and smiled at him, forgetting their enmity for a moment as she quoted, "The Silver Thames, her own domestic food, Shall bear her vessels like a sweeping train, And often wind, as of his mistress proud, With longing eyes to meet her face again."

Lord Peter's eyebrows rose, recalling their feud. "My dear Miss Jarrett! I beg you to remember Miss Melanie's innocence and tender years. If I had thought you were about to quote those loose lines, I would never have encouraged you, though I must compliment you on your knowledge. I was not aware that you were such a—such a *scholar!*"

His deep voice mocked her and Lorna silently cursed herself for letting down her guard, as Melly gave a silvery laugh. "Oh, Lorna is a great reader. She shows us all the way, but she is not a bluestocking, m'lord, not at all."

She was so earnest in her defense that Lorna's heart warmed to her, but all the Earl would say was "Indeed?" in his most disbelieving voice as he shook his head at them both.

Sir Digby, who was looking astounded, recovered himself when he noticed Lorna's tiny shiver. Not realizing it was from rage, he insisted they leave the bridge at once. "Too cold by half for the ladies, m'lord. I must insist. Come away and let us drive to Grillon's Hotel for tea."

He held out his arm and Lorna was quick to accept it, allowing him to lead her from the bridge without comment as she fought to control her temper. Sir Digby was so busy promoting the coming tea party and telling her how much better she would feel when she was inside the hotel and warm again, that he did not notice her angry eyes and set expression. When the four of them were once again seated in the carriage, she had herself under firm control and was able to look into Lord Peter's triumphant eyes with cool indifference.

A few evenings later, as she was seated beside Melanie at a small dance given by Lady Jersey, Lord Peter came up to claim his dance with her cousin. Melanie was about to rise when she heard the musicians begin to play a waltz.

"You must excuse me, m'lord, for I am not allowed to waltz yet. I have not been granted permission by the patronesses of Almacks, and in Lady Jersey's own drawing room I should never dare."

Lord Peter nodded and was about to take the gilt chair beside her when she added, "But do ask Lorna, m'lord! Of course *she* can waltz, and she is so graceful."

Lorna did not know whether this altruistic gesture on Melly's part to find her a partner sprang from a desire to ease the tension between the two of them, or from a madcap sense of mischief-making, but she demurred quickly. "No,

thank you, Melanie. I have been on the floor almost continually and would be glad of the chance to sit out for a
while."

"But I insist," her cousin said, smiling from one to the
other and ignoring Lord Peter's frown and Lorna's indignant stare. She had seen Sir Digby bearing down on them
and was looking forward to a *tête-à-tête* with him as soon as
she rid herself of the Earl and her cousin.

Now she pointed at Lord Peter and added in a disappointed, small-girl voice, "You have often said you wish only
to please me, m'lord, but when I make a small request of
you, you hesitate. I will fear all your words are light, sir, and
not to be taken seriously."

The Earl rose and bowed to Lorna. "I should of course be
delighted to oblige you by dancing with your cousin, if that
is your wish, Miss Melanie, Miss Jarrett?"

His voice was carelessly indifferent and Lorna wished she
might still refuse, but something that she did not seem to
have any control over made her rise and take his hand. The
tingle she felt at his warm strength did nothing to prepare
her for the breathless shiver she could not control when he
put his arms around her to draw her close. As Lorna put her
left hand on his shoulder, she felt the muscles tighten under
his well-tailored gray evening coat and almost missed her
first steps. Neither of them had spoken a word since they left
Melanie's side, and Lorna knew that to continue silent
would bring them to the attention of the other guests and
cause comment.

Struggling to appear normal, she said, "What a lovely . . ." just as Lord Peter remarked, "How well you . . ."
And then they both stopped speaking together.

"How well you dance, Miss Jarrett," the Earl began again
in his deep voice, still carefully colorless. "But then, having
been out so many years, it would be a great surprise if you
had not mastered the waltz—and a great many other things
as well."

Furious, Lorna looked up into that dark, hard face so
close to hers, then lowered her eyes, all the angry replies in
her mind fragmented in a kaleidoscope of incoherence as his
grasp tightened a little so he could lead her in a sweeping
turn. She was very much aware of the hard buttons of his

evening coat, the massive expanse of his chest, and the muscles of his thighs as they brushed against hers. His warm breath stirred in her hair and she could smell the masculine scent of him over the faint cologne he used. She was more disturbed than she cared to admit to herself. Being held so close in his arms reminded her vividly of the day at Jarrett Hall when he had forced her to kiss him. Her high color faded a little as she answered in a low voice, "Thank you, m'lord." It was the only remark she felt capable of making.

She felt his hand tighten even more at her waist, the heat of it burning through her thin ball gown of ivory silk, and she steeled herself not to lean back against his powerful forearm. If she drew away, he would know how much he was affecting her. She could not know that he was remembering that December day as well, especially how she had felt in his arms, and that he could not help admiring her smooth bare shoulders and the full breasts half-concealed by the taut silk, so provocatively crushed against his chest. As they danced on, he noticed that the top of her auburn curls came just to the level of his jaw, and he wished she would look up again into his face, instead of refusing to meet his eyes. The silence between them continued until he controlled himself and said blandly, "I have made a perfectly innocuous remark, Miss Jarrett, and now it is your turn."

"What a lovely party! Lady Jersey is to be congratulated, don't you agree?" Lorna asked, her blue eyes seeking his gray ones for a brief second. She caught a tiny breath at the light she saw gleaming there, and lowered her lashes in confusion. I am behaving just as childishly as Melly does, she thought to herself, furious with her fast-beating heart, which he could hardly fail to notice, pounding as it was right against his ribs, and with the inane remarks she was making. It was as if all her wits had gone begging at his nearness and left behind only a simpering, silly girl.

"Very pleasant indeed. Do you think the weather will continue cold?" Lord Peter asked, as if determined to be just as socially inept.

"I have no doubt of it, unless it comes on to thaw," Lorna replied, thinking that not even sir Digby had ever subjected her to such an empty-headed conversation.

"How disappointed Melanie will be if it turns warm,"

Lord Peter remarked next, since it was clearly his turn. "She is looking forward so to the Frost Fair."

Lorna only nodded, wondering if the music would ever end. Lord Peter, disturbed by his reactions to this woman he had vowed to bring to her knees, said brutally, "I hope you will lend us your consequence that day, Miss Jarrett, for I would never expose Melanie to the rough element that is sure to be present or the gossip that might arise if we attended the fair alone together."

The music swept to a close, and Lorna was quick to draw away and curtsy. She felt much more herself now that he had released her, and too repay him for his insults, she said sweetly, "I doubt you have anything to fear, sir, for surely everyone will think you are giving your young daughter a special treat."

Lorna smiled when she saw the flash of anger in those disturbing gray eyes, but they were quickly shuttered by the Earl's bow.

"I thank you for the compliment, Miss Jarrett, but I can assure you I was not so precocious a lover at the age of seventeen. At least I do not think I was. It is hard to remember— so many women, so many love affairs, as I'm sure you, from your own experience, must agree," he added pensively.

She turned to leave the dance floor, indignant at this plain speaking. She might not be the little innocent Melanie was, but to treat her as a sophisticated woman who had been involved with countless lovers was insulting in the extreme.

As she reached her cousin's side, Sir Digby rose reluctantly and offered her his chair, and her smile for him was as warm as she could make it.

Across the room, Miss Eliza was finishing her account of the dance. "She has returned to Miss Melanie now, Your Grace, and she had a wonderful smile for Sir Digby. Oh, dear, do you think that perhaps—"

"Nonsense!" the Dowager snorted. "I am sure she is only using him to taunt Peter. How I wish I had been able to hear what they said while they were dancing."

"It is too bad," Miss Jane agreed, "but Eliza told you how close he held her, and how she refused to look at him most of the time, as well as how angry they both seemed to be as they left the floor."

"If only the gel would trust me," the Dowager mourned, peering across the room at the blurred figures they were discussing. "I have asked her to confide in me as she would her mother, time out of mind, but although she is all that is polite, she claims she has nothing to confide. What a farradiddle! It is impossible to insist she speak when she is not a relative. But I do not despair; I shall be more direct at next meeting, and then we shall see."

"But Mrs. Jarrett says it is only a matter of days before Lord Peter declares himself, so what good will that do?" Miss Eliza warned her, and then she sighed. Her visits to Mrs. Jarrett had been hard to bear. By this time she felt as knowledgeable as a physician in the diagnosis and treatment of any number of physical disorders, for when her new bosom bow was not crowing about her daughter's conquest, she was endlessly discussing her ill health. Miss Eliza did not find either topic intriguing.

"It is true he is often with the girl," Miss Jane agreed. "I heard him teasing her only the other evening at the musicale, and calling her Melly. If he has reached the stage where he uses her pet name, Your Grace, I fear Mrs. Jarrett is right."

"Pooh! Do not regard it; I will never permit that marriage. I will even kidnap my great-nephy if necessary to keep him captive until he regains his senses, but propose to Miss Melanie he shall not." She thought for a moment and then she tossed her head, causing some hairpins to go flying and part of her chignon to fall down. "I shall send for Peter tomorrow and insist he tell me what is on his mind. From what you have related, my dears, I do not feel we can delay any longer, and perhaps his explanation will give us a clue as to what direction we should now take in this frustrating affair."

Lord Peter was not pleased to receive his great-aunt's summons early the following morning. He wondered when the old lady slept, for her note was waiting for him beside his breakfast plate. He had seen her at the dance the night before and knew she had not left it until late; surely at her age she required a great deal of sleep to recoup her strength? He himself was feeling out of sorts this morning, dull and heavy and somehow disappointed.

His mind kept returning to that waltz with Miss Jarrett. Would the girl never lose her temper? How much longer would he be forced to play the suitor to her cousin before she took him to task and reproached him for his attentions? He knew he had disturbed her, though; he had noticed how her breasts lifted and fell in the ivory gown with her quick breathing. As this picture returned to his mind, he shifted in his chair and stared out the window of the breakfast room at the gray winter day, noticing that it looked like snow. There was that quiet stillness in the air that so often presaged a storm.

I will not think about her, he told himself. It was not as if he had not held many breathless ladies in his arms before, and been pleased to see the power he had over them. So why had he himself been so perturbed by Miss Lorna Jarrett's nearness—for if he were to be honest with himself, he must admit she had had a most disturbing effect on him. And why had he felt such a stab of anger when he saw her warm smile for Sir Digby, that smile that showed the deep dimple in her cheek that he found almost impossible to bring out of hiding? For one moment he had even thought of pulling her away from the man and forcing her to remain beside him. The foolish thoughts of a moonling, he reproached himself. Next I will be writing an ode to her left earlobe. How maudlin and how strange. She must be a witch.

He was prompt to make his call at the hour the Dowager had set, although he was a little dismayed to find her companions missing. When Great-aunt Agatha received him alone, it generally meant an unpleasant half-hour or so was in store for him.

She allowed him to pour them both a glass of Madeira, then she began her attack almost as soon as he had taken a seat across from her. "Now, my good man, I insist you tell me what you are about to do pursuing that silly little girl so assiduously?" she demanded. "She has more hair than wit and is not at all up to your weight. Ha! Might as well mate a hummingbird with a falcon."

Her nephew swallowed his wine the wrong way at her bluntness and was forced to resort to his handkerchief in a coughing fit as the Dowager plowed on. "And furthermore, I have told you that the match no longer has my approval. Are you trying to be deliberately difficult? Perhaps you think to pay me back for sending you to Dorset in the first place? Or perhaps it is because Miss Lorna was so disobliging as to refuse you and scorn your manly charms? I quite understand your chagrin if that is the case, but what does constantly seeking the company of her cousin prove? I fail to see why her admiration for you atones for her cousin's indifference. Well, man, have you nothing to say for yourself? Speak up!"

She leaned forward, her dark-gray taffeta gown crackling as she fixed him with a nearsighted eye.

"I should be delighted to do so, if I am ever given the chance," her great-nephew replied coolly, restoring his handkerchief to his pocket. "I hesitated to interrupt until you had, er, run down, ma'am."

"Well?" the Dowager demanded. "I have run down now!"

"I told you all this before, Aunt Agatha. I have discovered I have a definite *tendre* for Melanie. You yourself advised me to choose her because she was so young and compliant, and I could mold her to my will with ease. Your very words, ma'am."

He paused while his great-aunt raised her chin and gave him a darkling look, and then he added, "Besides, as you pointed out, I greatly dislike having my will crossed. I doubt Miss Melanie, unlike her saucy cousin, would even try."

"And so you will marry to spite Miss Lorna, will you? And spend the rest of your life being bored to death just to prove you could make her cousin accept you? Men!" The Duchess snorted in disgust, shaking her head at his folly.

Her great-nephew frowned at her, but the Dowager was not as easily intimidated as the rest of the world.

"Take that Friday face away at once, sir," she ordered, pointing her wineglass at him. "I have never thought you devoid of intelligence or of good sense either, Peter, but this latest start of yours makes me wonder."

Peter was becoming so angry at her interference in his affairs that he made up his mind not to tell her he had no intention of offering for Melanie, and never had had, and as she paused to sweep aside the wisps of hair that had escaped her cap, he said, "It is of course kind of you to concern yourself with my affairs, ma'am, but I go my own way. I will not be commanded, not even by you."

The Dowager put her wineglass down on the table beside her chair with a snap that threatened the delicate crystal stem. "I do not think I have ever seen a more unsuitable bride for you than Melanie Jarrett," she said, ignoring his independent words just as if he had not spoken at all. "She is weak and boring, and although I grant you she is a pretty little thing, her beauty is not the kind that endures. In twenty years she will still be weak and boring—and faded as well. That is, she will be if she survives that long. Being married to you, nephy, is more apt to send her into a decline than into raptures. Can it be possible that you really want a wife who spends her life on an invalid's couch in a darkened room surrounded by medicines and potions?"

"I suppose you consider Miss Lorna Jarrett to be more suitable, ma'am?" Lord Peter asked, his deep voice harsh with distaste. "She is certainly healthy."

The Dowager peered at him. Could it be possible that dear Peter suspected what she was about? It cannot be, she reassured herself as she took up her glass again and sipped to give herself a few moments to consider her reply.

"Infinitely more suitable, but then she refused you, has she not? A shame, because with her by your side you would never be bored or teased by trivia, or subjected to spells of ill health. And she would be so good for you, dear Peter. I'd wager she'd stand toe to toe with you and fight for whatever she felt was her right. You would not ride roughshod over that lady, and a very good thing, too, for you are beginning to tend toward arrogance."

Lord Peter started, his harsh face reddening at this insult, but the Dowager did not notice. "Yes, you are arrogant, wanting your own way in everything. Believe me, a little humble pie now and then has been the saving of many such a man as yourself before now. I advise you to forget the fragile bud and apply yourself to capturing the rose."

"I am of course desolate to be unable to grant you your wish, Your Grace, but I have no intention of trying to capture the rose. In fact, 'tis an interesting title for the lady, and not one I would have chosen myself. To my mind, she appears more a nettle or a thorn in the flesh. Physically we may be suited, I grant you that, but in no other way is she acceptable to me. I would prefer to be bored by Miss

Melanie, even as sickly as she may become, than to be constantly embroiled in the arguments and scenes that life with that ill-mannered shrew would be sure to produce. Thank you, but no, thank you!"

The Dowager felt a little thrill of exultation. So, he *was* attracted to Lorna, was he? She had known it all along! She allowed him to change the subject, and for the remainder of his visit he appeared to have accepted his ultimatum with a good grace he would not have believed possible of her. He did not question her interest in his activities for the coming week, especially the day he was to escort Miss Melanie to the Frost Fair. The Thames had frozen solid at last, and the booths were already being erected, and in better humor now, he invited his great-aunt to join his party if she should wish to see the sights. She declined this treat by inventing a touch of rheumatism that she claimed cold weather always exacerbated, the two parted company, peace between them restored.

For at least half an hour after Lord Peter left the house, the Dowager sat on in the drawing room by herself, deep in thought. At last she rose, putting up her chin and smoothing her taffeta gown with determination as she went to the bellpull to summon her companions. Yes, she would do it! It was risky, and failure would bring censure down on her head, but she had never let such paltry considerations sway her once she had made up her mind she was doing the right thing. Nor did the amount of preparations that must be made so the timing would be perfect deter her, for with dear Eliza and Jane to assist her, she was sure she could not fail.

And if Miss Lorna Jarrett refused in the end, she would find a way to make all right for the girl. The Dowager chuckled to herself. Somehow she did not think Miss Lorna would refuse.

5

Besides the Dowager, there were several other people very interested in the courtship of Lord Peter and Miss Melanie. However, none of them were as astute as that lady was, or as clever in interpreting information, and so they continued in even more ignorance of the true state of affairs than she did.

Lord Landford was having a difficult time these days speaking to Lord Peter with any degree of camaraderie. He found himself falling more and more under Miss Jarrett's spell each time they met. Melanie did not intend to depress his expectations; indeed, she encouraged any gentleman to dangle after her with complete impartiality, and it would have been a very dull young lady indeed who could not recognize from his fervent notes and tender smiles and sighs that he was well and truly smitten. Melanie liked Lord Landford: he was a pleasant young man and reminded her of her country beaux — that is, he did whenever she spared a thought for those distant gentlemen.

Sir Digby Fortescue also wondered what Lord Peter was up to. The Earl certainly appeared to be pursuing Miss Melanie with every wile at his disposal, but Sir Digby noticed he never drew any closer to the conclusion he appeared to seek so avidly. And then there was the way he treated Miss Lorna Jarrett. On many occasions in Sir Digby's company, he had been almost rude to her. This behavior caused a few vague stirrings of chivalry in Sir Digby's breast, though not the indignant feelings of a man in love. Sir Digby had discovered, after not too many hours spent in Miss Lorna's company, that she was not at all the woman for him. True, she was beautiful and spirited and intelligent, but it was not in the power of such an amazon, so sure of herself and so independent, to make him fall in love with her.

Instead, Sir Digby found himself falling head over heels in love with her cousin. Sweet little Melanie! So dear and helpless, and so in need of a strong supporting arm and masculine guidance. Sir Digby hoped he was not raising false hopes in Miss Lorna's mind by seeking her company so often, but there was no way he could make himself stay away from the Jarretts, not when the little darling was to be one of the party. He suspected Miss Melanie was not indifferent to him either, and on the evening of Lady Jersey's ball, he went home in a fog of happiness, after having the joy of sitting and conversing with her alone throughout what he was sure was the shortest waltz that had ever been performed.

Lorna, of course, would not have agreed with him. The waltz had seemed endless to her, and when it was over, she had wished she might go home at once. There was a faint shadow in her eyes, and an ache in her heart, for Lord Peter's haughty insults had made her miserable. It was the outside of enough to have to watch the man hovering over her cousin and once even raising her hand to his lips when he thought they were unobserved. *Not that it matters whose hand he kisses*, she told herself as she tried to find a comfortable spot in bed several hours later, *as long as it is not Melanie's!*

Lorna had been summoned to the Dowager once again, two days after the ball, and could not understand the suppressed air of excitement of the elderly lady, or the smiles and winks of her companions when they came in to join them for tea. The Dowager had tried to get her to talk of Lord Peter, a subject Lorna was aware took up entirely too much of her time when she was alone, but she had no intention of discussing the man with his great-aunt. After admitting he waltzed very well for a man of his height and build, and yes, she did find him astute and witty, and bang up to the echo as well, she firmly changed the subject. She was glad when the Dowager began to discuss the Frost Fair.

"I would advise you, my dear Miss Jarrett, to be on your guard while you are attending the fair," the Dowager said, holding out her cup for Miss Eliza to refill. "There is sure to be a rough element. Perhaps you have heard of the gangs of river thieves with which the Thames is plagued? Night-Plunderers, and Scuffle-Hunters, and Heavy Horsemen, they call themselves, and they say that the amount of larceny and looting of ships and cargoes that goes on is disgraceful."

Lorna accepted another piece of angel cake. "Indeed? But, Your Grace, surely there will be no danger now that the river is frozen. When I was there last, there were only a few small ships caught in the ice. Perhaps the thieves have been forced to abandon their evil ways for lack of prey."

"I hope you are right, but they may be up to new tricks now," the Dowager warned. "Of course, you will be with Lord Peter, and he, I am sure, is more than a match for any number of thieves."

"And Sir Digby Fortescue as well," Lorna was quick to add.

"Oh, thank you, I had forgotten him. Are there any more in your party?"

Lorna shook her head, wondering at the Dowager's interest and sudden agitated manner as her hostess continued, "Such a nice man, Sir Digby, I knew his mother. Jane, remind me to ask Sir Digby to call this week. I have not seen him for some time. We must do something special for him in the very near future, for it would be most remiss of us to leave him dangling."

Lorna was surprised to see the plump little woman take a well-thumbed notebook and pencil stub from her sewing bag and mark the name down. She could not help wondering what that was all about. The Dowager did not enlighten her.

Of course Mrs. Jarrett and Lady Morthman were more than just interested in Lord Peter's suit, although the younger of the two was beginning to get impatient.

"I am sure he has had more than enough time, Mama, to fix his interest," she said in her soft, die-away voice. "And I must tell you that Mr. Jarrett is becoming impatient with the length of our stay here and is beginning to make plans to return to the Hall in the very near future."

Lady Morthman drew herself up and all her chins quivered, a sure sign of strong indignation as she replied, "My dear, do not repine. If Mr. Jarrett feels he must return to Dorset, then Mr. Jarrett shall do so—alone! You are much too weak to make the journey as yet, and so I shall tell him, and of course Melly must stay with her mama. After all, she has Miss Lorna and I to take her about."

Mrs. Jarrett nodded and her expression brightened: her husband was no match for her mama. "Perhaps I should just put a hint in Lord Peter's ear, Mama? I know he would wish to apply to Mr. Jarrett for permission to address Melanie, and I would spare him that long tiresome journey to Jarrett Hall. It might be just the thing to bring him up to scratch."

Lady Morthman agreed, advising her daughter only to be careful how she went about it. "Gentlemen, as you know, my dear Mary, do not like to feel they are being led, or . . . *crowded* in any way. You must be subtle and just mention it in passing."

Just then Miss Eliza was announced, and Lady Morthman went away to oversee the fitting of a pale-green cloak and hood she had ordered for her granddaughter to wear to the Frost Fair. It had a matching gown and little half-boots trimmed with fur, as well as a huge fur muff. As Melanie modeled it for her, Lady Morthman did not see how any gentleman could resist the girl, so pretty was she with her hazel eyes sparkling in anticipation of the treat in store.

Melanie was not the only one who was busy preparing for the fair. Many visitors came to the Dowager's town house in Berkeley Square that week, some of them such strange types that any other butler would have referred them to the service entrance if he did not shut the door in their faces with hearty disdain instead. The Dowager's butler had been with the lady since her wedding, however, and consequently did not blink an eye at admitting the men she had summoned to attend her.

During this same period, Miss Jane could be seen leaving town in a post chaise. She was gone only for one day, which was most unusual for the amount of baggage she carried with her, although when she returned, the chaise was empty.

Lorna found Melanie already in the breakfast room on the morning they were to go to the fair. She was glad it had not come on to storm, for she knew her cousin would have been disappointed in any put-off. Although the sky was gray and wintry, and threatened snow in the not-too-distant future, at least it was not as bitter cold as it had been. Melanie chattered with her as she ate her breakfast, and she insisted on pouring them both another cup of coffee to warm them for the hours ahead.

Lord Peter was due to arrive at ten, for he considered the morning hours more suitable for ladies. By afternoon, all the more vulgar elements of London, the pickpockets and prostitutes and pot-valiant riffraff would assemble, and the bullbaiting and cockfighting, as well as the more unsavory gambling games, would be in full swing.

Melanie was ready well in time and looked entrancing in her new outfit. Once again Lorna wore her blue velvet cloak. Although it was the warmest garment she had, she hated to appear in it one more time in Sir Digby's company. But when Lord Peter's Town carriage pulled up before the door, only the Earl appeared to climb the front steps and bang the knocker. As he escorted the young ladies to the carriage, he explained that Sir Digby had been unable to attend at the last moment and had sent his most abject apologies. He had not said what the reason was for his defection.

"What a shame he has to miss the fun," Melanie pouted, her bright expression fading a little, for while Lorna had been dreading Sir Digby's oft-repeated compliments, she had been looking forward to hearing him admire her new outfit. She settled herself in the carriage with a little flounce. Lord Peter had not even noticed how the green complimented her hazel eyes or how beautiful her fur muff was. It was too bad!

Lord Peter insisted Lorna sit beside her cousin while he took the seat facing back. "I am afraid you will have to make do with me, ladies," he said with a warm smile for Melanie, making her wonder if he could see into her mind. "But I am honored to be the escort of such loveliness, Miss Melanie. You look like one of the tenderest shoots that bloom in April in that soft green—it is most becoming."

"And Lorna, too," Melly prompted, squeezing her cousin's gloved hand.

"Of course," Lord Peter said, glancing toward her companion with an uninterested expression. "I hesitated to mention your cloak, Miss Jarrett. It is difficult to know what to say when Sir Digby has been before me so many times in admiring it. He has such a polished address, it is hard for another to follow him with any degree of, er, originality, don't you agree?"

Lorna inclined her head, her heart sinking. Lord Peter had not abandoned his taunting, nor was his expression for her any warmer. Somehow she had thought that after their waltz, he might mellow a bit or cry truce, and she had been looking forward to meeting him halfway. She turned to look out at the street they were traveling, swallowing her disappointment.

Because Melanie could not believe it was safe, she begged the Earl not to have the carriage driven onto the ice, and Lord Peter banged on the roof with his cane as they neared Westminster Bridge.

"We shall leave the carriage here by Westminster Hall," he announced. "It will be farther to walk, but space has been set aside for the conveyances of the gentry."

"The walk will not bother us, will it Lorna? Isn't this wonderful?" Melly asked, sitting on the edge of her seat in her excitement.

Lorna thought she appeared to be about one and ten in her childish anticipation. Was she going to be disappointed when she discovered it was only an ordinary fair, much like the ones she was used to in Dorset? Did she think that because it was held in London on a frozen river there would be all kinds of magical entertainment even at this time of year, balloon ascensions, wondrous fireworks, and glorious trinkets to buy, and the Prince Regent with all his lords and ladies in attendance? She stole a look at Lord Peter and caught his eye for a moment as she shook her head. He nodded, seeming to know without her even saying a word what she was worried about.

The three of them, followed by a footman, made their way to the river, Melanie for once keeping up with her long-legged cousin and tall escort, for she fairly skipped along, chattering all the way. Lord Peter looked about him carefully, until he saw other ladies and gentlemen and several carriages with crests on their side panels already on the ice. Then he seemed to relax. He helped both girls down a slippery set of steps that ordinarily led to a boat landing, and then onto the ice. In spite of the crowds, the booths, and the carriages, Melanie squealed a little.

"I keep waiting to hear a crack, you see," she explained when Lorna asked her why she had grown so silent.

Lord Peter laughed and tucked her hand in his arms, patting it for reassurance, before he offered his other arm to

Lorna, almost as an afterthought. A dangerous light gleamed in Lorna's blue eyes for a second, but it was quickly veiled. From one side of the river to the other they strolled, greeting such friends as they chanced to meet, and stopping, at Melanie's insistence, at every booth. Lord Peter would not let her use her own money for the fairings she insisted she must have, and the footman was soon loaded down with packages of ribbon and lace, a commemorative fan, and other favors including a cunning glass ball that, when shook, showed a miniature snowstorm. The Earl sent him back to the carriage with the booty.

There were more people arriving at the fair every minute. Lorna could see that some of them were the type the Dowager had warned her to be on her guard against, and so she kept a close watch on Melanie. The child might not be permitted to open her reticule, but there were others there who would be glad to dip their hands into it.

As Melanie stopped to watch a game of bowls, declaring she had never seen anything so amusing as when it was played on the slippery ice, Lorna murmured to the Earl, "How wise of you to bring your footman, m'lord. No doubt your vast experience with women taught you that his services would be required as a cart horse."

She could have bitten her tongue when she saw his harsh features stiffen and his gray eyes grow stern. Of course he thought she was referring to his outrageous remarks the evening of Lady Jersey's ball. She could not help lifting one gloved hand in denial, but Lord Peter did not see the gesture, for he had turned away to her cousin, who wanted to bet a penny on the outcome of the bowling game. After Melanie lost her wager, he bought them all a cup of mulled wine and a seed cake from one of the booths selling food and drink. Lorna was amazed to see the pancakes, corn bread, and bacon being cooked over stoves set on the ice, and remembering the swift, dark current not so far beneath their feet, she could not restrain a tiny shiver herself.

Melanie was easily persuaded that she would not enjoy the bullbaiting that was about to get under way, as much as she would the Punch and Judy show and the dogsled race to follow.

"So charming, your cousin," Lord Peter remarked to

Lorna as Melanie clapped her hands and laughed at Punch's antics. "I do not see how any man could fail to love her, she is so artless and so lovable, and has such a sweet temper. How strange that members of the same family can be so different, don't you agree, Miss Jarrett?" He paused, but since Lorna did not seem inclined to reply, he continued, "It is plain that she needs someone mature and well up to snuff to take care of her in her innocence."

"Her father serves that purpose admirably, m'lord," Lorna could not help snapping.

"Yes, of course," Lord Peter agreed in an almost meek tone. Lorna looked at him, amazed, but then he added, "But in the near future, there is sure to be a husband to take her father's place. *She* will not wither on the vine, of that I am positive. One can only hope that her next suitor will be allowed to speak to Mr. Jarrett before he meets another, er, meddling member of the family."

As Lorna's face paled with anger, he curled his lip in a sarcastic smile, wondering if this thrust would be enough to make her fly at him, but although she opened her lips as if to speak, she just as quickly closed them a moment later and turned away, her head held high.

In doing so, she missed the neatly dressed groom who bowed to Melanie as he slipped her a note and whispered a few words before he faded away into the crowd. It was a simple matter for her to secrete the note in her muff, and only a few minutes later until she could read it, taking advantage of Lord Peter's engaging a friend in conversation, while her cousin, who had grown very silent, stared across the frozen Thames to Southwark.

Lorna was recalled to the present when Melly began to beg to have her fortune told, and Lord Peter replied, "And so you shall, my dear, but there is no need for you to listen to some dirty old hag. Even I can see your future. Shall I tell it to you, Melly?" he teased as they made their way to the gypsy's tent. "Let me see. Shall he be tall, dark, and handsome? I do hope at least two of those attributes will belong to your future husband and the happy ending you are sure to have. You must tell me if the seer mentions Beauty and the Beast to you—I cannot tell you how that would raise my spirits."

Melanie blushed and smiled even as she shook her head, and Lorna thought she had never heard anything so ridiculous as Lord Peter Truesdale playing the eager lover with her little cousin. He is impossible, she told herself. Thank heavens there is no chance that Melanie will ever have him.

Although Lorna had not expressed any desire to have her fortune told, Melanie insisted that she must be first, and she slipped into the tent, leaving her cousin and Lord Peter to maintain any uneasy alliance while they waited for her. Rather than remain by his side, Lorna went to inspect some jars of potpourri on display in a booth across the icy street, and Lord Peter was importuned by a seedy man selling snuff. The Earl sent him on his way in short order and turned to watch Lorna, his dark brows drawn together in a frown. When Lorna looked back and saw him staring at her, she tilted her chin and refused to lower her eyes. For a moment it seemed that all the noise and commotion of the fair, the laughter of the children and the cries of the vendors, faded away, and she was helpless, her eyes locked with his. Then suddenly she remembered Melanie. She put the jar of petals back on the counter and hurried across to join her tormentor.

"Whatever can have happened to Melly, m'lord?" she asked, glad to banish her unruly thoughts for ordinary conversation.

For a moment, Lord Peter did not speak. He continued to gaze down at her face with its direct blue eyes, but her words penetrated the spell he was under.

"You are right. It has been much too long a time for her, with her easily read future, to remain with the gypsy. Perhaps it would be best if you went in to her. I would hate to interrupt some girlish secret," he said, holding the flap of the tent aside so Lorna could walk in. He heard her gasp even before he let the curtain drop; he was quick to join her inside.

There was no one there, no fortune-teller and certainly no Melanie Jarrett, but the Earl strode around, investigating the two rush chairs and the woven baskets and trunk against the walls, while Lorna lifted the dirty gold cloth that covered a small table in the center of the floor. The only light came from a small oil lamp that hung over their heads, and in its flickering light Lord Peter could see that she was very disturbed, although she was trying hard to keep her composure.

"But where could she have gone?" she whispered. "Surely we would have seen her if she came out of the tent, as she must have done when she found no one within."

The Earl ran his hands down the panels of the tent and discovered a small opening that led to the back of the booths. Lorna was beside him in a moment, blinking after the dimness of the tent in the bright light that reflected from the ice.

Lord Peter stared up and down the row of booths, searching through the crowds. It was an attractive scene, full of color and happy sounds, and in the cold, crisp air as sharply etched against the frozen white background as a painting by Brueghel. Here were the revelers strolling about in their bright, colorful cloaks and mittens, there were the children sliding and laughing and throwing snowballs, and beyond them all, the carriages and teams of the *beau monde* clattered over the frozen surface, steam rising from the horses' nostrils and flanks. Even as he watched, one carriage left the ice while another waited to come onto it, but nowhere in sight was there a slender figure in pale green, nor were there any cries of alarm or disturbances to mar the merriment.

"We must assume that for reasons unknown to us, Melanie slipped out of the tent this back way," he said at last, his voice calm but the frown between his dark brows showing his concern. "Tell me, Miss Jarrett, is your cousin given to pranks? Could she be hiding from us as a joke?"

Lorna was about to exclaim that Melanie would never do such a thing, but then she remembered the girl's delight in mischief and was forced to nod her head. "It is possible," she said slowly. "Perhaps she has gone back to the bullbaiting that we would not let her see."

She started forward in that direction eagerly, and the Earl grasped her arm. "Steady, Miss Jarrett! That is probably the explanation, but you will fall if you rush about on the ice. We will inspect the baiting ring, and if she is not there, we will search all the booths and displays. Come, and do not worry."

But Melanie was nowhere to be found. By the time the

pair reached the final booth, Lorna could not control her fears and hung on to the Earl's arm with both hands.

"Oh, what am I to do? Mrs. Jarrett will fall ill again, if indeed she does not die of the shock, and my uncle will never forgive me. I was supposed to watch over Melly and now she has disappeared!"

Lord Peter stared down into her blue eyes, now glistening with unshed tears, and the strange feelings that rose in his breast caused him to speak more harshly than he intended.

"Oh, yes, one can see that you are imagining all kinds of dire events: a kidnapping or a rape or a murder. Or perhaps you envision all three? Come, come, Miss Jarrett! You disappoint me; I never expected one of your caliber to succumb to womanish hysteria." He paused until he saw Lorna's eyes begin to flash that familiar fire as she straightened her back, and then he added in a lighter tone, "If anyone is at fault, it is I, for as her escort she was my responsibility. But we are wasting time. Perhaps she met some friends and has gone off with them, or perhaps she became chilled and went back to the carriage, playing hide-and-seek with us. Shall we return there and see?"

Lorna did not trust herself to speak. What a hateful, insulting man he is, she thought, but since she needed his help, she allowed him to lead her from the ice and up the steps of the boat landing. She could not help remembering the Dowager's warnings about the gangs of river thieves, and picturing in her mind her childlike cousin in their clutches, she matched the Earl stride for hurried stride as he pushed their way through the crowds of merrymakers in the narrow streets. Hateful though he might be, it was comforting to feel his strong arm supporting her, and reassuring to know he was beside her, calm and determined and in complete control.

When they reached the carriage, Melanie was not there. The groom sprang to attention, and Lord Peter opened the door so Lorna could climb in and take a seat.

"I shall just question Paulding here, and if he has not seen Miss Jarrett, we must plan our next move. I rather think a visit to the Thames Marine Police at Wapping might be in order. I am somewhat acquainted with Dr. Patrick Colquhoun, who with the Reverend Mr. Bentham originated the force some years ago. He will help us, I am sure."

Lorna was glad to sink down on the velvet squabs and rest while he questioned his groom, but then she espied a twist of paper on the seat opposite, half-hidden by a fur rug. She reached for it eagerly. When Lord Peter joined her a few minutes later, he found her holding the paper in a trembling hand. Her face, normally so rose-hued and assured, was white and frightened, and her eyes stared at him blankly. Without trying to question her, the Earl took the paper from her nerveless fingers and proceeded to read it, his face growing darker and more forbidding as he did so.

Written in an uneducated hand, the note said that Miss Melanie Jarrett was safe, for the moment at least, but if the interested parties ever wished to see her again, they were to bring two hundred pounds that very day to the Spotted Dog Inn at Croydon, without telling anyone their errand or destination. Further instructions awaited them there.

The Earl read the note again, and now the faintest of smiles twisted his lips. Lorna did not notice.

"Well, now, Miss Jarrett, it appears that your worst fears have been realized. Melanie kidnapped, and by a group that calls itself the Scuffle-Hunters, too," he said in a mild way.

His deep voice, speaking in such ordinary tones broke into her stunned, shocked condition, and Lorna leaned toward him and put out her hand. "Have the goodness to take me home at once, m'lord! I must lay this information before my uncle and then hurry to Melanie's side."

"The note says you must not tell anyone, Miss Jarrett," the Earl pointed out.

"But I must! I do not have the money," Lorna admitted, "and there is no way I could get such a sum in a short time without my uncle's help."

"Miss Jarrett, if you please! It is my responsibility, not your uncle's. We will return to my rooms, where I keep more than enough money on hand for emergencies, and while I am making all ready, Paulding will harness my grays to my racing curricle. Croydon is not that far distant. I daresay we can reach it by midafternoon, collect Miss Jarrett, and restore her to her family by dinnertime with no one the wiser. You must allow me to assist you, for, as I pointed out, the fault for Melanie's disappearance must be laid at my door alone."

Lorna wished she could deny him, but it was such a relief knowing that she did not have to face her uncle with the terrible news, that she nodded. Before the Earl could signal his coachman to start, there was a rap on the coach door, and Lorna looked out to see the Dowager Duchess of Wynne waving and smiling at them.

"Dear Miss Jarrett . . . and my great-nephy, too," she said as her footman opened the door for her. "You see I have succumbed to temptation after all, Peter, and come to see this marvelous Frost Fair for myself."

Accepting the footman's arm, she climbed into the coach. "That will be all, Ames. Tell Miss Eliza that I will be with her in a moment and then wait for me without."

Lorna tried to look pleased, but she was so concerned for Melanie that she could have screamed at this delay. Turning to gauge Lord Peter's reaction, she surprised a grim little smile playing over his shapely mouth.

"Whatever can you find amusing, m'lord?" she asked in her most frigid voice.

"You would be absolutely astounded if you knew, Miss Jarrett," he said in a voice that she could have sworn trembled with inner mirth. "Dear Aunt Agatha, of course! Yes, do join us. I must tell you what has happened, although whether you will be able to believe the tale I do not know. It reminds me forcibly of one of Maria Edgeworth's more fantastic romances, but you shall be the judge."

"We must not tell her," Lorna explained. "Remember the note! We must not tell anyone!"

"But the Dowager Duchess of Wynne is not just 'anyone,' " Lord Peter reminded her. "I think you will find that although my great-aunt knows everything that occurs in London—sometimes even before it happens, you know— she is more than capable of keeping her budget shut. You need not fear her tattling, and somehow I have the strongest feeling that the Duchess is the very person we need to help us out of our dilemma."

"You are too kind, of course, anything I can do," the Dowager agreed, feeling a little flustered and carefully not looking into her great-nephew's face. His rallying words, although complimentary, caused a small, uneasy qualm. But having long before determined on her course of action, she was not to be deterred from it now.

The story was soon told, Lorna joining in after the first few sentences in her relief that they were to have this formidable dame as their accomplice. By the time the two had finished, the Dowager's nearsighted eyes had widened and she had herself in complete control.

"Fore gad, how very singular to be sure," she said. "You are right, Peter, you must both make haste to Croydon and rescue the gel without a word to anyone. The fewer people to know of this the better. Now Lorna," she added, turning to stroke the girl's hand, "it does not appear that Miss Melanie is in any danger, at least for today. Go along with Peter and try not to worry. I think it will be helpful if I went to Lady Morthman's town house and told the family that I have, on a whim, decided to whisk you both, along with the Earl and a few others, down to one of my brother's estates near Croydon, and that if it comes on to snow, you will be remaining there with me overnight. That will put paid to any fears they might entertain if you do not make London tonight, and I can collect such clothing as you will both require at the same time. After you find Miss Melanie, bring her to Tower Hill; Peter knows its direction." She turned back to her quiet great-nephew then and asked, "Are you planning to drive your curricle, dear boy?"

The Earl, who had not taken his eyes from his great-aunt's face, nodded. "With only a tiger up behind," he told her, somewhat irrelevantly. "But stay! Perhaps he would be in the way?"

Her Grace considered this question as she smoothed her gloves. "I do not see why that should be so — unless his extra weight would be a factor? Perhaps you would be wise to dispense with his assistance. Lorna is not missish, and I can see she is anxious to make all speed to her cousin's side."

As Lorna nodded, the Earl's lips twisted in another grimace. He was wondering how his tiger would take the insult, weighing as he did only seven stone, but he did not say anything more as the Dowager called for her footman and climbed down from the carriage. Indeed, he was very silent on the journey to Albany Street, but since Lorna was busy praying for Melanie's safety and trying to think what she must do if her cousin was not to be found at the Spotted Dog, she did not notice his abstraction.

The Earl insisted she rest in his sitting room while he made the preparations, and Lorna noticed that he bade a small maid attend her, while his landlady prepared them both a meal. Lorna would have refused him, for there was a lump in her throat past which she did not feel she could force a single mouthful, but the Earl would not heed her protestations.

"Spare me such foolishness, Miss Jarrett. You will be worse than useless if you faint with hunger later today, and since we do not know when we will be able to eat again, it is best to be prepared. Make yourself comfortable. Molly will get you anything you require. I will not be long."

Lorna did as she was bid, thinking how abrupt and autocratic he was. If there were any other way, she told herself as she sat down to her soup and cheese and bread and the large pot of tea the landlady placed before her, I would refuse all his assistance. How very uncomfortable all this is going to be, to be forced to bear his company alone all afternoon. But I must not think of that. I must remember Melly and put my own feelings aside until she is safe again.

And even if he is impossible and overbearing and arrogant, she thought suddenly, I can think of no other man I would rather have by my side in a situation as bad as this. Strangely reassured, she was able to make a good meal, and in a short time they were on their way, weaving through the London streets in the Earl's racing curricle.

Lorna noticed that there was no tiger up behind, but she did not comment on it, for she was busy wrapping a fur rug about her feet and legs and adjusting the heavy driving cape Lord Peter had thrown over her shoulders. His curricle was built for extreme speed, and there were no amenities like a hood to shelter them from the elements, or thick rugs beneath their feet to defeat the cold drafts that found their way through the thin floorboards. In fact, she thought as she clutched the side of the seat as the Earl took a corner at speed and she was thrown against his shoulder, there will barely be room enough for Melly in this narrow vehicle.

Few words passed between the rescuers until the outskirts

of London had been reached, and then the Earl settled his grays into a steady canter and turned to smile down at her. Lorna, determined to be pleasant, tried to return the smile, but the Earl noticed that that elusive dimple was nowhere to be seen.

6

"Are you warm enough, Miss Jarrett?"

"Quite, thank you, m'lord," she replied, mimicking his scrupulously polite tones, keeping her eyes on the road ahead. "Although what either of us could do about it if I were not, I fail to see."

The Earl smiled. "I am delighted to see that you have recovered your spirits, ma'am, but it is not that long a run to Croydon. I expect to have you drinking some hot coffee at the Spotted Dog by three in the afternoon."

He glanced sideways at her and saw a tiny frown between her brows.

"What will we do if Melanie is not there, m'lord?" she asked.

"I do not expect her to be there," Lord Peter replied calmly. As Lorna started, he added, "These Scuffle-Hunters could hardly keep a lady prisoner in a public house. Moreover, I am well acquainted with Mr. Broadbent, the owner, and I know he would never consent to becoming a party to the crime. No, what we will find at the inn will be another misspelled letter, telling us where to go next."

Lorna thought this over. "Yes, I see you are right. It was foolish of me to think Melanie would be there. I do so hope, however, that she is somewhere warm and safe nearby."

The Earl's lip curled. "I can almost guarantee that Miss Melanie is as safe as either you or I at the moment, Miss Jarrett, and a good deal warmer, and I would be very surprised if we find her more than a few miles from the inn or Tower Hill."

"You are reassuring, sir, but how can you be so positive?"

"I may tell you sometime, but not now. I am not entirely convinced even yet," was all the Earl would reply.

Each lost themselves in their own thoughts then, and they had passed through two small hamlets before Lorna spoke up again.

"Lord Peter! I hope you thought to bring your pistols with you in case we have need of them."

The Earl stared at her resolute face, considerably startled. "We, Miss Jarrett?"

"Of course! If you brought two, I think you should give me one of them so I can hide it in my reticule. Then if the robbers search and disarm you, I can still be of assistance."

The Earl appeared to consider this generous offer gravely. "My compliments, Miss Jarrett. Such foresight is commendable and I admire your spirit. But tell me, are you familiar with firearms? I have my dueling pistols with me and they have hair triggers."

Lorna thought that hair triggers sounded horrible, but she said gamely, "I am not in the habit of firing guns — to be truthful, I have never done so in my life, m'lord — but I am sure I could give a good account of myself if necessary. After all, all one must do is point them and fire, is that not correct?"

"An admirably brief description of shooting, Miss Jarrett. The rub comes in hitting what you are aiming at, and not hitting anything, or more important, *anyone* else. No, in thinking over all the ramifications of allowing a novice to handle one of my pistols, I think we would both be safer if I kept them in my possession."

"But I would be shooting at the kidnappers, m'lord," Lorna persisted. "You need not fear for your safety."

"Even at the expense of being thought of coward, I must refuse. Besides, I do not expect that guns will be at all necessary. Someday I will teach you to shoot, and shoot well, if you like. Would you care for that?" he asked, his voice milder than she had ever heard it before.

"I do not see how there could be any occasion for you to have the opportunity, sir," Lorna replied, putting from her mind the entrancing picture of herself leaning against Lord Peter's broad chest as he corrected her aim and taught her how to culp a wafer. She was so angry at her wayward thoughts that she added, "We are not likely to find ourselves very much in each other's company after today."

The Earl disregarded the conviction in her voice and said in his usual brusque and positive way, "I am desolated to have to contradict you, Miss Jarrett, but if what I suspect is right, we are apt to find ourselves very much in each other's company for some time to come if we are not careful."

Just then, a gust of wind blew Lorna's hood back, and she became very busy tying it again and tucking in the auburn curls that whipped about her face. Another mile thundered away under the grays' hooves before she spoke again, ignoring his last comment.

"How kind the Dowager Duchess is to help us, m'lord. She thought of everything, even to going herself to reassure my aunt and uncle that Melanie and I would be visiting her."

"Knowing my great-aunt, I am sure she has thought of everything," Lord Peter replied. "I do hope she will not be too disappointed if matters do not work out as she has planned."

All of a sudden, he sounded almost grim again, and Lorna stole a glance at his dark, harsh face.

"Yes," he added, "it will be such a pleasure for me to bring this adventure to a successful conclusion of my own making."

Lorna would have liked to ask him what he meant, but just then he pointed his whip at a signpost ahead, and she could see that Croydon was no more than four miles distant. She drew a sigh of relief. Even with the heavy cape and her own fur-lined cloak, she was becoming chilled as the afternoon lengthened. The low clouds above them seemed to be racing with the curricle, and she saw that they were heavy with snow, so that even though it was still only midafternoon, an early winter's dusk was falling.

"I hope we can reach the inn before the snow comes," she remarked, her eyes still searching the sky.

"Have no fear, we will. But I doubt very much if any of us will see London tonight. Well, never mind, there is always great-aunt and her two cronies at Tower Hill if we need a haven after we rescue Melanie."

He saw that Lorna was frowning again and twisting her

hands together, and he said gently, "No harm will come to her or to you, my dear, no harm at all. My word on it."

Her blue eyes sought his steady gray ones for a moment and then she lowered them to her lap again. "Why, sir, how can you make such a rash promise about me, or Melanie either?" she asked, trying for a light tone. "Surely that is boasting. We must pray that no harm will come to any of us, but I myself would prefer to put my trust in Providence rather than in a mere man."

"You have no good opinion of men, Miss Jarrett?" Lord Peter asked in his usual tone, concentrating on his leader as the gray stumbled a bit.

"Some of them, certainly, but I do not consider them infallible, nor do I think they hold the only answers to each and every situation. I have often found the ways of women to be superior to those of men, in fact. Their ways are more subtle and gentle, and they are kinder."

The Earl laughed in derision, the harsh sounds torn away to be lost behind them by the rush of their passage. "I do hope you are of the same opinion tomorrow, Miss Jarrett! Now, where you use the adjective 'subtle,' I am afraid I would substitute 'devious.' We are not like to agree on the superiority of either sex, are we? And since we have traveled so many miles in unexceptional accord without once ripping up at each other, may I suggest another topic? Perhaps one more innocuous? Yes, tell me where you learned to waltz so beautifully instead, Miss Jarrett. I cannot imagine how I missed meeting you if you have spent any time at all in London these past several years."

Lorna could not help the spark of anger that rose in her breast again, for she was sure he was taunting her for the sum of her years. She wished he had not remembered their waltz as she admitted that she had visited Vienna with her mother and father and had had special lessons in the Viennese dance. Her answer was stiff and brief, but the Earl did not notice, for he was forced to give his whole attention to his team and a herd of cattle that was crossing the road ahead of them. Even after all the miles they had run, the grays could not approve of cows, and he had his hands full. Lorna marveled at the strength of those hands in their thick leather gauntlets as he effortlessly controlled his high-spirited horses.

When they were able to proceed at last, they both fell silent again. Lorna had been trying hard to still the anxiety she felt for Melanie's safety as the afternoon wore on, and now she could not help leaning forward as the first small cottages of Croydon appeared on the high road ahead.

"At last!" she breathed in relief.

"Careful, Miss Jarrett! My grays would be insulted if they heard you: we have made very good time. See there on the left ahead is the yard of the Spotted Dog."

He drove deftly through the gates, calling for an ostler in his powerful voice, and in a short time Lorna found herself being lifted down in his strong arms. He held her close for a moment to steady her, and she felt a weakness that had nothing to do with the cold and her exhaustion. She was so angry with herself that she pushed him away much more vehemently than she had intended. One of Lord Peter's eyebrows rose, but he turned to give his orders to the ostler without commenting on her rudeness.

"Do not unharness them as yet, for I am not sure we stay."

"Aye, m'lord." The ostler grinned, leading the team away, and the Earl turned back to find Lorna already mounting the shallow step to the doorway where Mr. Broadbent stood ready to welcome them.

"M'lord? Is it you, then? Come in, come in, and the lady too. A private parlor, m'lord?" he asked, bowing and holding the door wide.

Lorna nodded to him as she stepped into the hall, but her eyes were busy searching for any sign of her cousin.

"Yes, thank you, Broadbent, and some hot coffee for the lady as soon as it can be contrived. But first, has there been any message left for me or perhaps Miss Jarrett? If so, it is important that we see it at once."

Mr. Broadbent stared. "So this be Miss Jarrett! Aye, m'lord, a ruffian, for I can call him nothing less, left a paper for the leddy this noontime. Follow me, sir, and I'll fetch it for you."

He ushered them into his best parlor and bustled away, calling for the fire to be made up, and some hot coffee and a mug of mulled cider brought for m'lord as he did so.

Lorna stood in the middle of the room, making no move to remove her gloves or outer garments, her eyes dark and worried with suspense.

Lord Peter threw his greatcoat and gauntlets on a chair and then strolled over to where she stood. Without asking permission, he calmly took the heavy cape from her shoulders, loosened her hood, and removed the blue cloak as well before he led her to a chair near the fire.

She looked at him as if she did not really see him, and he said in a calm voice, "Steady, Miss Jarrett, steady. If you remember, I told you we would not find your cousin here."

Lorna sighed and held out her hands to the blaze gratefully. The ordinariness of his words seemed to recall her to her own customary good sense, and she nodded. "I remember, m'lord, but still I could not but hope you might be mistaken and Melly would be here to run into my arms, full of the tale of her adventure."

Just then, Mr. Broadbent knocked and entered, followed by a small maid, who set the tray she carried on the table near Lorna. Lorna ignored the steaming coffeepot as she reached for the note her host held in his hands, and she eagerly tore it open to see what was written inside. It was left to Lord Peter to converse with Mr. Broadbent and oversee the pouring of the coffee. By the time he had done so and seen the two out of the door again, Lorna was rereading her note, a deep frown on her face as she did so.

"Bad news, Miss Jarrett?" Lord Peter asked.

"Not exactly . . . I cannot tell . . . but surely it is just as you suspected, and we have only to—. But somehow I cannot like it," she said, and then she looked up and held the note out to him. "But here, you had best read it for yourself."

"I am sure you are right," Lord Peter agreed as he took the note. "Especially since I cannot make head nor tails out of what you say." He read the note out loud as she listened.

Miss Lorna Jarrett;

The lady that you seek is at Rose Cottage, High-woods. Come there at once and bring the money with you and she will be restored to you. It must be today— or else!

"Well, I see nothing so difficult or unusual in that, Miss Jarrett. I do not know this Rose Cottage, but I am sure Mr. Broadbent can assist us. Drink up your coffee and we will be on our way again as soon as you are warm."

"No, let us go at once," Lorna cried, jumping up to put on her cloak and hood again.

"Do try for a little common sense, Miss Jarrett. Rushing about before we know where we are going is fruitless. We have no idea in which direction we must set off or how long a journey we must undertake until I speak to Mr. Broadbent, so you might as well take advantage of this chance to rest and warm yourself. Drink your coffee and be as good as to curb that impetuous nature of yours."

Lorna glared at his retreating back, even as she had to admit he was right. But why did the man have to put up her back almost every time he spoke? He was impossible! She forced herself to take her seat by the fire again and drink her coffee until he returned. The hot, steaming drink laced with brandy calmed her and revived her spirits. Surely she would see Melly soon, it was only a matter of a little more time.

A few minutes later Lord Peter came back and nodded in satisfaction at her empty cup as he tossed off the rest of his hot cider.

As he helped her back into her cloak and hood, he told her what he had learned. "Mr. Broadbent says that Rose Cottage is up beyond the village of Peasely, which is some two miles west of Croydon, but of its precise location he has no idea and suggests we inquire at Peasely. He did say he was sure the cottage was unoccupied and had not been lived in for some time."

Lorna looked up at him anxiously as he tied her hood. "Come, Miss Jarrett, of course it is unoccupied. You cannot be such a goose as to imagine the Scuffle-Hunters would take your cousin to a cottage full of people. Let us be on our way. This adventure becomes a little tiresome, don't you agree?"

By that time, Lorna was in the hall again, thanking Mr. Broadbent for his kindness and smiling at him, so she did not hear the Earl's last murmured words, which was just as well for their continued accord and temporary truce. When she stepped outside the door of the inn, she was dismayed to find that it had begun to snow. The thick white flakes were drifting to the ground in an almost lazy fashion, but she had lived in the country long enough to know that this was no mere flurry and might very well come on to snow all night. Shivering a little, she climbed into the Earl's curricule and tried not to show her impatience when Lord Peter remained to exchange a few quiet words with Mr. Broadbent.

They took the high road out of the village and then turned into a narrow lane. Lorna would have missed the crooked sign that said PEASELY, for not only was it old and faint, it was beginning to be obscured with snow, but Lord Peter seemed to know exactly where he was going. Almost at once, their way led upward as the lane wound through the tall thick hedges with which it was lined. It was impossible to see beyond these hedges, and Lorna hoped they would not meet a farm cart, for there was no room for another conveyance to pass. Still, when the Earl slowed his team to a walk, she asked in impatience, "Can we not go any faster, m'lord?"

"Impetuous as usual, Miss Jarrett. No, we cannot. The lane is narrow and steep and my team is tired. Besides, it is hard to see through the snow, and since the road is strange to me, discretion must be our watchword. If the curricule were to overturn, you would find it most unpleasant at the very least, to say nothing of the fact that it would then be impossible to reach your cousin with any degree of facility or comfort. No, Miss Jarrett, in a word, no."

Lorna subsided, for once again she knew he was right, and besides, from his sarcastic tone she could tell that he was becoming short of temper.

They almost missed the village, if two or three tiny cottages set beside a crossroad could be designated as such. Fortunately there was a light in one of the cottage's windows, and as Lorna grasped the Earl's arm and pointed in its direction, the door opened and a man came out, holding a horn lantern above his head to light his way. As he marched out to the lane and proceeded to make his way down it, completely ignoring the smart London carriage and its two occupants, Lorna cried, "Stop him, m'lord! He can tell us where Rose Cottage is and perhaps even guide us there."

"Ho, there, my good man," the Earl called, and as the farmer turned and waited for the carriage to catch him up, he added, "I would be astounded if he could not, Miss Jarrett. My, how very, er, opportune this meeting is, to be sure. Almost as if it had been planned somehow, don't you agree?"

Lorna ignored him. Surely they must be very close to Melanie now. Lord Peter questioned the farmer, who in broad dialect allowed that, aye, he knew where Rose Cottage was; no, there baint no one livin' in it; and, aye, he supposed he could take them there, this last expression of Christian charity being prompted by the sight of the gold guinea the Earl was holding out to him. Tugging his forelock, the farmer grasped the bridle of the Earl's leader and, holding his lantern high in his other hand, proceeded at his own slow pace up the lane. He turned into a rough cart track some minutes later, and all at once the oppressive hedgerows were left behind, although the track still rose slightly as they proceeded. They had passed no house, no farm, not even a tumbledown shed since they left Peasely, and Lorna whispered to the Earl, "What a lonely place this is, m'lord. With the dusk and the snow falling, it is as if all the world had disappeared but our small cavalcade."

Lord Peter smiled down at her as if amused by her fantasy. "A perfect spot for an abducted victim, in fact, Miss Jarrett. If only we could hear a bloodhound's mournful cry, it would be perfect."

"We seem to have come quite a distance from the village, sir," she said next. "I am so glad we met up with this man, for we would never have found Rose Cottage by ourselves."

Lord Peter had no comment to make to this and they continued on their way in silence. Lorna found herself dozing a little from the cold and the hypnotic movement of the grays' heads as they plodded onward, their breath steaming with their effort, and the bobbing of the farmer's lantern going before.

"Miss Jarrett," Lord Peter said suddenly, startling her into attention, "I must warn you that there is no assurance even now that Miss Melanie will be at Rose Cottage. I would not have you disappointed if you find we must go on, for it—"

"There she be," interrupted the husky voice of their guide as he pointed with his lantern a little way ahead.

Lorna could barely make out the stone wall covered with the bare canes of the rose bushes that gave the cottage its name. It seemed to be set in a small garden of fruit trees at the edge of a larger wood. There were no lights visible, but Lorna could smell wood smoke and she could not help tightening her grasp on the Earl's arm as he helped her down. He turned to speak to the farmer, and alone, she made her way through the gate and the deepening snow and up the front path.

"Take them around to shelter, my man, and the guinea is yours," Lord Peter began, but then he noticed Lorna already at the cottage door and hurried to follow her, checking to be sure his pistols were ready to hand in his greatcoat pocket and cursing the girl's impulsive, independent nature once again. Most women he knew would have been on the verge of hysterics by now, clutching him and crying with fear, but she would probably not even bother to knock before she charged inside, he thought as he caught up with her and took her arm to deter her. If there should be someone inside who would prefer not to be surprised in such a way, who knows what might not happen to her, but she does not think of that. Before he could advise caution, Lorna was banging on the knocker on the cottage door, crying out as she did so, "Melly? Melly? Are you there? It is I, Lorna."

There was no answer, and in a minute the Earl picked her up bodily with two strong hands and deposited her on the path behind him. Lorna gasped at his audacity, but when she saw the dueling pistol in his right hand as he stood slightly to one side of the door and opened it slowly with his left hand, she understood he only wished to protect her.

"Miss Jarrett?" he called, and when no one answered, he stepped inside, followed closely by Lorna, who grasped one of the capes of his greatcoat now as if she were afraid she might lose him. Peering around his massive shoulder, she could see a good-sized room, sparsely furnished, but with a fire burning low on the hearth. Its flickering light disclosed a room empty of human presence, and her heart sank.

Lord Peter strode inside and put his gloves and pistol down on a rough wooden table before he lit the branch of candles conveniently placed there. The room was more cheerful with the additional light, but Lorna was so depressed that they had not found her cousin at last that she sank down on the wooden settle before the fire and swallowed hard to control the tears that were threatening to fall.

Lord Peter took the candles and inspected the only other room on the ground floor, a rough larder and kitchen, and then he climbed the steep narrow stairs set against the side wall of the main room. There were two bedrooms on the second floor set under the sloping roof, but no Melanie Jarrett was to be found in either one of them. The Earl turned back the counterpane on one of the beds and he curled his lip when he saw the linen sheets and warm quilts with which the bed had been made up.

When he came back to the main room of the cottage, Lorna rose to her feet.

"What do we do now, m'lord?" she asked in a tired voice that seemed devoid of hope or useful suggestions. He could tell that this new disappointment had lowered her spirits and he spoke kindly. "We search this room for the third letter, of course," he said, and suiting his actions to his words, he inspected the table and two armchairs carefully before he went and ran his hand over the high mantelpiece. When she saw the familiar white paper in his hand, Lorna drew closer to read the contents with him.

The letter instructed them to leave the ransom in the wood box by the hearth, assuring them that when they returned to the Spotted Dog they would find Miss Melanie there waiting for them, safe and well.

Lorna drew a deep breath and snapped, "It would be wonderful indeed if this were true. I begin to feel as if someone is making mock of us, m'lord, involving us in a child's game while they laugh as we struggle from one place to another, never getting any nearer to Melly or coming to any successful conclusion."

The Earl considered her flushed face. "I do not think they are laughing, not yet at any rate, but I agree with you, Miss Jarrett, this is hide-and-seek indeed. However, he who laughs last laughs longest, you know. Tell me, do you feel able to make the trip back to Croydon?"

His voice was so concerned and kind that Lorna bit back

her sharp retort and said almost meekly, "Of course."

"Good girl!" The Earl smiled, squeezing her shoulder in camaraderie on his way to the door. "I shall have the yokel bring the horses around. At least the way lies downhill now. I fear the grays are almost spent."

He went out, slamming the door behind him, and Lorna amused herself by inspecting the ground floor. She was surprised to see the amount of food in the larder. There were cheese, eggs, and butter, a cold chicken, a large pot of soup ready to heat, and a fresh loaf of bread. In a caddy was tea and there were three bottles of wine as well, and remembering how long it had been since that last hurried meal in London made her realize how hungry she was. She was just about to cut the heel from the loaf when she heard the Earl returning, and taking it with her, she went back to the main room, a smile on her face for her discovery.

The Earl stood there glowering at her with his hands on his hips, the rugged planes of his face so taut and dark with anger that she took a step backward in dismay. As she watched, speechless, he threw his gloves on the table so furiously that they knocked the pistol to the floor, causing it to skitter across the bare wood.

"M'lord, what is the matter?" she asked, one hand going to her throat. "Are we ready to leave?"

"Only if you feel able to walk back to Croydon, Miss Jarrett," he said between gritted teeth.

"Walk?" she asked, confused. "Are the horses so done up, then, sir?"

"They are not there! I suppose I should have thought of it, but it never occurred to me that anyone would dare to play tricks with my grays. By God, they had better come to no harm or I will not answer for my actions."

Lorna sank down on the settle again, the knife she had been holding to cut the bread slipping to the floor to join the pistol. "Do you mean the farmer has taken them away? But why would he do such an infamous thing?"

"I do not think that this is the time to enlighten you with my theories, Miss Jarrett," Lord Peter said stiffly, coming to warm his hands by the fire. "Suffice it to say the team, curricle, and our oh-so-helpful guide have all disappeared."

Lorna waited for him to continue, but he just leaned

against the mantelpiece deep in thought, with one booted foot on the raised hearth as he brooded down at the dying flames. At that, she rose and with a determined air said, "In that case, m'lord, I suggest we get started. It will take us quite a while to get even as far as Peasely, but I am sure we can find someone there who would be willing to give us a ride to the inn, even if we must go in a farm cart. Come, let us be on our way."

The Earl looked up at her from under his frowning dark brows and laughed, that harsh, jeering laugh that had so little amusement in it.

"I suggest you look outside, Miss Jarrett, before you make any plans. Even someone as redoubtable as yourself might find it unnerving. The crowning touch to this ridiculous farce!"

Lorna went to the front door of the cottage, and the sight that greeted her caused her heart to sink. The storm had intensified, along with the wind, and it was impossible to see even as far as the gate in the blowing snow. She could barely make out the Earl's footsteps and she knew that even if they started in the right direction, their tracks were fast being covered so there was no way they could follow them back to the hamlet. Her shoulders slumped as she quickly closed the door.

"Just so," Lord Peter said grimly. "We appear to be trapped here with no hope of escape."

"I wonder how long the storm will last?" Lorna pondered as she came close to the fire again.

"We will be rescued in the morning, Miss Jarrett, depend on it," the Earl informed her. As she stared at him, he added, as if to himself, "Yes, early tomorrow will serve the purpose admirably."

"In that case, m'lord, I suggest we make ourselves comfortable," Lorna said as she took a log from the wood box and put it on the fire.

The Earl watched as she knelt beside him, adjusting the wood.

"I do not understand what is in your mind, sir, but I know we will both feel better after we have had some food. You would be amazed at the provisions I found in the larder of this supposedly empty cottage."

"I would not be amazed in the slightest. The food was left for us. The purpose of this plot would in no way be served should we starve to death. Oh, no." He laughed again harshly, and then began to pace up and down.

Lorna added the last log to the fire and watched as it flared up, and then she rose to remove her cloak and lay it over the settle.

"No good will come of all that striding about, sir," she said briskly, brushing back a curl that had come unfastened and leaving a streak of soot across her cheek as she did so. "It would be more helpful if you would fetch in some wood. I will begin to prepare a meal for us while you do so."

As Lord Peter stopped to frown at her giving him orders as if he were a servant, she added, "Do you prefer the burgundy or the claret with your supper, m'lord?"

For a moment he gazed at her dirty face and tousled curls, admiring the steady way she held her shoulders and straight back; and then the absurdity of their situation was borne in on him, and the hard angry glare left his eyes. She was behaving like a trooper, and he respected her for it. No hysterics, no weeping, no spells. No, Miss Lorna Jarrett would scorn such weakness. He would do no less than behave as well. He wondered if all the evil of their situation had occurred to her as yet, and he suspected it had not. Well, time and enough to tell her when she was warm and rested and had had something to eat.

"Is there enough water in the larder, Miss Jarrett?" he asked mildly as he put on his gloves again. "I only ask because you are in such dire need of it."

Lorna went to look into the dusty cracked mirror that hung on the wall, and when she saw her reflection, she laughed out loud before she went and fetched the bucket and handed it to him.

"If you would be so kind, m'lord," she curtsied, the dimple in full display now. "How unappetizing to sit down to eat with such a ragamuffin. I look as if I have been sweeping the chimney, do I not?"

"You look delightful," he said in a gruff voice, and then, as if he wished he had not spoken, he turned and left the cottage in a rush.

7

The Earl brought in a full bucket of water and several arm-loads of wood while Lorna put the kettle on and hung the soup pot on the iron spit above the flames. There was little conversation between them as they worked, for Lorna was pondering the meaning of his last remark after all his previous insults, and Lord Peter was cursing himself silently for speaking the irrelevant thought that had come unbidden into his mind at the sight of her lovely face dirtied like an urchin's and her tumbled curls glowing with such fire in the candlelight. Somehow the picture she made moved him more deeply than any woman's appearance had ever done before, even that of ladies dressed in satin and jewels with not a hair of their elaborate coiffures disarranged. But he knew that the situation was delicate, and he also knew he must not do anything further to startle her.

Accordingly, when they sat down to their simple meal, his remarks were terse and commonplace. Lorna drank her soup and watched the fire. She was well aware that they should not be here alone together, but since there was no way to change their location, she was wise enough to accept it and deal with the consequences later. Since the Earl (up to that last incomprehensible remark) had always taken her in such aversion, indeed with often expressed dislike, she did not fear that he would try to take advantage of her. The question of how she would react or what she would do if he tried, she put firmly from her mind and instead bent her thoughts to her cousin Melanie.

Aloud, she expressed the hope that Melanie was safe at the inn as the kidnappers had promised. "Surely, sir, it was not our fault that we could not leave the money and go away. How could we possibly know the farmer was dishonest? You do not think they will hurt her, do you?"

Lord Peter paused from his task of cutting them some chicken to study her concerned face for a moment. "I am sure they will not. In fact, I told Mr. Broadbent just before we left the inn not to be surprised if your cousin arrived before we returned, and to extend her every courtesy, but I doubt that will be necessary. I would wager you anything you like she is sitting down to dinner at Tower Hill right now, with my dear, *dear* great-aunt. My grays had better be stabled there as well."

He snorted and returned to his carving, attacking the chicken as if it were his mortal enemy. Lorna's eyes widened a bit, but she accepted the mangled piece he presented to her without comment.

For the remainder of the meal, they discussed friends in London and parties they had attended, and the Earl bestirred himself enough to relate several *on-dits* of the Ton she had not heard before. When he broached the second bottle of claret, Lorna watched him with some little anxiety. Gentlemen, she knew, were capable of consuming a great deal more wine than ladies without any ill effects, but still she had had only one small glass of the first bottle. When Lord Peter gestured with the new one, she nodded and held out her glass again, determined to match him swallow for swallow.

The simple meal was soon consumed, but when Lorna would have cleared away, the Earl commanded her to remain seated, and he himself took everything but the wine and their glasses back to the larder.

Lorna busied herself wiping the table and making up the fire. She was very tired from all the excitement and worries of the day and their long traveling in the cold, and besides, the wine and the hot fire were making her drowsy. She forced herself to sit up straight in her armchair. There was an old clock on the mantel, but its hands had stopped at four o'clock, and she had no idea what time it was. Surely it could not be very late, for they had reached Croydon at three. If, as she assumed, they had come to Rose Cottage by five, it could not now be much later than seven in the evening. The long hours to be spent in the Earl's company stretched before her, and she clasped her hands tightly in her lap. Their uneasy truce had lasted this long; she would do her best to see that it continued.

When Lord Peter returned and poured himself another glass of wine, she forced herself to say pleasantly, "If there were a pack of cards in the cottage, m'lord, I would challenge you to a hand or two of piquet."

The Earl nodded, but he seemed to have sunk into abstraction again, and soon he turned away from her toward the fire, and propping up that determined jaw with one large hand, he stared into the flames as if she were not there at all.

Lorna was affronted. "I have now made a perfectly innocuous remark, sir, and it is your turn," she said in exact imitation of his comment at the ball.

Lord Peter set his glass down on the table before he leaned forward to rest both arms there while he studied her face. Lorna had never seen him so serious and grave.

"I fear we have reached the stage, Miss Jarrett, where innocuous remarks will not serve our purpose," he said in his deep voice, his accents clipped and harsh. "You must understand that our position here places a new light on our relationship."

"How so, m'lord?" Lorna inquired, her heart beginning to pound.

He tapped his fingers impatiently on the table before he went on. "You cannot be so naive as to think we can remain here overnight alone together without paying the consequences. Why, you have not even a maid to attend you — not, I am sure, that any number of servants would serve the purpose of chaperones."

"I will not pretend to misunderstand you, Lord Peter," Lorna said, never taking her blue eyes from his face. "But I am sure you are unduly concerned. Who is to know? We have only to say that we were at Tower Hill, as indeed we would have been, except for our misfortune with the farmer and the storm. Who in the Ton is to know otherwise? You may be sure I shall not mention our being stranded here together, and I am positive you have no desire to make mischief either."

A crooked little smile of amusement twisted the Earl's lips. "And what of the Dowager Duchess? Miss Eliza and Miss Jane? And more important, what of Miss Melanie? I would not accord her much discretion or forbearance when she is in possession of such a juicy bit of gossip as this, would you?"

Lorna frowned, for she knew he was right. Melanie had a tongue that ran at both ends, and even if she promised to be discreet, Lorna knew she would be unable to restrain herself. And even if she only let it slip to her mother or Lady Morthman, the damage would be done.

Lord Peter pushed the table back and rose to pace the room again. Lorna watched him, her eyes troubled and a little bit afraid.

"No, my dear Miss Jarrett, it will not serve. Fortunately I know my duty as a gentleman as well as any man." He paused before her and looked down into her flushed, rosy face. "You will do me the honor to become my wife, Miss Jarrett, as soon as it can be arranged."

His voice was harsh and his words so sarcastic in spite of their correct formality that Lorna cringed. As he waited for her to reply, a million thoughts tumbled in her mind. Of course he had to offer for her, but he did not want her. Heaven knew he had spared no pains to show his dislike for her, and the mocking words of his proposal showed that that aversion was as strong as ever. She put up her chin and looked straight into those piercing gray eyes.

"Of course I thank you for the honor you do me, m'lord, but I must refuse," she said as formally as he had spoken.

"You cannot refuse, Miss Jarrett," Lord Peter said in a cold, positive voice, as if he were not much interested in her denial.

Lorna rose and clenched her hands. "Yes, I can! I will not marry you just to satisfy some ridiculous notion of propriety."

"You have made it quite clear to me on an earlier occasion in what light you regard me, and it is not necessary to reiterate your distaste for such an ugly brute, but there is no need to cringe from marriage to me. I do not offer you a union of love. No, there will be no danger of that between the two of us." Here Lord Peter barked that jeering laugh that Lorna was beginning to hate. "You need not fear any unwanted attentions from me. Ours will be only a marriage of convenience. Once the ring is on your finger and you have the protection of my name, you may go your own way, if that is what you desire."

Lorna's temper exploded. "What a marvelous marriage

you are offering me, m'lord. It hardly tempts me, you may be sure. The Ton, indeed the world, can say what they like. I *will* not marry you."

"Your aunt and uncle will have something to say about that," Lord Peter snapped, his own temper rising at her obstinate refusals.

"You seem to forget, m'lord, although you have twitted me about it time out of mind, that at my advanced years, my uncle is not my guardian. In fact, there is no man who holds me under his jurisdiction, no man who can tell me what to do. No, and I say again, no!"

"Better for you if there were some man to guide you," Lord Peter growled. "You have grown conceited, Miss Jarrett, too positive of your own omnipotence for your own good. But in this instance you will do as you are bid. You will marry me!"

He came and pulled her from her chair to grasp her arms and shake her a little. "Fool! Do you think for one minute that I will be made a laughingstock? Do you imagine that I will ever consent to being mocked and reviled for my ungentlemanly behavior in allowing your name to be disgraced? You do not know me very well, Miss Lorna Jarrett, if so you think."

Lorna tore herself away, and now it was she who paced the room while a coldly furious Lord Peter glowered at her from his place beside the hearth.

"I will go away," she said at last. "Yes, I will leave England and never return. You cannot stop me, for you have no power over me, not now or ever! I have relatives in Bermuda who will be glad to take me in."

She stopped and threw him a triumphant glance, and the Earl gave his hateful laugh again. "I believe there is still communication between England and Bermuda, Miss Jarrett. The news of your downfall will come on the very next ship after yours, if indeed it does not travel with you. There is nowhere on this earth that you can go and escape it. You will be as snubbed and reviled in Bermuda or China or Africa as you would be here."

He watched those proud shoulders slump in her neat merino gown, the defiantly held head bow until all he could see was the top of her auburn curls, and he went to her and led her back to her chair. He had not failed to notice the tears glistening in her eyes or the helpless gesture she gave as he spoke, and knowing he had won, he said softly, "No, my dear, it must be as I say. Distasteful as it is to both of us, we must marry. You will soon grow accustomed to the idea, and you have my word that I will not bother or distress you." Taking her hand, he pressed it gently. "It is not, to be sure, the marriage you may have dreamed of, but I will care for you and honor you all our lives. No one will know that we are sharing a marriage in name only, and you shall have nothing to complain of, on my word."

Nothing but a loveless farce of a marriage, Lorna thought bitterly. Lord Peter turned away and went to his greatcoat, and from one of the capacious pockets he extracted a silver flask. He poured them both a tot of brandy and put Lorna's in both her hands, closing her nerveless fingers around the stem.

"Drink that. I know this has been a shock to you," he said as he turned away to sip his own brandy. "So great-aunt has won," he murmured, as if to himself. "I said that he who laughs last laughs longest, and if it had not been for the abduction of the grays, which I did not foresee, we might have won through, in spite of all her scheming. Surely, the woman must be in league with the devil, for how else could she predict this storm? It is useless to fight such power! Lorna, I give you the victor, the Dowager Duchess of Wynne."

He raised his glass and tossed off his brandy.

Lorna put hers untasted down on the table. "I do not understand, m'lord."

"You may call me Peter now, my dear Lorna. Surely the least we have won is the right to address each other familiarly. You see, I knew all along my great-aunt engineered this whole thing. She was determined that I should not marry Melanie, and in her place she meant to set you. I refused, and so she concocted this elaborate plot to force us together in such a way that we would be compelled to marry."

Lorna sat up straighter, her blue eyes dangerous. So, he had refused to marry her, had he? It was just what she had always known. But to speak so of his great-aunt, the man must be mad! "I refuse to believe such a terrible tale," she said rapidly. "To kidnap Melly, to put us both to such anguish and concern! I cannot believe it of the Dowager. Surely you must be mistaken."

M'lord shook his head. "No, I do not think I am. You will see if dear, *dear* Aunt Agatha does not arrive here first thing in the morning. One hopes she will contain herself to the point of not bringing the local vicar and a special license with her, though I cannot be sure even of that. There will be a perfectly logical explanation of this adventure, in which her part will appear only as savior and advisor. There was no doubt a gang who kidnapped Melanie and led us on this wild-goose chase, but there will be no way to connect them with my great-aunt or to prove that it was at her instigation that they acted. But you will see."

"I think the events of this day, to say nothing of the amount of wine and brandy you have imbibed, have made your mind unstable," Lorna snapped.

Lord Peter's head came up and that dangerous light came back to his eyes again.

"How very wifely you have become, so suddenly," he purred, one eyebrow raised as her face flushed red. In a different tone he added, "Perhaps you had better learn right now, my dear wife-to-be, I do as I please and I do not take kindly to being instructed by anyone. Learn that lesson well, my dear, and do not interfere with me. You will do so at your peril."

Lorna put up her chin. "Of course, you must always have your own way, and what you wish must always prevail . . . I understand. You are arrogant, m'lord, and I dislike you intensely."

Her scornful words were still echoing in the room when he laughed at her. "You may dislike me as much as you wish, dear Lorna, but marry me you must. No, no!" he added when he saw she was about to speak. "No more protestations! Come, let me light you to your room. It has been a tiring day, but you will feel more the thing in the morning, and after you have rested and considered, you will see that I am right."

Taking her arm, he led her to the stairs. Lorna would have liked to refuse this new example of his high-handedness, to show her defiance in even this small instance, but that would mean she must remain in his company unless she went and sulked in the cold larder, and she did not know how she could do so without ripping up at him, she was so angry. With tight lips and her head held high, she allowed him to escort her upstairs to one of the bedrooms and light the candle there, and she waited with her arms folded while he returned downstairs to bring her a pitcher of hot water before he bade her good night.

"Sleep well, my bride," he said from the doorway with a mocking bow.

Lorna glared at him, all six feet, three inches of muscled masculinity with those strangely lit gray eyes staring at her from his dark, harsh-featured face. Her jaw was set as ominously as his own, and Lord Peter continued to watch her, wishing he could go and kiss her until she lost her militant look and admitted her defeat. He shook his head at such a foolish fancy, and bidding her good night again, he closed the door behind him before he went back downstairs.

Lorna washed and removed her travel-creased gown and her boots. She did not undress any further, for in spite of his words about marriages in name only and letting her go her own way, she did not know what he might do, especially after all the wine he had had. Besides, look at the way he had forced her to kiss him at first meeting!

She climbed into the cold bed and pulled the quilts around her, determined to remain awake and on her guard, but it was only a few minutes before her eyes closed and she was fast asleep. She did not hear Lord Peter's soft footsteps when he came up to the other bedroom, nor notice how they paused for a moment at her door, and when she woke to a brilliant winter's day the next morning, she had slept so soundly that she could not imagine where she was or why she was not in her own bed with one of Lady Morthman's maids bringing in the chocolate.

As she lay there, it all came back to her in a rush, and she groaned and pulled the covers over her head as much to block out the problems she had to face as the bright sunlight that streamed into the little room. She was not allowed any time for reflection, however, for a moment later she heard a call from outside. She got up and went to the window to see liveried sleigh stopped at the gate and a groom busy clearing the path to the door. Recalling Lord Peter's remarks, he could not be surprised to see the Dowager step down from the sleigh, nor to hear Lord Peter's deep voice from the doorway beneath her window.

"Good morning, Aunt. What kept you? I have expected you anytime this past hour. Come in, come in! If there are any provisions in that basket, I should be glad of some coffee."

Lorna heard no more as they entered the cottage, and she knew it was only a matter of time before someone came up to find her. Hiding under the covers would be not only poor protection from the world that waited, but cowardly as well. She washed in the cold water that was left in the pitcher and dressed, arranging her hair as best she could with the tiny comb she carried in her reticule.

As she opened her door, she heard the Dowager exclaim, "But it was all a stupid misunderstanding, dear boy! Jenks did not perfectly understand that you wished the grays stabled. Poor man, he has always been a little slow and hard-of-hearing as well, and thinking that you and Miss Jarrett were keeping a tryst here, he took the team back to the Spotted Dog, where I assure you they are safe and well stabled. Mr. Broadbent sent a message to Tower Hill as soon as Melanie was released at the end of the village and had made her way to the inn, and of course I sent a carriage for her immediately. What you and Miss Jarrett were doing or where you were, I could only conjecture until I had spoken to Jenks when he came late last night to demand his guinea and to read me a lecture on the loose ways of the Quality. It would have been diverting, if it had not been so upsetting, for it was much too late and far too stormy to rescue you then. Poor dear Miss Jarrett! No doubt she felt the situation keenly, with no maid and no other servants here either. Dear, dear!"

Lorna grasped the railing, her eyes dark with anger, for it appeared that Lord Peter had been right about his great-aunt after all. She was about to start down the stairs when she heard his deep voice, and his words made her shrink back against the landing again.

"There is no need for such mealymouthed piety, Aunt

Agatha. I have asked Lorna to marry me already, so it will not be necessary for you to remind me of my duty. You may however, have to remind Lorna of hers, for she is determined not to have a thing to do with me, no matter how her reputation suffers, and mine as well." His harsh laugh floated up the stairs before he added, "What a glorious thing an unwilling bride will be. What rapture we are sure to share as we travel life's path together."

"Peter, you are distraught, and no doubt so is Lorna. She is much too sensible a young woman to be so silly and so stubborn. I am sure it is only the agitation of the moment the distress she must have felt at her predicament that prompts this reluctance. Go and fetch her, dear boy, and I will be glad to bring her to a more agreeable frame of mind. One must do one's duty, after all."

"I am sure you came on purpose to do so, Aunt," the Earl snapped. As he neared the stairs, he added, "But where is the vicar? I was sure he would be beside you, prayerbook in hand."

Lorna did not dare remain where she was for another minute. Taking a deep breath, she descended the stairs in a rush. Lord Peter watched her from the bottom of the flight, his face as unsmiling as her own. She nodded to him and let him lead her to his recently vacated chair. She could not help the stiffness of her shallow curtsy to the Duchess, nor her cool words of greeting, but the older woman did not appear to notice any reticence.

"My dear," she exclaimed as she poured out a cup of coffee quite as if she sat in her own grand drawing room, "you are not to worry anymore. All will be well, and Melanie is quite, quite safe. She was a little fearful at first, she tells me, but she soon came to see her abduction as a kind of game. What a thing it is to be so young and resilient! I am sure I would have been frightened to death, but Melanie assures me the two men who captured her were very polite and kind, and told her of her safety over and over again."

"What a shame they will not gain their ransom, paltry though it was," Lord Peter sneered, coming to lean against the mantel. "But somehow I am sure they will be reimbursed."

"Hmmm?" the Dowager asked, peering at him with her

nearsighted eyes. "Cream? Sugar, my dear?" she asked Lorna. "Do have a scone, they were fresh baked this morning." Then she turned to her great-nephew again and continued, "Of course I came as early as I could, and as soon as you have finished your coffee, we will return to Tower Hill. My dear Lorna, Peter tells me you are reluctant to marry him, but on that subject we must speak seriously. You must be brought to see how impossible it would be to ignore what happened here last night—"

"Nothing happened!" Lord Peter snapped, two streaks of red slashing his cheekbones.

"How you do take one up, Peter! Of course I did not mean *that*. You are still a gentleman, I hope. I meant only that in the eyes of the world, it does not matter what occurred or what did not. It is a sad fact that people always put the worst possible interpretation on things—even perfectly innocent things—but so it has always been. Lorna, my dear, allow me to speak to you as your mother would, and give you my guidance—"

Lorna put down her coffeecup, and without thinking said in a quiet voice, "That will not be necessary, Your Grace. I will marry Lord Peter."

As soon as she spoke, she wished she might call back her hasty words and was about to cry, "No, no, I did not mean that!" when she heard the Earl's sudden indrawn breath and felt the way he leaned toward her, although she kept her eyes firmly on the Dowager's suddenly beaming face.

"Good gel! I knew you would see reason, for although this has not been the most conventional of beginnings, it is the happy ending that counts, is it not? May I be the first to wish both you dear people happy? I can hardly wait to tell Eliza and Jane, and of course Melanie is so anxious to see you. Come, let us quit this squalid cottage. I am longing to hear all your adventures, and we have so many plans to make."

The Dowager continued talking of weddings and announcements and honeymoons as they gathered their cloaks and belongings, which was just as well, for both Peter and Lorna had fallen strangely dumb. Lorna only dared to look into his eyes for a fleeting moment when he took her arm to help her into the sleigh, and she quickly turned away from the question she read there. She could not answer him, for she did not know why she had spoken as she did. Her mind was in tormoil and refused to conform to logical thought.

The Dowager did not appear to notice her abstraction, or how silent she was on the ride to Tower Hill, and she could not know that the only thing Lorna was aware of was Lord Peter's firm arm and shoulder pressed against hers in the sleigh and the nearness of his muscular thigh which the tiny vehicle made it impossible for her to avoid. She noticed he stared straight ahead of them, his lips compressed, and she wondered if his thoughts were as chaotic as her own.

When they reached Tower Hill, a recently modernized house that was named for the Norman keep that still rose at one corner of the manor, the Dowager bustled her upstairs to a large bedroom, calling for a hot bath to be prepared and a more substantial breakfast, after which she was ordered to climb into the huge four-poster hung with velvet curtains for a really good sleep.

"I shall tell Miss Melanie that you must rest, my dear," the Dowager twinkled at her. "Time enough to satisfy her curiosity later, for, after all, it was her naughtiness that caused the contretemps. A few hours of suspense is little-enough punishment, but these modern misses! Tchh!"

She closed the door of the bedroom behind her and went away, leaving Lorna to wonder if Lord Peter had been wrong, after all, and they were both doing the Dowager an injustice.

She dozed for an hour or so, more to escape the reality of what she had promised to do than from any further exhaustion, and she was wide awake when Melanie was permitted to enter the room at last. The two cousins were forced by the presence of the maid, who had come to help Lorna dress, to chat of ordinary matters, but as soon as she had been buttoned into a morning gown of figured primrose muslin with matching sandals, and had had a ribbon threaded through her now smoothly brushed, immaculate curls and the maid had curtsied and left the room, Melanie threw herself into her cousin's arms.

"My dearest Lorna! How worried I have been for you, and how frightened! You must tell me everything, especially how you came to accept Lord Peter's proposal. You can imagine how I stared when Miss Eliza told me you had done so. Never did I suspect that you had a *tendre* there, you sly puss. You should have told me, Lorna, and I would have taken my claws out of him ages ago."

"Melly, cut line," Lorna ordered, leading her volatile cousin to a chair by the fire. "We will get to my side of the story later, but first I insist you tell me what happened to you. Why did you leave the gypsy's tent in that clandestine way? Or were those two men waiting for you there and did they force you to go?"

Melanie colored up and looked a little conscious. "Well, not exactly. You see, a groom slipped me a note as we were leaving the puppet booth, and it instructed me to slip out the back of the tent, where a coach would be waiting for me."

"And you did so, Melly?" Lorna asked as if she could not believe her ears.

"I had to! You see, the note was from Lord Landford, and all he wanted was for me to join him in his carriage for a few moments, and he swore you would never know I had been gone. And, Lorna," she added in a hushed, awed voice, "he vowed to shoot himself if I did not. I could not have that on my conscience, now could I?"

Lorna stared at her young, romantic cousin. Of course you could not, my dear, she thought wryly, although why you imagined Lord Landford would do any such thing when he can call on you in St. James's Place and see you freely anytime he likes, I have no idea.

"And then what happened?" Lorna asked when she could control the quiver in her voice.

"Oh, then it did get a little frightening, for Lord Landford was not there, only two young grooms. One of them put his hand over my mouth so I could not scream, while the other kept telling me no harm would come to me, and the carriage drove away. I fainted," she added proudly.

"It was unnecessary to tell me that, Melly, I was sure you did," Lorna could not help remarking.

"When I came to myself again, I discovered we had left London. How I pleaded and cried, Lorna! But it was all to no avail, and soon I came to see from their nice manners and concern for my comfort that they meant to do me no injury. And one of them was so handsome, too, and he kept calling me m'lady, too diverting! They brought me to a cottage quite near here, where there was a pleasant older woman to wait on me and bear me company until the time came that they drove me to Croydon and told me to walk up the road to the inn and tell the landlord my name. It was quite the most exciting thing that has ever happened to me," she added naively as Lorna wondered if even once during her thrilling day she had thought how much her disappearance must be worrying her cousin and perhaps distressing her doting father and ailing mother as well.

"But what of you, Lorna? Tell me everything, especially all about Lord Peter."

Lorna related the events of the previous day, and Melly's hazel eyes grew wide. When she told her how they had been trapped at the cottage and forced to spend the night there, which circumstance had prompted the Earl's proposal, tears came to Melanie's eyes.

"My dear, I did not understand. Oh, Lorna, how terrible for you. But perhaps you might come to like Lord Peter in time. I myself have discovered he is nothing like the monster I pictured, although of course I could never bear to marry him myself, he is so quick-tempered, and so ugly and old . . . Oh, dear, I did not mean to say that, when you are forced to it. Dear, dear, Lorna, what a charge I have been on you, and now I see I have ruined your life. I am quite overcome."

Lorna was so busy for the next half-hour, soothing and petting her weeping cousin, that she had little time to think of her own unenviable position, and when a footman knocked and presented her with a note from the Earl, begging a few moments of her time in the library, she was almost relieved to make good her escape.

The footman escorted her to the book-lined room and, after announcing her, bowed himself out.

Lorna came forward slowly, feeling a little breathless, to find the Earl bowing before her, dressed for traveling, his greatcoat over his arm. "You are leaving, sir?" she could not help asking, for somehow this surprised her.

"As you see. I have much to do in Town, and since Aunt Agatha plans to remain here for another day, she has charged me with calling on the Jarretts to report the change of plans. I must also insert an announcement of our coming wedding in the newspaper, of course."

Lorna looked away from his face, and he took her chin in his big hand. "Look at me," he demanded, and she forced her eyes to return his gaze as steadily as she could. She noticed he was frowning as he said, "This is all most uncomfortable for you, I know, but I cannot tell you how exceedingly relieved I was when I heard you agree to marry me this morning." Still looking deep into her eyes, he released her chin and raised her hand and kissed it. "You will have no cause to regret it, my promise on it," he said softly.

Lorna made an impatient gesture and he released her. "How gallant, my lord! But such distinguished attentions and handsome words are unnecessary in an arrangement such as ours. I trust you will not regret our marriage either, but at least my acquiescence has saved both our reputations, and now you can be easy on that head."

The Earl frowned again at her words, but then, as if determined to be pleasant, he begged her to be seated. "A glass of wine?" he asked, a little devil in his eyes that Lorna ignored as she nodded.

"And what did Melanie have to say about her abduction," he asked in his normal harsh tones when he was seated across from her and they were both sipping an excellent canary.

Lorna told him the story, a great deal more briskly and unemotionally than her cousin had.

The Earl snorted when she reached the part about Lord Landford blowing his brains out. "If only she had asked me, I could have told her Percy couldn't hit a wall, never mind so small a target as his head," he snapped.

Lorna stiffened, sure he was showing his disgust at the silly way he had been trapped, as he continued, "But you say she was not afraid of her kidnappers? How strange."

"Not when you know they were both young, well mannered, and handsome, and called her m'lady every other word," Lorna told him, and he laughed.

"An adventure of the first order, then. I wish you would advise your uncle, when you reach London, that he should bend all his skill to marrying little Melanie off as soon as possible. Let us hope she manages to restrain herself from indulging in any more excitement until after our wedding.

Granted she is more prone to romance than either you or I, but still . . ."

Lorna lowered her eyes to her glass of wine.

"But that was unkind. Forgive me," he said. After a moment's silence, he asked, "What say you to a February wedding, Lorna? I see no reason for a lingering engagement, do you?"

" 'If it were done when 'tis done, then 'twere well it were done quickly,' you mean m'lo—Peter?" she asked, wishing she did not feel so miserable and uneasy. "As you wish, of course."

"Comparing our marriage to a murder is hardly complimentary, ma'am," the Earl snapped, losing his temper a little for the first time since she had come into the library. "I shall make arrangements for the first calling of the banns to be made next Sunday, and now I must be on my way. And even though I know there is no need to ask his permission, I will wait on your uncle to apprise him of our plans. I prefer to offer him every courtesy."

Lorna could not help smiling a little then, for she suddenly remembered her aunt and Lady Morthman. "May I suggest you avoid the ladies of the house, sir?" she said, picturing Mrs. Jarrett's inevitable spell, and her mother's chagrin when they learned that the big fish had escaped their net. She could not restrain a small gurgle of laughter as their horrified faces came to her mind.

Lord Peter admired the sparkle it brought to her looks. She looked especially beautiful in her smart London gown with her hair so perfectly arranged, but somehow he missed the unkempt urchin she had appeared last evening. Reluctantly, he dismissed the memory of her in the cottage as he bowed.

"I wish I might assure you I am not as cowardly as that, but to tell the truth, your advice is well taken. I will let Mr. Jarrett break the news."

He came toward her and she rose, setting her glass down on the table beside her chair, all smiles and laughter stilled. Her heart was beating a little faster now he stood before her. Would he touch her? Attempt to kiss her? Surely not, for he had made no demur when she spoke of their "arrangement." She looked into his eyes, her own cool and controlled, and a mask came over his face. "Adieu, my dear. I shall expect you in London tomorrow afternoon, at which time, having this little space apart, I expect you will be more easy in your mind," he said.

Lorna curtsied. "I wish you a safe journey, sir, behind those matchless grays," she said, clenching her hands in the folds of her skirt and praying he would not notice how distraught she became whenever he was near her.

In a moment he was gone and Lorna went to the window to watch him swing up into his racing curricle and give his team the office to start. When he turned his head to look back at Tower Hill, she stepped back out of sight quickly.

She spent what was left of the morning alone in the library, grateful for the delicacy of manner with which the Dowager had arranged for her to be undisturbed. She did not think she could bear to listen to Melanie's chatter right now, or anyone else's either.

In thinking over the meeting with Lord Peter just past, she had to admit he had behaved very well—better, in fact, than she had—but she still wondered why she had given in so easily and agreed to marry him. She had had no intention of doing so, especially not without taking time to consider any other options that might be open to her, but like the evening of the ball when he had held out his hand to her and she had risen to waltz with him, helpless to refuse, so this time, too, she had been unable to deny him.

She crossed her arms and hugged herself, feeling a little shiver in spite of the blazing fire and warm library. She had always been so sure of herself, so independent, up to now. Was this some kind of magic he was able to perform? Did he have her in his power to the extent that she would do as he bade her every time he made a demand? That could not be! She must be careful and keep up her guard; it would not do to give the Earl any advantage in their relationship. For what must he already think of her surrender, especially after all her former expressions of disgust for him? How it must amuse him to know that he had won, even though the outcome of their battle was a matter of such indifference to him. No, the man was autocratic and overbearing enough without any added superiority. She would continue to be independent just as he had promised she could be, her own mistress, as calm and sure of her position as he was of his. But allow him to order her about, to know of the weakness she now acknowledged, she would not.

And if this loveless marriage that neither of them had wished for became too difficult a facade to maintain, she could always go away, for hadn't he promised her that as well? She considered taking ship for Bermuda a short time after she became Lady Truesdale, protected by the title Countess Norwell. It had been a long time since she had been there with her parents, and she remembered how she had enjoyed the warm air, the abundance of flowers, and the aquamarine ocean that deepened from palest green to almost navy, but instead of feeling any anticipation, she decided that the tropical air would be too languid for her mood right now.

She sighed. She did not know what the future would bring after that day in February when she married Lord Peter, or whether there would be any happiness in it for her. She must wait and see.

Unbidden, his powerful, frowning features came to her mind, those gray eyes glowing with a light she did not understand, and she remembered the words he had spoken in this room just a little while ago. His leaving Tower Hill so quickly showed a kindness and consideration she would never have expected of him. He seemed to know instinctively that she needed time to be alone, time to become accustomed to the idea of a lifetime spent by his side. And his intention of calling on her uncle and showing her every sort of homage and deference, just as if he really did desire their marriage, was more than kindness, it was a protection from the jeers and gossip of the Ton, which she would have found impossible to bear.

She straightened her shoulders and resolved to behave as well as he had. Lord Peter would have no reason to be displeased with her behavior, for she would be just as much the "gentleman" as he had shown he intended to be.

8

Lorna determined to begin at once on this noble resolution, and by the time the luncheon gong sounded and she was forced to rejoin the company, she was much easier in her mind. She was able to accept the breathless good wishes of the Dowager's companions and quiet her cousin's worried look with a warm hug and a smile. The Duchess nodded her admiration for such control and kissed her cheek as a compliment.

Taking the seat the butler was holding out for her, she said, "Come, we are almost family, Lorna. Sit here by me so we can bend our minds to the preparations that must be made. You must allow me, my dear child, to serve as your mentor since you have lost your own mother, for somehow I do not think Mrs. Jarrett will care to undertake the task, and as for Lady Morthman, it is not to be thought of."

"Indeed, no," Melanie chimed in, helping herself to the tureen of soup the footman was presenting to her. "Mama will be far too ill almost immediately, and as for Grandmama—well, she will be mad as hops."

She paused and blushed, but the Dowager only laughed at her and bade her to eat up her soup. Lorna thought Melanie seemed to have lost all her terror of the old lady in just the short time she had been at Tower Hill, and she wondered at it, even as she thanked the Duchess for her kindness, and said she would be pleased to have her advice on wedding matters. Miss Eliza and Miss Jane assured her they were at her service as secretaries as well, and she was not to worry her head about any of the thousand or so nagging details that must be resolved, for they would see to everything.

"Peter mentioned a Febraury wedding, I believe," the Duchess said next. "That does not give us much time, m'dears, so we must bustle about. Melanie, you of course will serve as honor attendant, but we should have at least eight bridesmaids and two flower girls and a page as well."

Lorna put down her soup spoon. "Your Grace, that is far too many. I do not know that many girls in London or even in Dorset that I would care to ask. Besides, I would much prefer a smaller, more intimate affair, especially in this instance."

The Dowager accepted some veal in a brown sauce and waved away the braised carrots. "I am sure you do, but, alas, it cannot be," she said in a positive way that reminded Lorna vividly of Lord Peter. "No, you will marry my great-nephy with all the pomp and circumstance that we can bring to bear. There must be no hint of hurry or irregularity to give rise to conjecture. Think, Lorna! And as for you, Miss Melanie," she said, fixing the girl with her severest stare and pointing her knife at her for emphasis, "I had better not hear that a single word has escaped your lips about this affair. You may be sure you would be very, very sorry if that happened. I would see to it."

Melanie paled and promised she would not tell a soul, not even her mother, and the Dowager nodded.

"Do not worry about bridesmaids, Lorna," she said next. "Heaven knows there are enough single girls in our family alone to outfit any number of weddings, isn't that so, Jane? I shall put you in charge of selecting them, dear friend, but whatever you do, avoid Grace Allendon and Lady Jennifer."

As Miss Jane nodded and took out the inevitable note-book, Lorna could not help looking askance at her hostess. The Dowager explained, "They are inseparable friends, and as one is too short and plump and the other too tall and thin, imagine the picture they would present. Jane, try for some uniformity of size and coloring so they will not detract from Lorna's auburn hair and glorious figure."

Lorna was amazed that such a tiny detail was given importance, but it seemed that this was just the beginning. Nothing was too minute to escape the Dowager's attention, and when they all sat in the drawing room after luncheon and made their plans, Lorna felt she was watching the orchestration of a Royal Command Performance in the theater, rather than such a simple matter as a wedding.

The color of the bridesmaids' gowns was discussed and the flowers to be chosen for their bouquets and headpieces, the church was selected more for its size and importance than because it was in anyone's parish, and the style and fabric of Lorna's gown took over an hour to decide to everyone's satisfaction. The Dowager peered at her for a moment before she said at last, "Ivory satin. Yes, a creamy ivory will be much more flattering with your high coloring. But stay! Eliza, do you think that anyone might make an unpleasant assumption because the gown was not pure white? Never mind," she added as she noticed Melanie looking perplexed and leaning forward to ask a question, "we can resolve that later, after we find out what people are saying. Mme Thérèse will advise us as well."

The number of invitations to be sent seemed staggering to Lorna, but since the Dowager had decreed that in addition to every member of the immediate family on both sides, all the Ton must be invited, up to and including the Prince Regent, she could do nothing but agree. The only member of Society who was to be neglected was Prinny's estranged wife, Princess Caroline. Lorna did not think she would even be missed in such a crush of people. She wondered what Lord Peter would think of all this.

"Bridal clothes," Miss Jane interrupted her musings, "bridal clothes and the groom's gift."

"And a gala ball," chimed in Miss Eliza, clapping her hands.

Miss Jane smiled and nodded as she wrote down these items, while the Dowager said once more she did not know how she would go on without her friends to help her.

"I will give the ball, of course, as well as a small dinner party and dance to announce the engagement. That I am sure we can manage by the end of the week, for it will be mostly family, and if meeting Peter's doty Uncle Connie and eccentric Cousin Bess does not give you pause, Lorna, all will be well. I beg you to remember that every family has its share of dirty dishes."

Lorna was not allowed time to contemplate these in-laws-to-be, for the Dowager rushed on, "I think we might allow your uncle to give the wedding breakfast and reception," she said grandly, in the manner of one conferring a tremendous boon. "Poor man, he must be allowed to do something for you besides help you up the aisle and give your hand to Peter. And I think we can allow my great-nephy to manage the details of the wedding journey by himself. It is always well to give the groom something to do during this period. It keeps their minds occupied. It must be something that is not too important, yet permits them to feel they are contributing the major share. Ha! The only important thing that is required of them, as we all know, is to present themselves at the church on time, properly dressed and ring in hand, but it does not do to let them know it. Men's feelings are so easily hurt."

They remained talking in the drawing room throughout the afternoon, but even so, the Dowager continued to make plans at dinner.

."An early bedtime is in order for us all," she decreed as she rose from the table. "We must return to Town as soon as possible so we can begin our shopping and all the other preparations without delay. Of course, I shall go in with you, Lorna, when you reach St. James's Place, to personally tell Lady Morthman and Mrs. Jarrett how ecstatic I am with Peter's choice of bride."

She nodded decisively as she led the way along the hall, her back stiff and straight, and Lorna could see that Lady Morthman had better not dare to show any disappointment in the outcome. Where the matriarch of the family—and the Dowager Duchess of Wynne at that—gave her blessing, who could disapprove?

In the drawing room, the Dowager asked Melanie to play the piano for them, and as her companions led the girl to the instrument, she beckoned Lorna to a seat beside her some distance away.

"You are behaving very well, Lorna. Good girl!" she said, patting her hand. "Of course, I knew you would, for I am seldom mistaken in people's character, and when I said I would tell the Jarretts of my approval, I meant every word of it. You and Peter are perfect for each other. I am, of course, sorry that, thanks to your silly little cousin, this has been such a ramshackle affair, and your liaison with Peter had such an unfortunate beginning, but since no one will hear a breath of scandal, what can that signify?"

Lorna wished she could ask the Dowager outright if she had taken part in the plot, but she could find no way to pose such an impudent question. However, she could not resist saying, "How unfortunate that I agree so hastily then, ma'am. If I had only realized your power in suppressing gossip, it would not have been necessary for me to accept Peter, nor for him to ask me to marry him."

The Dowager looked amazed. "Can it be that you do not realize you are in love with him and he with you?" she asked in an incredulous voice. "Coming it much too strong, my dear, for I have known it this age."

Lorna opened her mouth to hotly deny any such thing, but once again the Dowager was before her. "But you will see before much longer that I am right." She chuckled and nodded her head, wisps of gray hair flying, and Lorna was tempted to tell her of the pact she and the Earl had made for a marriage of convenience only. "As for suppressing gossip, I am not so omnipotent. In this instance, where there is an engagement, to be followed almost at once with a wedding, any idle chatter can be denied. If you had continued to refuse to marry him, I am afraid even my influence with the Ton would not have been enough. No, Peter was quite correct. His immediate proposal was the only course possible, after Miss Melanie's escapade. That child should be spanked, by the way. When I have a moment, I intend to put a bee in her Grandmama's bonnet about her flirting, flighty ways before it is too late. Tell me, Lorna, is there no one among her admirers that she prefers above the others?"

Lorna considered. "No one that I can be sure of, for she seems to enjoy her popularity too much. Sometimes I have suspected she likes Sir Digby's company more than the rest, but since he was always my escort, it is hard to say with any certainty."

"How charming if it were so . . . the perfect solution, and so tidy," the Dowager enthused. She seemed abstracted for a moment, and then she turned back to Lorna.

"Your eyes are still shadowed and troubled, my dear. Will you take an old lady's advice? I assure you it is given from the heart." She said, leaning forward and peering at her.

Lorna nodded, unable to speak for the kind concern in her voice.

"Do not regret your promise to marry Peter, for you did the right thing, and do not worry too much about your marriage or the future you will share. It will all work out, given time, and I know you and my great-nephy will be as happy together as I was with my dear Reggie, you'll see! As for the

Ton, no scandal will touch either of you. I am determine that your marriage will not begin under a cloud."

Lorna was glad Melanie was finishing her étude just then and the butler was bringing in the tea tray. Her heart was full of doubt and nameless fears, but she knew she could not voice them to the Dowager, sympathetic though she was. The lady seemed to sense she could say no more, and squeezing her hand, she went to talk to the others.

Later, after Lorna had dismissed her maid, she wandered over to the window to gaze out at the moonlit snow. She was restless and knew she would not be able to sleep. Recalling the Dowager's words, she realized that she was right on one count at least: the Ton must be made to accept this marriage as a perfectly ordinary event. There must be no whispering about the length of time the Earl had courted Melanie, nor how suddenly his eyes had turned to her cousin. There must be no one to question their absence from Town or wonder what they had all been doing, and above all, Lady Morthman must be silenced. Lorna was sure the Dowager would manage it very well.

She wondered what the Earl would think of the elaborate wedding plans, the dinner party, and the ball, and whether he would allow his great-aunt to sweep all before her without protest. Somehow she was sure he would try to assert his own will, but she questioned whether he would succeed, for she had never met anyone like the Dowager. She was unique.

Lorna shook her head as she remembered that the lady had told her her marriage would be happy. In that area the Dowager was not as perceptive as she thought she was. Look what she had said about knowing that they were in love with each other! Lorna sighed and rested her cheek against the soft velvet of the drape, a little frown on her face. I wish I could tell her about Dr. Fell, she thought, and that the Earl has never made any secret of the fact that he considers me the personification of Miss Fell. At last she went to bed, but her sleep was restless and troubled with fragments of dreams she did not understand when she woke.

It was early when they rode up to Town in the Dowager's coach. Fortunately this was an old-fashioned, roomy vehicle, so the five of them could take their places without undue crowding. The Dowager whiled away the journey by instructing Melanie in how she was to behave, echoed by Miss Jane and Miss Eliza, while Lorna watched the passing countryside.

"You must appear to be delighted with the good match your cousin is making, and perfectly content, and if you could manage to act as if you had had a hand in promoting it and for that reason have allowed Lord Peter to escort you so he would have the opportunity to be near Lorna, it would be quite a coup."

Melanie assured the Dowager with her sunniest smile that she would do her best, saying she had always liked charades and amateur theatricals.

"Hmm," the Dowager replied. "No doubt you are a good actress, then. I am glad to hear it, for if it is seen that you feel at all slighted by my great-nephy's change of affection, you can only appear ridiculous and an object for pity. And if you go about claiming that you never wanted him anyway because he was too old and domineering, it will sound like sour grapes. That will not add to your consequence."

Melanie's smile disappeared and she seemed much struck by this advice, and Lorna saw that the Dowager stressed just the right things to ensure her cousin's wholehearted cooperation.

They were back in London by early afternoon. Lorna learned that Mrs. Jarrett had retired to bed with a bad spell and refused to see her. Lorna was reviled by Lady Morthman, until the Dowager drew her aside and spoke to her severely, and had to bear a painful interview with her uncle, who, out of his love and concern, asked her so many times if she were quite sure she wished this marriage to take place that she did not see how she could lie about it one more time. It is all so much more difficult than I imagined, she thought as she left her uncle's study, hoping that she had calmed his fears with her smiling delight in her future husband.

As she took her leave, the Dowager bade them all to remain at home that evening, and Lorna was glad to obey. She had the headache and she did not feel up to the stares and whispers that were sure to come. As she crossed the hall, Lady Morthman's butler presented her with a bouquet and a note that had just arrived. She buried her face in the flowers, inhaling their fresh scent, while she tried to ignore the fatherly beam of the old butler before she carried them upstairs. Of course they were from the Earl. She recognized his distinctive handwriting at once from the many teasing cards and notes he had sent her cousin. But this note had nothing of the admirer in it: it was only a few brief lines, telling her he would do himself the honor of calling on her tomorrow afternoon, when he hoped she would be able to join him in a drive through the park at the fashionable hour all the Ton assembled there. He signed it "Norwell" and Lorna threw it into her fireplace in a fit of pique. She told herself she did so so that no one would read it and discover their secret, but she admitted she was hurt by his casual, business-like manner. How foolish I am, she thought, when I know he does not care for me, or I for him.

The Dowager called for her and Melanie the first thing next morning and swept them away to her dressmaker. The ivory satin wedding gown was bespoke, and a number of other gowns and ensembles, and Mme. Thérèse promised to have all ready in time, as well as the bridesmaids gowns as soon as their measurements had been obtained. The next stop was for bonnets and reticules, sandals and lingerie and gloves. Lorna's head was in a whirl, and not once did she try to impose her own tastes or voice any preference.

The Dowager watched her closely whenever she could. There was something wrong, that much was sure. Well, the gel would be too busy preparing her trousseau, attending parties, and answering notes of congratulations to brood about it, but perhaps it would be wise to question Peter again. Lorna had never really confided in the Dowager; there was no reason to believe she would let down her guard now.

After a late luncheon in Berkeley Square, Lorna was driven back to Lady Morthman's while Melanie went on to an afternoon party. Another basket of flowers had been delivered in her absence, causing her maid to sigh over this romance as she dressed Lorna for her drive in the park. The Earl had asked for a few minutes alone before they went out, and when she was dressed, she went to the gold salon, where, the old butler informed her with a knowing smile, they would be quite undisturbed. She tried to look pleased.

Peter, when he came in, inspected her with his searching gray eyes before he bent over her hand and kissed it. "What is wrong?" he asked, his deep voice intense.

"Why, nothing, Peter," she began, and then, when he would have spoken, she added quickly, "Was there some particular reason you wished to see me privately?"

The Earl scowled, and for a moment she was sure he would insist on pursuing his question, but then she saw him shrug and take a small box from his pocket.

"Surely it is proper for us to be alone now, my dear bride, and all the servants expect it. Besides, I could hardly give you this in the hall," he said, coming to stand close to her and put the box in her hand. "It is your engagement ring."

Lorna was glad the tiny clasp allowed her to lower her eyes. When she had the box open, she could not restrain a gasp, for there, on a bed of dark-blue velvet, was the most beautiful sapphire she had ever seen. It was a domed oval in shape and surrounded by a score of brilliant white diamonds, but the flashing fire of the main stone was not a bit overpowered by them.

"How very beautiful!" she exclaimed, and then he took her left hand and slipped on the ring.

"I am glad you approve my choice. Rundell and Bridge would have been delighted to exchange it for another if it had not met with your approval," he said, his deep voice stiff.

Lorna raised her hand and looked deep into the sapphire. "I have never seen anything so lovely," she assured him. "Thank you."

Her voice for once had lost all its cool authority and seemed about to break, and he took the opportunity to say, "It is not quite the color of your eyes, ma'am, but there is a fire in it that reminded me of them when you are angry."

Lorna looked up at him, her high color deepening as she asked, "Shall I cultivate anger, then, sir?"

Lord Peter grinned down at her. "But there is no need to cultivate it, my dear. It has seemed to me it is an emotion you can all too easily call into being almost at will. I know you wish to dispute that remark, but come, I cannot keep my team standing on this cold afternoon."

Lorna allowed him to help her into her blue cloak, but she was quick to draw away and fasten the ties herself. She wanted no repetition of the way he used to button Melanie into her cloak with such a tender air.

They spoke very little until Hyde Park Gate had been passed, and then Lord Peter began to question her about her stay at Tower Hill. Lorna was glad to have such an easy topic of conversation introduced, for it gave them something to do in between nodding and greeting all their acquaintances. The Earl did not appear to be too distressed when she told him the style of the wedding the Dowager planned; in fact, he did not even seem to hear her, and very soon her voice died away.

"Now what is wrong?" she asked in a tight, angry voice.

"We have made a complete circuit of the park, Lorna, and not once have you smiled at me. Don't you realize that everyone is watching us? Your attitude toward me is hardly that of an ecstatic bride . . . No, do bother to defend yourself. I know this is abhorrent to you, but we must appear at ease with each other, delighted to be together, and indifferent to the world; otherwise all will be lost. I realize it will be difficult, but surely you can playact a little. I am prepared to do my part."

Lorna sat up straighter, her eyes flashing with the same fire as her ring, and she determined to stun him with her show of emotion. "It shall be as you say, sir," she said through gritted teeth, and then espying Lady Jersey coming toward them in her small landau, she put her hand on his arm and, melting against him, gave him her most caressing, lingering smile.

Lord Peter appeared stunned for a brief moment, but he returned it equally, his gray eyes lighting up and his harsh features relaxing. "Excellent!" he said in a gruff voice. "You look as if I were your sole delight, and Sally will be sure, as Lady Silence, to tell everyone she knows."

He ignored the lady's wave, bending over Lorna as if to whisper in her ear, and they continued around the park. Lorna straightened up as he said, "It is too bad I cannot recall any jokes or stories that might make you laugh, but keep telling me about our wedding plans and do remember to smile."

It was the most ridiculous hour Lorna had ever spent. In between descriptions of the eight bridesmaids and their gowns, she laughed and acted the flirt. She was telling him about the grand ball the Dowager was honoring them with when he turned his head and kissed her lightly on the cheek where the deep dimple he remembered was in full display. For a moment, she faltered in her story, and her smile faded away.

"I suppose that will have to do," Peter remarked, his attention back on his team. "I am sure the Countess and her party saw me kiss you, and perhaps she will put down your agonized look of distress to the fact that we are in public and you are simply regretting you cannot throw your arms around me but must wait for a more private occasion."

Lorna hesitated, controlling her temper before she snapped, "You told me once before how expert a lover you are. Perhaps the Countess thinks me stunned by my great good fortune in attaching you. No doubt most girls would swoon away at such distinguished attention."

"Smile, m'dear, smile," he reminded her. "No, they do not swoon."

"I am surprised you admit it," she replied, waving and beaming at Lord Landford, who was walking with a party of friends.

"You see, they are afraid of missing what is sure to come next," he explained kindly, turning to grin down at her clenched fists and brilliant eyes.

"You are conceited and boorish! How dare you tell me these things?" Lorna demanded.

"But I thought you wished to know," he replied, flourishing his whip and allowing the team's pace to quicken. "After all, you were the one who brought 'em up."

Lorna gasped, and then in a tight, angry voice she demanded to be driven home.

"Yes, I think just about everyone who is anyone has seen us now, and those who did not will hear about it from their friends," Lord Peter agreed as he turned the team toward the gate. "Now let us consider, Lorna. My aunt tells me her dinner party is set for Friday evening, but before that we

must surely meet. Let me see. I do not suppose Lady Morthman would care to entertain me at an evening party?"

At Lorna's incredulous look, he nodded. "No, of course
not. The woman is so stupid she does not realize what a
great gabby she appears, but let that go. I know! We shall go
to a play and then on to supper. Would you like that?
Besides, in the theater you shall not have to converse with
me, but can stare at the stage in rapt attention."

"I do not care to go alone with you, sir," Lorna was swift
to say.

"Fear not, my dear, you shall be accorded all kinds of
protection from my passionate, impulsive advances. Let's
see. I shall ask Melanie and Lord Landford and Sir Digby
. . . that is, I will if you can bear to meet him, realizing he is
lost to you forever."

"You are ridiculous," was all Lorna found to say. The
Earl seemed to be possessed of a devil this afternoon, the way
he was teasing her. "Besides," she added when she saw his
lips curling in a triumphant smile, "the numbers are
uneven. Pray ask another lady to join us, m'lord."

"You would leave that to me?" he asked, as if incredulous.
"Aren't you afraid that my choice might be one of my
former flirts?"

"I believe Miss Mary Warren is a pleasant addition to any
party," Lorna said, ignoring this raillery. "And although
you have not asked, I would very much like to see *Macbeth*
at the Drury Lane."

"I had it in mind to choose another play," Lord Peter
remarked in deep disappointment. "Somehow *The Taming
of the Shrew* seemed most appropriate, but let that go. We
can see it another time. I am sure you would find it most, er,
most educational."

Lorna was delighted to see that they had reached St.
James's Place. Since the Earl had not brought a groom or
tiger with him, she told him she could get down without any
help, for she was sure he could not leave his horses. Peter let
her slip down to the cobblestones, wondering if she were
going to march into the house without another word, but
Lorna was not to be betrayed into incivility.

Smiling up at him, she thanked him for a delightful drive
as she dropped him a little curtsy. Lord Peter looked down

from the high perch into her rosy face and tipped his hat. She turned away, and then whirled around again and held out her hand. "My dear sir, allow me to thank you again for the beautiful ring," she said. "I never expected anything like it, I assure you."

"But we must follow the usual form, must we not, Lorna?" he asked. "If we were in love, it is just the style of ring that I would choose for you and expect you to delight in. Even something as small as this must not be overlooked if we are to be successful in tricking the Ton into thinking us mad for each other."

Some of the light in her blue eyes died away. "In that case I must also thank you for the flowers you have sent, must I not?" she asked quietly, and then added, "You think of everything, sir," before she nodded and went up the steps.

The Earl wondered as he drove away why he had thought to put it in quite those words, as if the matter were of little account and done solely to fool Society, and he wondered also at her reaction, so formal and wooden. It was most unlike her! He had visited the Dowager the previous afternoon, and she had told him of Lorna's strange meekness, but he had had no explanation that he could give for it. He had been on the lookout today and noticed that she had been quiet, her voice lacking animation when she did speak, until he began to tease her. He had continued to do so, for it appeared to be the only way to stimulate and rouse her, and since it had worked to perfection, he planned to continue to behave that way. It had become very important to him to remove the awkwardness she felt when they were alone together.

As he drove back to the mews behind his rooms, he continued to think of her. His first feelings in Dorset of dislike and revulsion had gone long ago, and his admiration for her had grown, especially now that he had witnessed her behavior all through the upsetting day that had begun with their attendance at the Frost Fair. Never once had she complained of the cold or her tiredness, and not once had she shown any fear, even offering to take one of his pistols so she might help him if they ran into any trouble. He grinned to himself at the memory. And then her behavior in the cottage, setting him to fetching wood and water while she prepared their meal, all without tears or hysterics or hand-wringings, which he would have found impossible to cope with without losing his temper.

The Earl failed to notice old Lord Howland, waving his cane in salutation as his mind went back to the violent way she had refused to marry him. He frowned. It was perfectly obvious she still held him in the greatest dislike. Perhaps that was why she was now so uncharacteristically cold and controlled. He shook his head. It was a ridiculous fiasco, that was certain, but he was sure they would manage to rub along tolerably well as soon as the ceremony had been performed and she became used to being at his side. After all, she had years ahead to accustom herself to it.

The Earl refused to think what their lives would be like, trapped in this marriage of convenience that he had promised her, or whether at some future date she might come to care for him, and he for her. He was experienced enough to know that his physical presence disturbed her, in spite of her aversion to him, and honest enough to admit that she had a very disquieting effect on him as well, but that kind of attraction was not love, as he had, at the age of thirty-five, every good reason to understand. His former mistresses, not as numerous as he had given her to believe, had all been able to excite him with a seductive glance or a passionate embrace, but he had not loved them, nor they him.

Lord Peter drew up before the stables and his groom hurried to take the grays' bridles, but his words of greeting died away when he saw how preoccupied his master was.

As the Earl strode around to Albany Street, his frown deepened, for he realized that Lorna had never tried to be seductive in her manner, and still he had experienced that familiar sensual warmth every time she was close to him. He remembered his reaction when she pressed against him in the phaeton. His right arm had seemed to burn from the contact with her soft, full breast, and he had felt a stab of regret when she moved away. And that warm, alluring smile! It had made him catch his breath in his struggle to appear normal.

You are a fool, Norwell, he told himself as he took the stairs to his rooms two at a time. She behaved that way because she had to, and at your express command. Strive for a little common sense, man! She had made it very plain, over and over again, that she thought him an ugly brute, with no sensitivity or charm, or any gentle, redeeming aspects to his character. The frown in his bleak gray eyes deepened, and for a moment his rugged face was distorted with pain. He had always known he was not the embodiment of any maiden's dream, as Sir Digby and Lord Landford were, with their open, handsome faces and trim physiques; and even though he dressed well, he knew his strongly muscled build would never show off his clothes to advantage, as theirs did. No, it was plain that she found his physical attributes as unattractive as she found his character.

But no matter what she thought of him, she had to marry him, and he knew it was up to him to take control of their predicament and guide her safely through it with all the expertise he could bring to bear. And he knew he must not do anything to upset her or cause her to feel any uneasiness of mind or spirit until their wedding had taken place and they could leave the prying eyes of London for their honeymoon. And what a farce that would be!

He remembered that the Dowager had inquired about his plans for this trip, but he had it in mind to ask Lorna if she would care to go into Kent with him and see Norwell House, her future home. Somehow it seemed absurd to whisk her away on a journey to Greece or Paris or Rome. Besides, they would be too much together, traveling alone. At Norwell he could ride out and interest himself in estate matters, and she could take up the reins of the household and busy herself with any changes or decorating schemes she cared to initiate, and with any luck, the only time they would be alone was at the dinner table, and even there surrounded by servants.

As he put his beaver and gloves on the hall table and allowed his valet to assist him from his greatcoat, he resolved to ask her if she would dislike Kent in February, without explaining his reason for foregoing a trip abroad. He asked if there had been any messages delivered in his absense and then did not wait to hear the answer before he shut himself up in the library. Mr. Swinnerton thought him distracted, but he smiled, for, of course, much must be forgiven a man who was about to enter the holy state of matrimony.

The evening of the theater party, Lorna dressed carefully in one of her new gowns. She was spending a great deal more time on her toilette, for knowing she looked beautiful and was fashionably gowned seemed to give her courage. Melanie squeezed her hand when the Earl was announced, but soon forgot to pay any attention to the engaged couple when she saw Sir Digby come in behind him.

Lord Landford had arranged to collect Miss Warren and meet them at the theater, and Lorna was delighted to see they had arrived at the box before them. In the exchange of greetings and best wishes for their happiness, she was able to appear composed and content as she took the seat the Earl was holding for her next to his own. The box was crowded, even though the other two gentlemen took seats behind, allowing the ladies the better view of the stage.

Lorna stared down into the smoky, noisy pit. The gentry exchanging greetings, the cits and beaux all vying for attention, and the orange sellers crying their wares made it impossible to carry on any normal conversation. She settled back in her chair and relaxed, but only a moment later Lord Peter took her hand in both of his and held it in a firm, warm grasp. Miss Warren peeked at them and nudged Melanie, rolling her eyes as Lorna stared straight back.

"Cultivate a warmer expression, if you please," the Earl reminded her as he bent closer to whisper in her ear. His warm breath stirred her hair and she steeled herself not to pull away.

Even then the lamps were being dimmed and the curtain pulled aside as the three witches came onto the stage amid sounds of thunder. Such was Kean's genius that Lorna soon forgot Peter's nearness and strong hands in her absorption with the great actor and Shakespeare's enthralling lines.

At the intermissions there were friends to wave to in other boxes, punch to sip, and the play to discuss with the others, and Lorna became quite animated with her delight in the performance. The Earl smiled and nodded, looking as infatuated as anyone could wish. The only time Lorna felt a qualm of unease was when Kean began Macbeth's moving soliloquy that she had quoted herself only a short time before. Her hand quivered in Peter's at his opening lines. The Earl frowned a little and she knew he was remembering too.

The delicious supper of lobster in a sherry sauce and woodcocks in pastry that the Earl had arranged for them to enjoy after the performance seemed endless to Lorna, and the toasts of Lord Landford and Sir Digby in the ever-flowing stream of champagne caused her to clench her hands under her napkin. Her head was aching with the effort to appear normal, and she wondered how she could ever have thought Mary Warren a sensible companion when she simpered and giggled in the ladies' withdrawing room, where the two had retired for a moment.

"Lucky Miss Jarrett," she crooned, primping before the glass, "Lord Peter is so . . . so virile, is he not? Anyone can see how he adores you. And that lovely sapphire ring, and all his wealth and title besides. Lucky, *lucky* you!"

When the Earl escorted Melanie and Lorna back to St. James's Place, Melanie excused herself at once, and Lorna, conscious of Sir Digby preparing to reenter the carriage to give the lovers a moment alone, gave Lord Peter a pleading glance. In the flickering light of the flambeaux that lit the doorway, she could see his frown plainly.

"You are tired, my dear," he said in a tight, barely controlled voice. "Go in with your cousin and sleep. I will see you tomorrow when I shall do myself the honor of escorting you to the Dowager's dinner party."

Lorna bowed her head and nodded. "Thank you, m'lord," she whispered. "That will be very kind of you."

Lord Peter spoke very little during the short drive to Sir Digby's lodgings, and his good nights were perfunctory and distracted.

For the Dowager's family party, Lorna chose to wear a gown of pale blue silk, with a matching silver net overskirt caught up in knots of silver ribbon. With it she had a matching stole to drape over her arms, and her maid had dressed her hair in soft waves that ended in clusters of curls. The Jarretts and Lady Morthman had already gone ahead in their carriage when the Earl was announced, and as Lorna came down the stairs to greet him, she caught her breath in that now-familiar gesture of first meeting. He looked more imposing and powerful than ever in his clinging knee breeches and silk stockings, his faultless white cravat anchored with a black onyx stickpin, and his gray moiré waistcoat fastened with onyx buttons. Above all this splendor, his harsh-featured face seemed dark and threatening, and no smile softened his well-cut mouth.

After bowing and kissing her hand, he helped her with her stole and they left the house. The Earl's groom, dressed in his livery, was there to assist her into the carriage, and the two settled back for the short drive to Berkeley Square.

"You are looking lovely this evening, Lorna. I admire you in blue," Lord Peter announced after a moment of silence, his voice so quiet he seemed bored.

Lorna felt that familiar spark of anger. "Indeed, sir? One could hardly guess from your expression that you were pleased at all. And if I may say so, it is no use to tell me to smile and appear happy all the time if you intend to walk about the world looking like a thunderhead."

Lord Peter turned sideways on the coach seat to stare at her rigid profile. "Perhaps I have decided that there is no sense in all this playacting?" he asked mildly. "It has been a great deal of bother, and in return all you can manage is a frightened, agonized look. You might just as well wear a sign saying you were forced into marriage. Why, even Sir Digby noticed the change in you last evening, and I had to tell him you were not feeling well. It is strange, for I never thought you a coward or a quitter, yet you prove me wrong every time we meet. And who would believe this fearful, cowering, whey-faced girl that you have become is the same positive and independent Miss Lorna Jarrett? Bah!"

Lorna turned swiftly to face him, one white gloved hand raised in anger, but Lord Peter was too quick for her and gathered both her hands in his. "No, you will not strike me, Lorna. I advise you never to try. I have a dangerous temper that is not always perfectly controlled."

"I am not fearful or cowering. And how dare you call me whey-faced?" Lorna panted, trying to free herself. They were approaching the Dowager's town house now, and Lord Peter tapped on the roof. Lorna subsided in her corner as the coachman opened the trap and the Earl ordered him to drive around the square until told to stop, before he turned back to his enraged fiancée. In the light of the oil lamps he could see her cheeks enflamed with her anger, and it made him smile to himself.

"Not whey-faced now, when you are furious, but at every other time you parade an insipid gentility and maidenly reserve that is most unlike your normal behavior. Tonight you are to meet my family, and there is not a one of 'em who will believe that I would ever have chosen such a prim, prudish puritan to wed, unless it was against *my* will. Coming it much too strong, m'dear! And if their tongues start wagging, all we have tried to do is for nothing."

"I am not a prude. You are insulting," Lorna interrupted him, beginning to struggle to free herself again now that the coachman had shut the trap and they were alone in the dark.

"Then behave yourself as you ought to," the Earl ordered in a clipped, authoritative voice, as if she were no more than two and ten. For the entire length of the square there was silence between them, and Peter wondered if he had pushed her too far. At last he felt her hands relax in his, and he released her.

Lorna moved away from him, smoothing her gown with shaking hands. "I advise you to prepare to be astounded, m'lord," she said through gritted teeth, and Peter turned away before he dared to smile and order the coachman to pull up at the Dowager's front steps.

That evening Lorna met member after member of the Earl's family, from second cousins twice removed right down to his doty Uncle Connie, who giggled from behind his hands as he subjected her to an inch-by-inch inspection and who seemed about to say something distinctly naughty to her before he was removed by a forceful Miss Eliza. There was worse to come, however. Cousin Bess, who spoke in the piercing voice of the hard-of-hearing, announced in what she considered a whispered aside to Miss Jane that she approved Peter's choice. "Never mind that the girl is handsome; what is more to the point, she is well developed and appears to have the makings of a good breeder," she said as Miss Jane bore her away to the other side of the drawing room. Lorna's color was as high as Lord Peter could wish for after this encounter.

She also met her bridesmaids, although they were so alike she was sure she would never be able to distinguish between them, and all through the crush of company and numerous introductions, she stood at Peter's side with a proud, assured air, an open smile, and laughing remarks that could not help but earn his gratitude and admiration. When she was forced to address him directly, she did so with such warmth and intimacy that he knew he was the only one present who was not fooled, for while the others might admire her sparkling blue eyes, they could not know they were lit only with anger and a desire to prove him wrong.

Lorna had been placed on the Dowager's right hand, and Peter on her left, as guests of honor, and all through the long formal dinner she was careful to smile and flirt with him over her glass. The Dowager peered at them and nodded in a contented way.

Nor did Lorna falter when the dancing began after the gentlemen rejoined the ladies. Peter wondered if he had it in his power to make her perpetually angry, it was such an improvement. He held her close in his arms for a Viennese waltz and bent his head close to hers as they danced, and many an old lady grew misty watching the happy couple. Even Mr. Jarrett was reassured at last, and conversed with Lord Peter in a friendly manner for some time; and since Melanie had confided to her Grandmama that she would never have accepted the Earl if he were the last man on earth, Lady Morthman managed, as far as it was possible for her to do so, to look moderately pleased.

Lord Peter congratulated Lorna for her performance when he escorted her home. Lorna sniffed and turned away.

"No, no, my dear, I mean it! You were superb," he assured her. "Breathtaking, in fact. Even Uncle Connie remarked your beauty and spirit, though I'm afraid it would not be seemly to repeat his exact words."

"I am no more interested in his outrageous remarks than I am in your compliments, m'lord," Lorna said with cold disdain. "I did only what I had to do, and now, if you would be so kind, please stop talking to me. You are giving me the headache."

She turned her shoulder and stared out the window, seemingly fascinated by two young peers who were wending their way home after a convivial evening, half in and half out of the gutter, and singing at the top of their lungs. The Earl prudently allowed his fiancée the victory.

But when they reached St. James's Place and he took her up the steps to the front door, she saw Lord Landford leaning against the wrought-iron fence that separated the park from the street, some little distance away. He had been there for some time, first waiting for Melanie to arrive home so he might have a glimpse of her, and now finding it difficult to leave when he was sure that the right front windows that had lit up shortly after she entered the house were those of his beloved's bedchamber. He would have felt the fool if he had known he was mooning over Lady Morthman's room, but he was spared that indignity.

Lorna, however, knew she was not to be spared a continuance of her masquerade. Lord Peter nodded his head slightly at the lovesick peer, his eyebrows raised as if he waited to see what she would do in this situation.

"Dearest Peter," she cried, throwing herself into his startled arms and causing his look of amusement to vanish in an instant, "kiss me before I must go in, my love."

The Earl was delighted to comply, though astounded by the ardor of her kiss. Lorna put her arms around him and nestled closer, and her warm lips opened under his in complete surrender. Peter responded fervently, lost in this unexpected but delightful embrace, and for several moments he forgot Lord Landford and his interested groom and coachman. Indeed, Wellington's army could have lined up in ranks across the street and he would not have noticed them either.

When Peter reluctantly raised his head at last, he was speechless. Lorna leaned back in his arms, her mouth quivering so it tempted him to kiss her once again. But before he could succumb to this enticement, she spoke in a quick, breathless whisper.

"You will have the honesty to admit, m'lord, that I am not

a prude or a prig, I hope, and as for being a puritan, I beg to be excused."

"No, you are not at all prudish, I see," the Earl agreed meekly, his intent gray eyes never leaving her blue ones.

Lorna stepped back and sounded the knocker. "But be that as it may, m'lord, you have agreed to a marriage of convenience. Know and remember henceforth that I hold you to our bargain and your promise still."

She glared at him, her breath still coming as fast as his as Lady Morthman's butler opened the door wide.

"A delightful evening, dearest Peter," she cooed. "Until tomorrow, my love?"

9

But on the morrow she woke to discover that Lord Peter had left London. When the maid brought up her morning chocolate, there was a bouquet of roses, accompanied by a letter from her fiancé on the tray. Lorna dismissed the interested maid, but she did not read her note immediately. Instead, she drank the hot, steamy brew as she went over the events of the previous evening in her mind, and her lips curved in a triumphant little smile before she opened his letter at last.

It was longer than his previous communications had been, but just as formal, telling her that he had been called to Kent on a matter of estate business and regretted that he would be unable to wait on her until the evening of the Dowager's ball. Since that was a week away, Lorna knew she had vanquished him. The mighty Lord Peter had fled and did not intend to spend any more time with her until the ball and their marriage, which would follow in two days' time. Her smile was scornful as she continued to read.

The rest of the letter informed her that he was taking her to Norwell House after the ceremony and he hoped she would not find the countryside too dull after all the amusements of Town. She was pleased to see he signed his letter "Peter" instead of using his cold title, but she could not be pleased with his postscript.

> My sincere congratulations, ma'am. Even Mrs. Siddons could not have matched your performance last evening. It was perfect from beginning to sophisticated end. One could almost say a drama acted by a veteran. Brava!

Lorna crumpled the letter in anger. So, he was sneering at her again, was he, and calling attention to her "experience" and "sophistication." She told herself she did not care; then she jumped out of bed, threw the letter in the fireplace, and summoned her maid. She felt marvelous. She would have a big breakfast and then she would go for a canter in the park before she had to meet the Dowager Duchess at Mme. Thérèse's for a fitting on her wedding gown. And, she reminded herself, there was her ball gown as well. Mme Thérèse had outdone herself with that, and Lorna was sure it was the most beautiful gown any girl could ever wear, a simple sleeveless column of ice-blue satin with a deep neckline and absolutely no lacy frills or knots of ribbon to distract from its pure, perfect lines.

She was still feeling marvelous when she entered the modiste's shop, and was joined by the Dowager Duchess of Wynne some minutes later as she was being hooked into her wedding gown.

"That ivory satin is perfect with your skin, Lorna," the older lady said. "There will be no other bride who can touch you."

Lorna laughed, her eyes twinkling in amusement. "But, then, there will be no other brides about, isn't that so, dear ma'am? In that case I must win by default."

"Naughty chit," the Dowager said as she took the little gilt chair one of the dressmakers was holding for her. Mme Thérèse herself was supervising this fitting and the room was crowded.

"I must thank you, Your Grace, for the lovely party last evening," Lorna said more formally. "You have been so good to Peter and to me."

"It pleased me to see you enjoying yourself, dear girl," the

Dowager nodded. "And I am delighted that the behavior of Uncle Connie and Cousin Bess did not give you a disgust of the family. I shall see to it that you do not meet them again until your wedding day."

Just then, another woman brought in Lorna's ball gown, and the Dowager clapped her hands. "Perfect! Madame, you are a genius. And, Lorna, although I should not tell you this, Peter has confided that his gift to you is to be a magnificent diamond and sapphire necklace and matching ear bobs. How splendid they will look with this gown. I am sure he will be showing them to you soon. When do you meet next?"

"Not until the evening of the ball, Your Grace," Lorna said, and although her voice was even, she felt a moment's pang of disquiet. There was a stunned silence in the fitting room, broken only by the orders of the modiste and the murmurs of her minions. "The Earl has gone down to Kent this morning," Lorna felt compelled to add. "Something to do with the estate, I believe. But that is not surprising, since we are to go to Norwell House for our honeymoon. It may be that there are some special arrangements—"

"Peter has left you for a week? And you will be going to Norwell House?" the Dowager asked in a stunned, disbelieving voice. Lorna was glad to turn at the dressmaker's urging so her train could be adjusted, and the Dowager could see only a bit of her averted profile. "Madame, please clear this room, if you would be so kind. I wish to speak to Miss Jarrett alone. I shall call you the minute we are ready to resume the fitting."

The modiste shooed the dressmakers out and shut the door behind them all as Lorna turned to face the Dowager, a question in her eyes.

"Now let us have no more of this farradiddle, if you please, my girl! I was sure Peter would take you to Greece, or perhaps the West Indies. It is so romantic there with the soft breezes and flower-scented nights. What is this foolishness about driving down to Kent instead, and in this cold and dismal month of February, too? You are not some little nobody to be treated to a stay in the country. No, you will be Countess Norwell and, as such, you should have a grand wedding tour. I did not look to see you in England for six months at least."

Lorna struggled to keep her expression calm. "Then you will be delighted to hear that you will see us much sooner than that, Your Grace. Going to Norwell House was Peter's choice. He did not ask me if I preferred another location, and to be truthful, it does not matter to me in the slightest where we go."

The Dowager was leaning forward in her chair, peering at her intently, and Lorna essayed a light laugh. "Besides, Your Grace, it is the outside of enough for you to take over the planning of our lives after the wedding. You have done everything that had to be done to bring about that event, but you must allow the Earl and I to muddle through without any further assistance. When we are married, I am sure the Ton cannot gossip about the length of our honeymoon or where we choose to spend it. Your part in this is over."

The Dowager looked thoughtful as she lowered her eyes. There had been something in the tone of Lorna's voice that told her of Lorna's suspicion that the Dowager had played more than just a little role in uniting her with Lord Peter, and this caused the old lady to pause and consider her next words carefully.

"Of course you are right, my dear, but how disappointing! And how sad for you that Peter must leave Town right now. I am sure you will miss him most dreadfully."

Lorna's expression did not change. "Of course, but as you know, there is still so much to be done—so much shopping, so many fittings, and Melanie's luncheon party, and the receptions and breakfasts, as well as the ball to prepare for, why, he would only be very much in the way. And that reminds me, should we not be getting on with this fitting? There are several pins sticking into me and it is most uncomfortable."

She went and rang the bell and nothing more was said, although Mme Thérèse noticed with her sharp black eyes that the Dowager Duchess looked very thoughtful and was a bit absentminded for the remainder of the morning.

When that lady had dropped Lorna off in St. James's Place, she ordered her coachman to drive her home, completely forgetting that she was expected at Mrs. Driscoll's for luncheon and cards, for she was thinking hard. Although Lorna had been pleasant and talkative, not once had she mentioned Lord Peter again. The Dowager was puzzled. Could it be that the girl was still upset at the way her engagement had begun? She would never had thought her so missish! And it was hard for her to believe that Lord Peter had not been able to bring Lorna to a blissful acceptance of the situation, happy with her bridegroom and looking forward to all the raptures that were sure to come.

The Dowager went to sit alone in a small salon. She had to admit that Miss Lorna Jarrett was different from the other young ladies she had dealt with before. Not only was she reticent about her feelings to the point of secrecy, but she appeared to have very definite ideas of her own when she did speak. The Dowager had chortled in the past when she wondered how her great-nephew would deal with this tendency; she had not imagined that she would find herself in similar straits. And of course it was too awkward, even for her with her blunt, outspoken ways, to tax the girl with any direct questions. She was not a relative—not yet, at any rate. However, she would not shirk her duty if she saw it plain, she told herself, and if necessary, she would be much more direct the next time they met. She sighed and wondered if Agatha Allendon were getting too old and past her prime to be manipulating others for their own good.

She heard Eliza and Jane come into the front hall then, and went to join them, hoping that they might be able to suggest something.

The ladies were shocked, but at the end of a long discussion, they persuaded the Dowager that no good would come of her confronting Miss Jarrett, and as for posting down to Kent or even writing to Lord Peter, they were both horrified.

"No, no, dear ma'am," Miss Jane exclaimed, her little eyes wide in her earnestness, "you must not, indeed you must not. It is only a few more days until the wedding, and nothing must upset the apple cart before then."

"Do consider, your Grace," Eliza chimed in. "We cannot know why Lord Peter left so suddenly, and while it is not perhaps the common thing for a groom to absent himself in this way, perhaps he did go to straighten out some problem. Or perhaps they have had a lovers' spat, and being separated will bring them to their senses. We must not meddle now, ma'am, not with the ending we seek so near at hand."

The Dowager agreed, albeit reluctantly, to forget her first impulsive solutions and to pretend that nothing was wrong, but in the following days she was careful to observe Lorna every chance she got. The girl was blooming, full of laughter and good spirits; she did not seem unwilling to marry or to be regretting her choice, and with that the Dowager had to be content.

She would not have been so easy if she could have seen the black look her great-nephew wore as he wandered about his estate, counting the days until he had to return to Town for that fateful wedding day. Of course there had not been any problem on his well-run acres, and he admitted to himself that he had bolted from Town, and Lorna's disturbing presence, as soon as he could after that passionate moment on Lady Morthman's doorstep. He did not know whether to be grateful to Lord Landford for inadvertently bringing it about, or whether he should curse him for provoking it. All he knew was that he needed some time alone, a little space apart to accept once again the fact that he was about to marry a bewitching, seductive, maddening woman who wanted nothing more from him than his name and who intended to hold him to his promise that he would not touch her or try to consummate their marriage.

He did not know how he was going to restrain himself, but he put that worrisome problem from his mind. One way or the other, he would have to manage. He knew he loved her now, that he had loved her for a very long time, for, otherwise, why would he have gone to so much trouble, courting Miss Melanie just to be near her and trying so hard to make her admit she returned his regard? Other women in the past had scorned him, and he had been able to shrug and turn away, but with Lorna such a course was not possible. And since he was being honest at last, he admitted that he had fallen into the Dowager's trap simply because it would bring him what he most wanted—Lorna, as his wife. He could have affected Melanie's rescue a dozen other ways, but, no, in tearing after her with Lorna beside him, he had gone willingly, a most unlikely lamb, to the slaughter.

He inspected the rooms he had ordered prepared for Lorna, his late mother's suite, which adjoined his own rooms and consisted of a bedroom, dressing room, and a salon. They were gracious rooms located on the front of the manor overlooking the park and the ornamental water. The morning sun streamed in through the many large windows and there were sizable fireplaces and old but comfortable furnishings of the early Georgian period: graceful Chippendale chests, a Bombé writing table and a fold-top dressing table from Ince and Mayhew his mother had particularly liked. He hoped Lorna would not want to change them, even if they were not in the current mode, but there was no doubt she would wish new hangings, for the green figured silk his mother had chosen was worn and faded. Wandering into the bedroom, he wondered if a pale-blue damask or perhaps a primrose silk would become her best; then he stared at the huge four-poster bed that dominated one end of the room.

His scowl was even blacker as he strode from the room, calling for his horse to be brought around from the stables immediately. Perhaps a hard, bruising ride would cure his puerile fantasies, he told himself viciously.

Couch, his butler, sighed as he saw him out the door and went to consult with his wife, the housekeeper. Mrs. Couch gave it as her considered opinion that the Earl was not a happy man, and she herself was most anxious to see this bride he had chosen. "Why is he hangin' about in Kent and not in Town with the young leddy, Couch, answer me that?"

Lorna, in the meantime, was delighted to be free of the Earl for even this little time. Knowing that she had caused him to flee gave her confidence, and somehow thinking about the wedding did not bother her nearly so much when she did not have to be near that tall, masculine figure with those piercing gray eyes and authoritative, forceful manner. She could do as she pleased, for now there was no one to order her to smile or to taunt and tease her, and it was pleasant to hear the envious comments of her bridesmaids at Melanie's luncheon and see the wistful smiles of the older ladies when they pressed her hand and told her how happy they were for her. Weddings were really feminine occasions after all, she told herself as she opened yet another gift or thanked Melanie for the lovely silk peignoir that she herself had embroidered for her cousin.

But of course her reprieve came all too soon to an end. The Earl posted back up to London early on the morning of the ball, and after changing to Town clothes and stopping at Rundell and Bridge, he made his way to St. James's Place.

The elderly butler bowed and smiled and showed him into the gold salon without announcing him, shutting the double doors softly behind him as he went away to allow the happy couple the privacy that they were no doubt yearning for after their separation.

Peter stood just inside the door, staring at Lorna's back where she knelt on the carpet surrounded by boxes and papers and ribbons. She was struggling to open a large carton and muttering to herself, and without thinking he said in his deep, distinctive voice, "Allow me to help you, ma'am."

She seemed to jump straight up into the air for a moment, and he heard the little shriek she gave before she turned to face him, one hand to her heart, her face white and strained.

"You!" she cried in a choked voice.

The Earl strolled to the center of the room. "Even accepting the fact that I am not your heart's dearest delight, ma'am, I find that greeting—hmm, shall we say—less than civil."

Lorna was struggling to her feet, for kneeling at his put her at a distinct disadvantage. Her heart was still jumping, and she was furious that he had found her this way, with her hair all untidy and wearing one of her oldest gowns. She had set aside this afternoon to open the flood of wedding gifts that had been arriving and that she had been too busy to attend to till now.

"How dare you burst in on me unannounced?" she demanded when she had caught her breath. "And how dare that stupid butler allow it? Why, I . . ."

Lord Peter took her hand in his and patted it, "I am sure it was his idea of a romantic gesture, Lorna. Surely you would not disillusion him?"

She looked up into those mocking eyes and her heart sank. He was back, the ball was tonight, and on Saturday at nine in the morning they would be wed. Her all-too-brief interval of freedom was gone. Still, she squared her shoulders and put up her chin. "My apologies, Peter," she said in a voice she tried to make light and careless, "it was just that you startled me. Should you like to go out so we can begin again?"

She smiled as she spoke, the dimple peeking out briefly, and he pressed her hand and led her to a chair. "Well done, ma'am. No, I will accept your excuse if you will allow me to pour you a glass of wine." He waved his hand at the cluttered floor and tabletops as he went toward the decanter. "But what on earth is all this?"

"Wedding gifts. Hundred of wedding gifts, it seems," she answered, nodding as she accepted the glass he brought her.

"Why do you not employ a footman or a maid or two to help you?" he asked, going to sit across from her and swinging one booted leg gently.

"Why, I suppose I felt it my own special task. These gifts are all expressions of good wishes from our friends and relatives. However, now that you are here, I see no reason why you should not assist. Come," she commanded as he raised his brows, "perhaps you can tell me who some of these people are as we unwrap."

Lorna rose and went back to her carton, and after a moment the Earl put down his glass and came to assist her. It was the most lighthearted hour they had ever spent together, for there was plenty of talk about and work to be done, and no time to be spent remembering their last encounter.

Finally, they reached the last gift, a large wooden carton tied with silver ribbon. Lorna opened the card. "Who is Sir Constantine Truesdale, m'lord, and why does the card say 'but not to compare with the original in any way'?"

Lord Peter removed the heavy carton from her reach. "That is my rakish Uncle Connie, and knowing the old gentleman as well as I do, I think you should allow me to open this gift unassisted." He set to work, and Lorna settled back on her heels to wait.

The Earl peeled back the silver tissue paper inside the carton and slowly withdrew Uncle Connie's gift. It was a three-foot-high pink marble statue of a plump nude, holding a lamp above her head with both hands, looking coy as she did so, and it was truly hideous by anyone's standards.

Lorna covered her mouth with her hands to hide her giggles, her eyes dancing at the Earl's pained expression.

"How very unusual, sir! I wonder where we should display it?"

"We are not going to display it," Lord Peter replied with obvious revulsion. He stuffed it back into the box and crumpled the paper on top of it, and Lorna noticed the reddish tinge on his high cheekbones and realized that he was embarrassed.

"But, my dear sir," she persisted, "surely Uncle Connie will expect it to have a prominent place when he visits Norwell House. It is too bad it is not a pair, for then we could set them on the mantel in the drawing room. But perhaps in the center of the hall? Or in your library? And although I could not see much from the hasty manner you put it away, I am sure the lamp can be used. How clever! A functional as well as artistic gift. But you do not seem pleased. Can it be that you are not a patron of the arts, dear sir?"

"Be very careful, Lorna," the Earl threatened, frowning at her when he saw her laughing. But Lorna only shook her head at him, lost in amusement, and Lord Peter retreated to finish his wine, thinking what a congenial time they had spent. As he set his empty glass down, he saw the scarlet velvet box that he had brought with him, and he picked it up before he went to help Lorna to her feet.

"There is one more gift that you must open, ma'am," he said, placing it in her hands.

Lorna looked up into his eyes, all laughter gone. She undid the clasp and raised the lid slowly, and once again her first reaction was a gasp of astonishment. "No, no!" she cried. "It is too much!"

"Too much for Lady Truesdale? You must strive not to be so silly, Lorna," the Earl commanded. Since she appeared unable to answer him and only stared down at the jewels in the case, he took it from her hands and, placing it on the table, lifted out the diamond-and-sapphire necklace that it contained. It looked fragile in his large hand, but it glittered and shone with a hundred diamonds of different sizes, interspersed with deep-blue sapphires that formed the flowers that made up the design. With his other hand he took out the matching diamond-and-sapphire drops for her ears.

"Do you like the set?" he asked in a gruff voice. "You are not to think I only intend to bedeck you with sapphires, ma'am. There is a diamond tiara I have my eye on, and two perfect strands of pink pearls, and—"

"No, you must not," Lorna interrupted, putting her hands to her hot cheeks. "You are too generous, sir, and all these gifts are not at all appropriate in our situation. I did not expect . . . I mean, I never thought to be an expense to you."

Her voice died away as the Earl came and fastened the necklace at her throat. She felt shivers on the back of her neck as he swept her hair to one side to fasten the clasp. Even against the navy merino of her old gown, it looked splendid.

"Behave yourself, Lorna! There will be no more comments about the gift's unsuitability. Remember you will be Countess Norwell, and as such, I expect to be proud of you in your beautiful gowns and jewels." He flicked her chin with a careless finger and added, "I must be off. I shall call for you in plenty of time this evening for my great-aunt wishes us to help her receive the guests. I insist you wear my jewels. Is that quite understood?"

Lorna nodded, still speechless, and he went and picked up the carton that contained his uncle's gift. "This monstrosity, however, you will not have to see again. Until tonight, ma'am."

From that moment on, time began to race by for Lorna. It seemed no time at all before she had bathed and had her hair done and had been dressed in her ice-blue satin gown, her awestruck maid clasping the glorious necklace around her throat and fastening the eardrops on with trembling hands.

Melanie was thrilled when she saw the magnificence of the

Earl's gift, and Lady Morthman and Mrs. Jarrett could not help one last heartfelt sigh in unison for everything their side of the family had forfeited, while her uncle told her she was more beautiful tonight that he had ever seen her.

When Lord Peter arrived and she came slowly down the curving stairs, he bowed low and kissed her hand in homage, and a few minutes later, in Berkeley Square, Miss Eliza and Miss Jane clapped their hands together while the Dowager Duchess beamed her approval.

Dinner took no time at all, or so it seemed, and then Lorna and Peter opened the ball. There were over a hundred guests in the Dowager's ballroom and salons, all of which had been decorated with blue silk hangings and bowls and vases of delicate hothouse flowers from Wynne itself. Lorna moved as if in a dream into Peter's arms as the waltz began, and the guests applauded them. It seemed strange to be all alone on that huge shining floor, but held secure in his strong arms, she did not falter.

"You are stunning, the envy of every woman here," the Earl told her, his deep voice a little unsteady.

"Such conceit, m'lord," Lorna could not help replying, but she was careful to smile at him as she did so. "Will you never stop boasting of your conquests?"

For a moment, she thought he would frown and make some cutting remark, but then he smiled back and whispered as they turned, "I should have said I am the envy of every man, should I not? I only meant that none can touch you tonight for presence and beauty."

Lorna smiled again, trying to ignore how close he was. We are really doing very well, she told herself, and I must not spoil it.

"We are doing very well, don't you agree?" he asked, and she caught her breath in a little gasp. Surely he could not read her mind? That would be fatal!

"I most certainly do, Peter, and I shall do my best to see that this happy truce continues. But if there is any envy felt, it is surely for these magnificent jewels." She inclined her head to the necklace that glittered on her throat and breast, and Lord Peter was careful to give it only a cursory examination. Lorna's gown was cut very low, and half her creamy breasts swelled above the cool ice blue of her gown.

They were joined shortly by the other dancers, and after that their ways parted as each was required to stand up with others. Although Lord Peter took her in to supper, he was called away by some of his cronies immediately afterward. Lorna noticed the Dowager's companions watching both of them carefully, and wondered at it, but then there was Lord Landford, Mr. Wilson, Sir Digby with his banal compliments, and a score of others all clamoring for a dance, and she forgot their scrutiny.

When the ball ended at three in the morning, she realized that her feet and legs were aching: she had not sat out a single dance. Lord Peter was there to help her into her blue velvet cloak, and she went and kissed the Dowager Duchess more warmly than she had ever done before.

"My dear ma'am, what a magnificent evening! How can we ever thank you enough for this ball and all your help?"

She looked to the Earl as she spoke and was surprised to see the cynical look come back over his craggy features, and his well-cut mouth twist in the briefest of smiles.

"How, indeed," he murmured sarcastically as he bent over his great-aunt's hand.

Her Grace appeared flustered for a moment, but then she tapped him with her fan and told him to take Lorna home, and entreating Lorna to be sure and curtail her activities on the morrow, she bade them good night. As they took their seats in Peter's Town carriage, Lorna was reminded of the previous occasion when they had ridden home together from the Dowager Duchess's, and she was quick to chat of other things. She had a number of questions about her trunks and when they were to be collected; she wondered if they would be coming back to town for the Season and if Lord Peter intended to hire a house, and in no time at all he was helping her down and taking her up the steps in St. James's Place.

She tried not to look as if she were thinking of what had happened the last time they stood together in the flickering light of the flambeaux, but she need not have worried about Lord Peter's calling it to her attention. He was almost brusque as he bade her to sleep well, and in a moment he was gone.

Lorna, worn out from the dancing and the excitement,

fell asleep at once, but the Earl was not so fortunate. The ice-blue ball gown had been too much of a success for that.

In spite of the Dowager's instructions to curtail her activities the day before the wedding, Lorna found herself in the center of a great bustle. Besides instructing her maid in how to pack her trunks, there were cards to read, flowers to acknowledge, last-minute gifts to open, and the preparations for the wedding breakfast to oversee. Mrs. Jarrett claimed fatigue and retired to her room, and Lady Morthman, secretly indignant that her house was to be the scene of such merriment, and not even for a member of her immediate family at that, washed her hands of the whole proceedings.

And so Lorna, once again dressed in her old merino gown, supervised the floral arrangements, soothed the butler about the amount and quality of the champagne and other wines, approved the caterer's menu, and checked the setting of the tables and the number of little gilt chairs that had been ordered to supplement the usual furnishings. Melanie tried to help as best she could, but by late afternoon Lorna wished she would stop chattering, for it was not only distracting, it was giving her the headache. She was grateful, however, for the rush of activity, for it kept her mind from the morrow.

She climbed into bed with a grateful sigh shortly after dinner, for her maid was to call her at six, wondering where the time had gone. In a moment, she was asleep.

By eight-thirty the next morning she was dressed and ready. The ivory satin gown looked beautiful. Its high choker collar was embroidered with seed pearls, and the tight bodice was fastened with tiny pearl buttons. The cuffs of the long, tight sleeves had matching embroidery, and below the waist the gown fell in graceful folds to the floor, ending in a wide, sweeping train.

Melanie had come to help as soon as she was dressed in her blue maid of honor's gown, and she looked lovely with the roses that matched her bouquet crowning her hair. Lorna stood quietly while her cousin and the maids fussed around her, and the door opened and closed bringing new people in to assist at every turn. Lord Peter's bouquet was delivered, a huge spray of creamy lilies and roses to match her gown, her mother's delicate lace veil was placed tenderly over her head, and Uncle John came to fasten a magnificent strand of pearls at her throat, his own personal gift to his beloved niece. Lorna felt tears coming to her eyes as she kissed him, and a weak quivering in her legs.

She had a moment of panic then, for her marriage to the Earl was happening after all in just a little while, and the progression to that ending that neither of them really desired seemed so inevitable, so relentless that for a moment she wished she could run from the house and disappear where no one would ever find her again. Then she straightened her shoulders and tilted her chin. She had made a promise, and for these last few minutes that she was Lorna Jarrett, she would keep it. She always kept her promises.

Just before she went down the stairs, a footman brought in a large box. Melanie opened it for her and cried out in delight when she saw the magnificent sable cape the box contained. She held it up for everyone to admire while Lorna read the card that accompanied it.

> It is not that you have not always looked entrancing in your blue velvet cloak, my dear, but I could not bear to see you wear it again. It would remind me too much of the "parfit gentil knight" who is now lost to you forever.

The note was signed "Peter, Earl Norwell." Lorna did not know whether to smile or stamp her foot, but then she saw the single word of the postscript. "Courage!" it said, and she could not help smiling after all.

And then they were at the cathedral, with crowds of servants and seamstresses and passersby oohing and aahing as her uncle helped her down from the carriage, and then they were waiting at the head of the aisle as the bridesmaids made their slow way to the altar to the resounding chords of the great organ.

Immediately before Lorna and her uncle were the page and two young flower girls with their baskets of petals. One especially, little Sarah Truesdale, kept turning to stare at the bride, her blue eyes wide and a little frightened, and Lorna smiled and winked at her. When she saw the child's shy answering smile, she felt better, and the long walk down the aisle on her uncle's arm did not faze her in the slightest. Over the organ music and the pure sweet voices of the boys' choir, she could hear the guests murmuring as she passed them, but she looked straight ahead to where Lord Peter and his groomsmen waited for her, his harsh features somber and his powerful body held stiffly erect and motionless. He looked like a caged tiger in his faultless wedding clothes, and Lorna lowered her eyes.

As she reached his side, she stole a glance at him and saw his gray eyes serious and intent as they searched her face under the delicate veil, and then he turned to the bishop. Her hands tightened on the stem of her bridal bouquet.

He said his vows in a deep, calm voice that was impossible for her to read, and her own replies were given in a soft murmur that could not be heard beyond the first pews. When Melanie took her flowers and her uncle put her hand in Lord Peter's, she could not stop its cold trembling, but the warm pressure of his clasp seemed to steady her, even when he put the gold band on her finger that signified their union.

As the organ swelled in the recessional and the boys' voices soared again, he faced her and turned back her veil, and looking down into her eyes for only a few brief seconds, he bent his head and kissed her. Behind them, Lorna heard Miss Jane sigh, her aunt's quiet weeping, and the rustles and whispers of the guests as they waited.

Peter lifted his head and said softly, as if they were alone, "Shall we leave now, wife?"

She smiled at him. "As you wish, husband," and he tucked her hand in his arm while the bridesmaids helped her with her long train before they began the walk together up the aisle.

The wedding breakfast was a blur of noise and laughter, congratulations and kisses, and then, in what seemed only a moment or two later, she was running down the stairs after throwing her bouquet straight to Melanie, to join the Earl, now dressed for traveling, at the front door. Lorna was wearing the new sable cape over a gown of sapphire-blue silk with a saucy matching bonnet.

As they went down the steps to the carriage, they were

pelted with rice, and when several of the tiny pellets struck her face, Lorna was glad to gain the safety of the carriage. The steps were swung up, the grooms jumped on behind, and they were off to the last waves and cheers of the wedding guests. Lorna sank back on her side of the seat and uttered a heartfelt "Whew!" and the Earl, his tall beaver tipped arrogantly over one eye, gave her a tight smile.

"My sentiments, exactly, madam, and yet I think we muddled through in tolerable fashion, don't you?"

"Yes, it all went very well. At least no one fainted and none of the bridesmaids had hysterics, and there was plenty of champagne, in spite of the butler's fears," Lorna answered breathlessly, stealing a glance at her new husband, who was leaning against the squabs and watching her.

"You are warm enough?" he asked in a courteous manner.

"Thank you, yes. Who would not be in these lovely furs? I am forever thanking you, it seems."

She reached down to smooth the sables and noticed that some of the rice had been caught in the soft fur. Frowning a little, she began to brush it away. "I wish they had not thrown rise," she said. "Look how it clings, and it hurts so when it strikes you."

"Besides being entirely inappropriate in this case," Lord Peter agreed.

Lorna flushed and turned her eyes to the passing street scene. She felt a flash of anger at his sarcastic words and had to make an effort to swallow a sharp retort.

"I beg your pardon, Lorna. That was not kind," the Earl said after a few moments of silence. "I think this day has been more of a strain on both of us than we realize, but when we reach Norwell House and have had a chance to rest and recover, our spirits are sure to improve."

Lorna changed the subject abruptly by asking about her new home, and the Earl obliged her without further comment. When he learned she had never been in Kent except when traveling through it to another destination, he told her tales of the white cliffs that guarded its seacoast; of Romney Marsh, once the den of smugglers; of Canterbury, with its magnificent ancient cathedral; of the Weald, an enormous well-timbered forest; and of the miles and miles of orchards and hop fields that turned the countryside into a fragrant garden every springtime. Norwell House, he said, was located some ten miles from Royal Tunbridge Wells, and if she was not too tired, he intended to drive straight through to it.

Lorna had no desire to break their journey along the way and assured him she would be glad to press on, for she was not at all weary.

"Of course! I should have remembered how indefatigable you were that day of the Frost Fair, even as cold and as bruised as you must have been from riding in my racing curricle," Lord Peter said, and then he fell silent as if brooding over that fateful day.

"But you have not told me of Norwell House itself, sir," she reminded him, for the silence between them was not at all the easy pause that occurs in a conversation between good friends.

Peter roused himself from his revery to tell her about his home. From his warm description of its sprawling brick exterior, set in a spacious park and surrounded by fields of apple trees, Lorna could tell how much he loved it.

"The interior, to speak plainly, has fallen into shabbiness since my mother's death some years ago, a problem that I trust, wife, you will take in charge. My mother would be horrified that I should bring you to see such old hangings and faded, worn rugs. But I thought you would prefer to choose new decorations for yourself, and to tell the truth, I like its old-fashioned air, for it looks comfortable and lived in. I despise these stiff modern rooms that look as if no one was meant to use them."

Lorna made a mental note to keep the Earl's home as much the same as it was possible to do, and then she asked about the staff. She learned that the butler and housekeeper were new since his mother's time, and that although new maids and footmen had been engaged recently as well, she was to add such staff as she felt necessary to their comfort.

It was quite dark when they finally arrived and turned into the gates of Norwell House and Lorna could not see anything of her surroundings and was forced to resign herself to waiting until morning. The carriage halted before the front steps and she was glad to take Peter's hand and step down to stretch her tired muscles. Indefatigable she might be, but it had been a long, emotionally tiring day and she would be glad to have a chance to rest and be by herself. But rest was to be denied her for a while, for all the servants were lined up in the hall to greet the newlyweds and stare at their new mistress. Lorna put up her chin and smiled her greetings, noting a soiled apron here, a shabby pair of shoes there, as well as the somewhat supercilious expression of Mrs. Couch, the housekeeper, and the fawning demeanor of her husband, the butler.

At last Lord Peter escorted her upstairs to her rooms. "Time enough to inspect the ground floor tomorrow, ma'am, although I am sure it would look better in candle-light."

The Earl had been noticing things about his home that had escaped him until he saw them through the clear eyes of his bride, and he was a little ashamed of the condition of the house.

"Ask Mrs. Couch to take you around if I should be busy," he said gruffly, a frown forming between his brows.

Lorna sensed his unease and guessed the reason. "I look forward to it, Peter. Your home is lovely. I see now why you are so proud of it," she said, and the frown left his face as he swung open the doors to her rooms.

There was a cheerful fire blazing on the hearth of the sitting room, and Lorna was quick to admire the furnishings, especially the Bombé writing desk.

As she turned to the other rooms, the Earl said, "I shall leave you to explore by yourself. One of the maids will be glad to assist you until your own dresser arrives tomorrow, and your trunks have been unpacked at my orders. And now, if you will excuse me, I shall rejoin you here for supper in an hour."

Lorna turned so quickly to stare at him that his eyebrows rose. "It would certainly cause comment if we dined apart, wife, or even in the formality of the dining room at that hour on our wedding night," he said stiffly. "A cosy supper à deux is not only expected, it is mandatory."

Lorna gripped the back of a wing chair. "I see, sir. Very well, I shall await you here."

She remained where she was until the Earl left the room, then she went to inspect the bedroom. Averting her eyes from the large four-poster, she entered her dressing room and saw her clothes hung neatly in the wardrobe.

She could not bring herself to approach that huge bed, so she lay down on the chaise, pulling a soft afghan over her, but she could not fall asleep or even doze. The events of the day kept running through her mind, and little fluttering warnings and premonitions about the future danced there as well; after a while, she got up and rang for the maid.

Josie was surprised that m'lady required only hot water and did not care for assistance, for she had been looking forward to helping her into one of those filmy nightgowns and beautiful peignoirs she had unpacked, each one as soft as a cobweb, but she grinned and bobbed a curtsy as she went to do as she was bade.

Maybe the leddy is bashful, she thought as she clumped down the backstairs. Coo-er, wonder wot it would be like to crawl into bed with the likes of 'im for the first time? Fair give a body the shivers, that would, such a big 'arsh man as 'e is. M'leddy can 'ave 'im and welcome, is wot I say!

In an hour Lorna was ready. She had remained in the bedroom while the servants set the table, and not until all sounds of preparation ceased did she come back to the sitting room. The table looked very cozy, placed, as it was, before the fire, although she could not help noting that the silver candelabrum was tarnished in spots and the crystal did not gleam as it should in the glow of the fire. Putting such housewifely considerations from her mind, she forced herself to sit down in one of the wing chairs to await her husband. It was only a few moments later that his knock came at the door, and she called for him to come in. She tried to keep her expression neutral when she saw he had changed into a scarlet dressing gown, and instead of wearing a cravat, had knotted a loose silk ascot around his throat. He seemed a little nonplussed to find her still attired in her traveling gown, but he made no comment as he rang the bell for the servants to bring in their supper.

Couch himself oversaw the meal and the pouring of the wines, and of necessity they were forced to chat of the same things they had already discussed, from the wedding guests, the bishop, and the boys' choir to the littlest flower girl, the reception, and their journey to Kent. Lorna was very tired now and felt that if she had to continue their farce for much longer, it would be more than she could bear, and she was relieved when the Earl dismissed the servants and waved the butler away. She could not remember what she had eaten, only that she had not had much appetite, and it had surprised her that Lord Peter as well had only toyed with his food, although he drank several glasses of wine. Now, he poured them both another glass, to finish the bottle.

"You have everything you need?" he asked in that gruff voice she was beginning to know meant he was not completely at ease.

"Thank you, everything is perfect. And thank you for giving me these lovely rooms, so large and comfortable," she forced herself to reply.

"These were my mother's apartments. You face the front, so tomorrow you will be able to see the lake and the park from your windows."

The Earl tossed off his wine and put the glass down on the table with a snap. "And now, my dear bride, I beg to be excused. I am sure you are tired and as sick of this playacting as I am. Until tomorrow?"

He bowed and came to kiss her hand, and Lorna felt that familiar weakening in her knees and constriction in her throat. "What . . . what time do you take breakfast, m'lord?" she asked.

"There is no need for you to bestir yourself to join me," he said abruptly. "I am always up very early, and plan to go out shortly thereafter."

Lorna was about to say that she was an early riser too, but then she realized that he did not care to see her at the breakfast table. Squaring her shoulders, she nodded. "As you wish, sir. Good night."

Without another word she whirled on her heel and went into the bedroom, closing the door firmly behind her, and then she leaned back against the door, her breath coming in dry sobs she tried to smother with her fists. This was awful, much, much worse than she had ever imagined it would be. But at least he was gone now and she did not have to pretend anymore, nor make silly conversation to show that everything was fine for the benefit of the servants.

She went into the dressing room and took off her clothes

herself, putting on one of her new nightgowns and wrapping herself in Melanie's silk peignoir.

Josie had turned down the bed—on both sides, she noted with a wry twist of her lips—but instead of climbing in, she went to stand before the dying fire. God grant me the strength to deal with this situation, she prayed, not only tomorrow but for all the days to come, and then she heard a sound nearby and, startled, turned to seek the source. There was a door leading from her bedroom that she had not noticed before, and she went to it and cautiously turned the handle. Pushing it open, she found herself face to face with the Earl, who was standing before the fire, a frown on his harsh-featured face and a brandy snifter in one big hand. From the heavy mahogany furnishings and his belongings lying about, it was plain to see that this was his bedroom.

For a moment there was no sound but the crackling of the fire, and then he exclaimed in an eager voice, "Lorna! Can it be that you . . ."

At exactly the same moment she said, "I beg your pardon, m'lord! I did not realize your rooms adjoined mine, and when I heard a noise, I thought only to investigate."

She sounded angry and indignant, and he replied in quite a different tone, "It is customary for married couples to have connecting rooms, is it not?" His eyes raked her face and then traveled up and down her figure, lightly concealed in the clinging silk robe. She saw a pulse at his temple begin to throb and her face paled as she put one hand to her lips, her eyes wary as if she suspected he had tricked her.

Before he could come closer or speak again, she lowered her eyes so he could not read her thoughts and said, "Of course. I was not thinking clearly, for I am tired. Forgive me, if you please, for disturbing you."

"It is of no importance, m'lady. Go back to bed. I may be quartered next door, but there is no reason for you to look so distressed. I will keep my word to you, of that you may be sure. The Truesdales always keep their word."

Lorna nodded and backed away, closing the door behind her, and then she sped across the room and jumped into bed like a child afraid of bogeymen. As she pulled up the satin coverlet, she wondered drearily if perhaps there was such a thing as being too much the gentleman, but of course his repeated assurances that theirs was to be only a marriage of convenience left no doubt in her mind as to how he regarded her. As she closed her eyes, she thought how easy it would be for him to keep his promise since he had no desire to break it, and she sighed.

In the room next door, the Earl refilled his snifter and cursed softly and at length. It was very late indeed before he sought his bed.

10

In the morning Lorna had her breakfast served in bed, and then she dressed with Josie's assistance. She had sent a message to Mrs. Couch asking for an interview in an hour, and when she went downstairs, she found the housekeeper, her keys at her ample waist, whispering to her husband. Couch bowed low to his new mistress, but his wife gave a very shallow curtsy, her expression militant. Lorna paid no attention as she asked to be escorted through the house. It was almost lunchtime before she had seen every room from the attics to the cellars, and although she had made few comments, her mind was racing with things that would have to be done before Norwell House was restored to its former magnificence. It was not the faded and worn furnishings that offended her, it was the careless housekeeping, the dirt and grime on the woodwork, the dusty unswept rooms and the dullness of the brass and silver, and the cloudy crystal of the chandeliers. The paintings that hung in the picture gallery were so dark with soot and filth that it was impossible in some pictures to distinguish whether you were inspecting a long-dead earl or countess, and Lorna could hardly wait to have them cleaned and rehung.

Mentally she had set aside for her own use in the mornings a small salon at the back of the house that overlooked the terrace and one of the gardens, and it was here that she repaired with Mrs. Couch to sink gratefully into a chair by the cold hearth.

"From now on, Mrs. Couch, I expect this room to be ready for my use at any time. Please set the maids to scrubbing it this afternoon. This carpet needs beating, and the windows are a disgrace."

Mrs. Couch bridled and said the library had always been good enough for the Earl, but when she would have continued to complain, Lorna raised a deterring hand.

"It is not good enough for his Countess, however. There are going to be a number of changes made here, almost immediately. After the maids finish in here, put them to work in the dining room and tell Couch that I expect the plate to be polished by dinnertime."

She rose to dismiss the housekeeper and was startled to see a gleam of hatred in the woman's little eyes. "That will be all. I shall see about hiring more maids this afternoon, for we will need them to set this house straight in short order."

As she left the room, she heard Mrs. Couch mutter something behind her back and checked for a moment before she went into the hall. The woman was insolent and she could see she was going to have trouble with her. It was plain that the Couches had had an easy time of it, keeping house for a bachelor who neither noticed the careless way his home was run, nor required anything special that would cause them to exert themselves. Since he spent so much time in Town, they had grown lazy and slovenly. Well, she would change all that, and if they could not adjust to the new regime, they would have to be discharged.

She went to the library and, sitting down at the big desk, drew a quill and paper toward her. For the next half-hour she was busy writing down lists. There was enough to do here to keep her busy for months, she realized, but first things first. When she had drawn up a cleaning schedule, she considered the servants. Some of the maids seemed honest, willing girls, but some had stared at her slyly, as if secure in their positions as the housekeeper's pets. The butler was a nonentity, and if his wife did not suit, it would not matter if he had to leave as well. She was tapping the quill against her cheek when the Earl entered and threw down his gloves and crop on the cluttered center table.

"M'lady," he said, bowing and coming to lean on the desk, "you spent a good night, I trust?"

Lorna forced herself to look straight into his mocking eyes, before she nodded and, putting down her pen, straightened her lists before her on the desk.

"And you have already set to work. Such industry!" he said, his lip curling as he went to pour them both a glass of sherry. "Now, I had intended to ask you to go for a drive this afternoon. It is not as cold as it has been and I thought to show you the grounds and the neighboring countryside. But, of course, if you are busy playing Madam Goodwife I shall understand."

Lorna ignored his sarcasm and said she would be delighted to join him. She thought Peter looked tired and he was most definitely out of sorts.

Later, as they sat at the table for luncheon, he asked what she had done that morning. Lorna wished Couch were not in the room, puttering around the sideboard, as she told the Earl of her tour of the house. "I am afraid, dear sir, that I find a great deal to do."

Peter nodded and said carelessly, "Apply to my agent for any monies you will need. Shall you send to London for fabrics? I do not know if you will find anything suitable in Tunbridge Wells."

"I am not speaking about new hangings, sir," Lorna said tranquilly, taking a slice of cold beef the footman was holding out to her and making a mental note to visit the cook as soon as possible. "No, before we can begin refurbishing it, we must clean this place from top to bottom."

The Earl's eyebrows snapped together at her criticism, but Lorna pretended not to notice. "You find my house dirty, ma'am?" he asked.

"By no means, sir," she contradicted him. "Rather I would say it was filthy. But perhaps our standards in the West are higher than yours in Kent."

The Earl's fork clattered against his plate, and she gave him a sweet smile. "Do not be distressed, Peter. In a short time I will have all in order, and you will see how much more comfortable you will be."

Luncheon was finished in silence, the Earl glowering at

his plate and Lorna trying not to look amused. That afternoon, after asking the agent to employ four more village girls to help with the cleaning, Lorna put on her sables and went out to drive with her husband. She admired the park and the silvery frozen expanse of the lake as they bowled down the drive.

"Does it remind you of the Thames, madam?" Lord Peter asked, busy with his frisky grays. "I am sure you have some learned quote for me, bluestocking that you are."

Lorna ignored this last statement. "It is hardly large enough to compare with the Thames, but perhaps we could skate on it before spring. What a charming wood! Beech, is it not? And I am so anxious to see the gardens, for I have it in mind to plant a herb knot if it should not displease you."

Lord Peter subsided. His lady was not to be provoked into a quarrel, not this afternoon at any rate. They came back to Norwell House in the late afternoon, Lorna's cheeks rosy from the fresh air and her eyes sparkling.

At dinner she inspected the silver carefully and nodded to an anxious Couch before she pointed to the massive chandelier that hung over the table. There were several cobwebs visible and the crystal drops were dull. Couch sighed as he shuffled away.

In the days that followed, Lorna set to work with a will, and her days and Peter's assumed a routine that was almost pleasant. They met only for luncheon and dinner, and then sat together in the library, Lorna busy with her sewing, and Peter either deep in a stud book or planning improvements to the outbuildings and fields. How domestic we look, Lorna thought one evening as she glanced up to where her husband sat before the fire, notebook in hand.

She sighed and lowered her eyes to her needlepoint. She had begun a new set of covers for the breakfast-room chairs in a cheerful design of golds and soft greens.

"What a domestic scene, to be sure," the Earl's deep voice sneered, and she dropped her canvas. This was not the first time he seemed to have read her mind, and it disturbed her.

"So it is," she agreed, lifting her eyes from her work to look at him. "And if you would not dislike it, sir, I would like to speak of domestic matters."

Peter courtesouly closed his book, one long finger

marking his place. He thought she looked very lovely tonight in her violet gown with its deep neckline showing off her uncle's pearls and the first swell of her breasts. He forced his eyes to her face as she began to speak.

"I am afraid the Couches must be dismissed. I have tried to get along with them, but Mrs. Couch especially fights my orders at every turn and her work is shoddy. Besides, her authority over the maids is based on favoritism, so there is dissension among the servants. Would it distress you to see them go?" she asked, hoping it would not.

"I suppose not," he replied with a frown. "They have not been with me long, only since I had to pension off the last couple in the fall. But perhaps you are being harsh, ma'am. If you were to explain why you are not satisfied, perhaps they would mend their ways."

Lorna looked at him, perfectly aware that his reluctance stemmed only from his dislike of any further upheaval, and so she said, "I shall take care of it all, m'lord, and ask my aunt to employ a new butler and housekeeper and send them down to us from London. Do not fear that you will be required to speak to the Couches," she added kindly, just as if, he thought indignantly, she thought he was too much a coward to dismiss a servant. Lorna smiled to herself. How men hated change!

Only that morning, when she knew Peter was going to the market town for the day, she had gathered the maids with their buckets and mops, and wearing her oldest gown, she had attacked his library. For an hour they had all worked with a will, scrubbing and polishing and carrying items away to be washed or cleaned, while Lorna herself dusted the books and made sure everything was returned to its proper place.

She was sitting on top of the tall set of library steps when the Earl came in and halted on the threshold, his mouth falling open for a moment at the busy scene before him.

"Out!" he commanded the scurrying maids, and as they sidled to the door, he marched to the foot of the steps and glared up at his wife. "What is the meaning of this, madam? How dare you invade my library?" he demanded, waving his arm around his *sanctum sanctorum*, now in a state of severe disarray.

Lorna came down the steps, sneezing from the dust. "Achoo! As you can see, sir, this room has been neglected too long, and if we are not to sneeze every time we enter it, it must be cleaned. Besides, what are you doing here? I thought you were going to town today."

She put both hands on her hips, looking quite as indignant as he did. With a mobcap protecting her auburn curls and a smudge of dirt on her chin, she looked like one of the maids rather than Countess Norwell.

"I was not aware that I needed permission to return early to my own home," he snapped, clasping his hands behind him so he would not be tempted to tuck that one errant curl back in place with its fellows. "It is snowing hard and I was forced to turn back. But I find I must complain at your boldness, ma'am. I was not aware I gave you permission to upset my private rooms."

"I did not think I needed it," Lorna said quickly, her anger rising as fast as his. "This is a part of Norwell House and you put me in charge of restoring it, did you not? *Ergo,* all the rooms must be cleaned, including this one, *and* your bedroom, *and* the estate room, *and* the gun room, *and* the—"

But she got no further, for the Earl clamped one big hand over her mouth, and when she would have torn that hand away, he captured both of hers with the other hand and held them behind her.

Over this gag her blue eyes flashed fire.

"Be quiet, madam," he commanded, his gray eyes just as dangerous. "This is still my house."

For a moment they glared at each other, and then the incongruity of their position occurred to him, and he dropped his hand and backed away to bow ironically to his dusty, furious lady.

"I beg your pardon, wife. Of course it is your house too, and if you must have the library cleaned, I suppose I shall have to bear with it. But why on earth do you feel you have to help? You are filthy."

Lorna thought she detected a note of disgust, and she smoothed her old gown. "Of course I would not let the maids touch your books, sir, nor anything on your desk. Besides, they work better when I am here, and I had planned to have everything gleaming and back in its place for your return. I am sorry if my person offends you."

Lord Peter bit back a quick denial of any such thing. "Go and bathe. I have no desire to sit down to lunch with a tweeny. And you may call the maids back. I shall retire to the estate room until the coast is clear — that is, I will unless you have also turned it topsy-turvy?"

Lorna curtsied and went away, seething so that she was afraid to speak, and wishing she had given in to her first impulse and bitten his hand. Now she looked around the spotless library, its copper and brass shining and its gleaming furniture smelling of beeswax. Perhaps a scarlet drapery with gold trim would be nice in here, she thought. Peter would look well against scarlet: it would show off his dark hair. She blushed and bent her head over her needlepoint again.

There were other skirmishes in the days that followed as February gave way to March. One evening Peter objected to a new gown she was wearing, and a battle such as both had been avoiding arose to spoil the evening and cause even more stiffness between them.

Lorna had wondered if the ivory silk was not too formal for the country, too revealing for a quiet evening at home, but after she tried it on and admired its lines and perfect fit, she could not resist it. Nothing was said until the covers had been removed and Lorna prepared to leave Peter to his port, and then he motioned for her to remain seated, and waiting only until the butler shut the doors behind him, he began a tirade that left Lorna breathless and indignant.

He did not care to see her wear that immodest gown again, he informed her in an icy voice. He wondered at her sense of propriety that she should appear before the servants almost naked to the waist.

Here, Lorna gasped and put both hands to her breasts, half-covered with the despised ivory silk, as if she expected that it had fallen down during dinner, and she raised angry eyes to his face, but she was not allowed to comment on his words, for Peter rushed on, his voice still cold and biting.

Must he remind her yet again that she had a noble position to fill, and attiring herself in a gown that would make a tawdry bit o' muslin or even an expensive *demi-*

monde blush was not how he cared for the Countess Norwell to appear? Thank heavens there had been no company at dinner to observe her indecent, disgusting garb. And now he would appreciate it if she would leave him, and since it was too late for her to change her gown this evening, ask her maid to bring her a large shawl. A very large shawl. He would never forgive himself, he added sarcastically, if she were to catch cold or a fever from exposure.

"And since, madam, quite half of you is unclothed, there is every possibility of such a calamity occurring. You are excused."

Lorna clenched her fists and glared down the expanse of the now-polished dining-room table. A score of remarks came to her mind, each to be discarded at once as not nearly crushing enough. Oh, he would pay for this insult, of that she would make sure. How dare he criticize her taste and judgment? She had seen many gowns more revealing than this one, and besides, he had no right to dictate what she should wear. She would certainly tell him what she thought of him, and unfortunately for their fragile truce, she proceeded to do so.

Neither of them considered that their raised voices could be heard throughout the house, causing the maids to tremble and the footmen to smirk while Mrs. Couch remarked to the cook that things were not the way they used to be, so quiet and serene, since m'leddy had come to stir everyone up. The evening ended with Lorna flinging herself from the dining room and slamming the door in Lord Peter's face. He followed her to the hall, but when he saw his butler and the footmen there, he realized that their discussion must be curtailed, for now at least.

The following evening when Lorna came down to dinner, she was buttoned to the neck and wrists in a navy silk with a demure white collar and cuffs. Her hair had been scraped back in a severe bun that looked to Lord Peter as if it must hurt her scalp from the tension. He refused to comment, and for a week thereafter Lorna went about looking like an escapee from a convent. At length, tiring of the game, she began to dress again in her pretty gowns, although she never wore the ivory silk again. She told herself she was saving it for their first large dinner party, when she planned to wear it over thoroughly dampened petticoats. It never crossed her mind that the sight of her sitting there in that seductive gown had almost driven Peter mad. He was finding that their seclusion and his abstinence were harder to bear with every passing day, and his expression grew even blacker and more dangerous.

There were other, minor skirmishes. The Earl entered the drawing room late one afternoon to discover that the carved Adam commode that had always stood to the left of the fireplace had been moved between two tall windows, and now sported a collection of bibelots on its polished top. He summoned Couch and ordered it restored to its former place.

For a week the commode made daily trips back and forth across the drawing room, and finally Couch was emboldened to complain to Lorna in his whining voice that they wuz all become *quate* worn down with it, and could her Ladyship and the Earl decide between them the final resting place of the commode?

When taxed by his wife, Peter replied that his mother had always kept the commode against the wall and he saw no good reason to change it. Lorna's eyes flashed, but she answered him sweetly.

"But as the present Countess, this is my drawing room now, is it not? I prefer the commode between the windows. It is a beautiful piece of furniture and was quite wasted behind the sofa in that dark corner."

The Earl was forced to admit defeat, but a frown could be seen on his face every time he entered the room for some time to come.

Lorna also took him to task one morning at the breakfast table after he barked a list of orders of things he wanted her to attend to immediately. She barely waited until the door closed behind the maid before she said in a cold voice, "Of course I will try to take care of these things if it is convenient, but understand, husband, I will not be ordered about like a servant."

Peter buttered another scone. "No, of course not. Anyone can see you are not a servant. Their manners are so much better than your own."

Lorna's mouth dropped open, but just then Couch

announced the Earl's curricle was at the front, and he was able to escape before a major tiff could develop.

Eventually Mrs. Jarrett wrote to say that an excellent butler and housekeeper had been engaged, and would take coach for Royal Tunbridge Wells in a few days, and Lorna summoned Mrs. Couch to her morning room.

The woman took a long time to appear and, when she came in, gave an insolent smirk as she curtsied. Lorna was delighted to be able to tell her that her services and those of her husband would no longer be required. She added that although their year's salary would be paid to them in lieu of notice, she could not give either of them a letter of reference, for she had found their work most unsatisfactory.

Lord Peter, passing through the hall, heard this last statement and stayed to eavesdrop.

"And 'oo are you to discharge me, me foine leddy?" Mrs. Couch demanded, her voice rising and her accent becoming more crude in her anger. "I takes me orders from the Earl, and so do Couch."

"The Earl and I are in complete agreement on this head, Mrs. Couch," Lorna replied in a cold voice.

"Is that so?" the housekeeper asked in an insolent voice. "Well, that makes a nice change for you, don't it? 'Complete agreement,' indeed! Fight like cats and dogs you do, and if I wuz you, m'leddy, I'd be ashamed of meself. Not even able to keep a new bridegroom 'appy, you ain't! If you was to arsk me, I'd say *your* work has been 'most unsatisfactory,' for 'oo would expect a newly married man to go about with a face like a thundercloud unless 'e wuz being made plain miserable by 'is choice o' bride? Probably think you're too good for a romp in bed, eh, me foine leddy? I know the signs, I do."

Peter heard the scrape of Lorna's chair and pictured her rising to her feet, and an unholy grin crossed his strong-featured face. Now, how will she handle this, he wondered.

"That will be all, Mrs. Couch," he heard her say in a tight, controlled voice. "I shall expect you and your husband to be off the estate today. The coachman will take you and your trunks to Tunbridge Wells at three. Leave me at once."

She must have advanced on the housekeeper then, for

Peter heard the rush of Mrs. Couch's heavy passage to the door and he made good his escape.

Within two days Mr. Tramble was in capable charge of the front hall, the footmen, and the butler's pantry, and a Mrs. Lowety had inherited the bunch of keys that proclaimed her office, and it was soon obvious that the household was running more smoothly than it ever had since his mother's death.

Peter was not called to deal with the servants' arguments, nor required to replace the unhappy ones who had formally left his employ on a regular basis. In fact, he thought to himself as he looked around his home, noting its gleaming cleanliness, the bowls of flowers, and the sweet smell of lemon and beeswax and soap, Lorna had done wonders.

He was not an ungenerous man, and so he was quick to compliment her and applaud her wisdom in replacing the Couches, and for almost two whole days, perfect peace reigned at Norwell House . . . until they found something else to quarrel about.

Now that Mrs. Lowety had the reins of the household firmly in hand, Lorna found that she had much less to do, and since the weather was improving every day, she often set out on rambling walks of exploration. Lord Peter was quick to suggest she ride out with him as well, and after he had seen what an excellent horsewoman she was, he had instructed his head groom in her hearing that the Countess could ride any horse in his stable, with the exception of his own young gelding. He had started her on a placid old mare, with which choice she was quick to express her scorn, and she finally chose a spirited filly named Chessie as her favorite mount. The Earl could not help but admire the picture they made together, Lorna's auburn curls almost the exact shade of the filly's coat, and if sometimes he had to stifle a groan as he watched his wife riding ahead of him on a narrow track, her slim waist swelling to a pair of luscious hips and firm, round bottom, Lorna was unaware of it and his intense scrutiny as well.

They had driven over to Royal Tunbridge Wells one day, and Lorna was pleased to find a silk merchant and draper whose goods were suitable for some of the new hangings at Norwell House. She made arrangements to return the following week with exact measurements, and since Lord Peter was not interested in such housewifely pursuits, she set off on the day appointed in the landau with her maid in attendance, after informing Peter of her destination.

By three in the afternoon, the skies darkened and the weather turned stormy. From his desk in the library, Peter could hear the rain beating against the windowpanes and gurgling in the downspouts, and a look of unease came over his harsh features. The book he was reading soon lost his interest, and many times in the next hour he found himself going to the window to see if the landau was returning.

By six o'clock there was no sign of Lorna, and he was very concerned. He did not know whether to mount a search party, for if she had had trouble along the way she would be wet through before anyone might come along to help. And then he found himself thinking of the robbers and charlatans who might take advantage of two helpless women and an elderly coachman, and he clenched his fists.

He was about to order the horses saddled when Mrs. Lowety knocked and came in to ask what he wished to do about dinner.

"I am sorry to trouble you, sir, but do you care to eat in the dining room at the usual time? I don't expect Lady Truesdale to return, for she did tell me she might spend the night in town if the weather turned nasty." Here the housekeeper chuckled before she added, "I think we might call this nasty, m'lord."

Peter was furious, but he returned a civil answer, asking for a tray to be brought to him in the library, and when the housekeeper left, he got up to pace up and down the room. How dare Lorna make such a decision without discussing it with him? No, he had to hear her plans from a servant, and not until he had spent three hours worrying about her at that. It was rude and arrogant and inexcusable.

By the time Lorna had arrived late the following morning, the landau crowded with parcels and boxes of all sizes, he had worked himself into a cold, icy rage. Her sunny smile was met with a glowering look as he ordered her to the library and shut the door firmly behind them before he told her exactly what he thought of her bold, inconsiderate ways. Lorna was stunned, and she watched him with wide eyes as he towered over her, shaking his finger at her as he recalled in infinite detail, every fault and mistake she had ever made to his knowledge since that dreadful, fated day he had had the misfortune to meet her. At last he finished his tirade and went to pour himself a glass of wine, and Lorna rose to remove her stole and bonnet.

"I think you are absurd, m'lord," she said briskly, causing him to turn and glare at her anew. "Any sensible man would have realized in an instant when it came to storm that I would stay in Tunbridge Wells. What, drive home ten miles in an open landau, getting myself and all my purchases soaking wet, to say nothing of being so inconsiderate of the poor servants who were with me? Besides, I must remind you once again that what I do is my own business. I am perfectly capable of taking care of myself, and if you remember, you promised me that after our wedding I could go my own way."

"I realize I made that rash promise, madam," Lord Peter interrupted. "However, I did think some innate good taste would tell you that I might have a vague interest in your whereabouts. I was forced to hear of your plans from Mrs. Lowety. The housekeeper, mind you! Not a word to me from my dear wife before she left, oh, no! And I object to you staying in public houses alone, subject to lewd remarks and ogling from any Tom, Dick, and Harry in the taproom. See that it never happens again. I trust I make myself clear?"

"Now you are being ridiculous, Peter," Lorna said quickly. "Of course I had a private parlor. You cannot be so mad as to think I consorted with the locals in the taproom. And as for lewd remarks and leers, I should like to see any one try it in Mr. and Mrs. Williams' inn. Do try for some semblance of rational thinking, sir. After one night spent in the company of my maid in a respectable house that has always enjoyed your patronage, there is no need for you to accuse me of being indiscreet and depraved. In fact, such accusations insult me."

By now, Lorna was as angry as he was, and although Peter realized that he had perhaps overreacted to a very ordinary happenstance, he could not find any way to retract his words. They parted stiffly, and the conversation at lunch was stilted to an extreme.

It was unfortunate that a few afternoons later they received their first callers. Tramble came into the drawing room with a card on his silver salver just as Lorna was unfolding the gold brocade she had purchased for the new overdrapes. She frowned when she saw the card, but when she read it, her face broke into a smile and she bade the butler admit the Dowager Duchess of Wynne and her companions without delay.

"My dear ma'am, how delightful to see you, and Miss Eliza and Miss Jane as well," she exclaimed as the threesome entered the room. "But why did you give us no warning of your arrival? It was not kind of you, for now I shall have to bustle about making your rooms ready or I will be ashamed of my prowess as chatelaine here."

"Dear Lorna," the Dowager said as she kissed her, "we have not come to stay, my dear, but finding myself visiting in the vicinity of Tunbridge Wells, I could not resist coming to see how you and Peter were coming along. You must tell me everything."

Lorna begged her guests to be seated and went to ring for refreshments, wondering what the Dowager would think if she were to tell the truth about their life together, the cold formality and the frequent ugly quarrels. When the butler came in, she ordered tea and asked him to inform the Earl that his great-aunt had arrived; then she returned to her guests.

"No doubt you are longing for news of your family, and I will not keep you in suspense," the Dowager began. "As briefly as possible, Mrs. Jarrett continues sickly and I imagine will enjoy that state at least until the Season is over; Mr. Jarrett has retired to Dorset and estate concerns; and Lady Morthman, you will be surprised to learn, is sporting a very sunny smile these days."

"Melanie has found favor with a duke or a foreign prince?" Lorna asked.

The Dowager chuckled. "Nothing that exalted, but she has received a proposal from Lord Landford, Sir Digby Fortescue is forever in St. James's Place, and the Earl of Spencer has shown a definite interest. Of course, he is only twenty and I myself do not consider him at all a contender, but we shall see. Needless to say, Miss Melanie is thrilled at

the breadth of choice, and like a child in a sweet shop finds
it impossible to make up her mind."

"Her Grace favors Sir Digby," Miss Eliza confided to
Lorna.

"Then I am sure she will choose Sir Digby and I look forward to wishing them both happy," Lorna replied.

"But enough of that silly chit," the Dowager interrupted.
"What of you, my child?"

Lorna was glad that Tramble and a footman came in
then with the tea tray, for it gave her time to marshal her
thoughts.

"As you can see from this material, Your Grace, I have
been very busy. Norwell House was in a sad way when I
arrived, for it had not been properly cared for in years, and
besides needing new decorations, it had to be scrubbed from
top to bottom. I had to let the butler and housekeeper go
when I saw their work," she added, passing Miss Jane a plate
of cakes.

"But are you happy, my dear?" the Dowager asked,
ignoring the gold brocade and the servant problems, as she
peered into Lorna's face.

Lorna looked at her and lied without hesitation. "But of
course, dear ma'am. I find the married state most enjoyable."

"As do I, but how happy I am to hear you say it, wife,"
Lord Peter's sarcastic voice exclaimed from the doorway,
where he stood surveying these unexpected guests and the
flushed face of his wife. "Aunt, Miss Jane, and Miss Eliza—
somehow I might have known that you would be our first
callers."

"Too kind," murmured Miss Jane, and her sister nodded
as he came in to join them.

He remained there until they took their leave an hour
later, Lorna begging the Dowager to return for a luncheon
another day so she might show them all the improvements
she had made.

Her Grace chortled. "No, no, my dear, I shall come
another time. You and Peter do not want others about on
your honeymoon, I am sure." Her nearsighted eyes were
sharp as she looked from one to the other, and Peter found

himself going up to Lorna and sliding an arm around her waist to hug her to him.

"In a general way you are correct, Your Grace, but I assure you we would be delighted to receive you at any time."

"Very pretty talking indeed," his great-aunt said, allowing Tramble to help her into her cloak and wondering if either of her companions had noticed the way Lorna stiffened when Peter touched her. Or perhaps it was just her imagination or wretched eyesight?

"When do you return to Town, my dears? The Season will be sadly flat without you," she asked next.

Lorna looked up at Peter, a question in her eyes.

"I imagine we will be among the throng before too much longer," Peter replied. "We shall have to see about hiring a house, but I cannot leave Kent right now. There are business matters, the spring planting, some building I am having done . . ."

"In that case, you must come and stay with me, Lorna, until Peter is free. We would be delighted to help you in your search for a house, wouldn't we, my friends?"

Her companions were quick to offer their services and say how delightful it would be to have her with them in Berkeley Square, and Lorna promised to consider it, and after a final hug and kiss all around, the guests took themselves away.

As soon as the door closed behind them, Lorna pulled away from Peter's strong arm, for being so close to him was making her breathing uneven. He left the hall abruptly, saying over his shoulder, "Dear, *dear* Aunt Agatha, but I do not think she can have any reason to suspect that the idyll she was so afraid of interrupting is not an idyll after all."

So sure was he that he had lulled any suspicions that he would have been amazed if he could have heard his guests talking as they drove away.

"Well, my dears, never did I think in my wildest imaginings that two people so perfect for each other, so ideally matched and attuned, so equally intelligent and spirited, and so much in love with each other, could be capable of behaving so badly. It is obvious that he has not bedded her yet, and who would believe it?"

"Who, indeed?" Miss Jane asked, shaking her head in amazement. "And it has been at least a month since the wedding day. My, my."

"But why hasn't he?" Miss Eliza asked, getting to the heart of the matter at once. "Lord Peter is such a virile, masculine man."

"That is what is so inexplicable." The Dowager frowned, pushing away some wisps of gray hair that had escaped her bonnet. "Do you suppose they agreed to a marriage of convenience?" She looked thoughtful for a moment and then she added, "If that is so, we must take steps at once, and I believe I have the perfect solution. Now that he has returned from Vienna, we shall be able to enlist Lord Geoffrey Allendon's services."

"The very man!" Miss Jane exclaimed, her face brightening.

"Let us hope that Lorna does not delay her arrival in London, for it is most important that we get her established as Lord Geoffrey's latest flirt before Peter comes to join her, and if that does not make the fur fly, I do not know what will."

"You do not fear it might be too dangerous, Your Grace?" Miss Eliza asked timidly. "Do consider Lord Geoffrey's reputation and Peter's terrible temper."

"Certainly our object is to provoke Peter to bed, not to a duel, but we must do our duty as we see it, and any cowardice must be set aside when that duty calls," Her Grace said, looking stern and resolute, and her companions nodded in unison.

"Is it true that Lord Geoffrey was forced to flee the country because he killed his man last year, ma'am?" Miss Jane asked next.

"Yes, but it has all been hushed up and there is no need to dwell on such unpleasantness. Geoffrey is perfect for the part of chief cicisbeo, so tall and handsome, and of course so dashing and worldly. And his pockets are to let, which will make him all the more anxious to oblige me, not that there is any need to tell him precisely of the part we intend for him to play. It will only be necessary to put him in close proximity to Lorna and that is all we will have to do. Peter cannot accuse me of meddling here, for it is a well-known fact that Geoffrey has never been able to resist a beautiful woman, not that he has tried very hard, from what I can gather. He is such an accomplished rake. Jane, remind me to write to Lorna and urge her to come to Town at once, and Eliza, I expect you to explain to our hostess why we must leave for London first thing tomorrow. I thought our part in this affair was over, but since the happy ending continues elusive, we must continue to pursue it with all the skill and determination we can bring to bear."

The Dowager nodded and her companions sat up straighter, the little old ladies looking as indomitable as possible, and then Her Grace added, "I know Peter is in love with Lorna, and that Lorna returns that love, and I will make them admit it if it is the last thing I ever do."

11

Lorna was preoccupied that evening during dinner, for she was considering the Dowager's invitation to join her in Berkeley Square as soon as possible. She stole a glance at the Earl, who was, as usual, applying himself solely to his excellent dinner. Conversation between them had been stilted ever since her trip to Royal Tunbridge Wells, and now she never saw him except at dinner and only occasionally did he join her in the library afterward. Such coolness made her feel depressed and lonely. She knew he had not forgiven her for not informing him of her possible plans to remain in town overnight, but she found his attitude so possessive and unreasonable in a man irrevocably determined to maintain a marriage of convenience, that it was impossible for her to even attempt to bring their relationship back to its former state of careful neutrality.

Suddenly she nodded as she picked up her wineglass. Yes, she would go to London as soon as she could possibly contrive it. What sense did it make for her to stay here and be treated like a pariah? The household was running smoothly now, and there was little for her to do in the way of further improvements until she could visit the large warehouses in London for additional curtain and upholstery materials, and several new rugs as well. Besides, she thought, her blue eyes darkening as she observed the harsh planes of her husband's face out of the corner of her eye, it will serve him right—rude, impossible creature that he is—not to have her at his beck and call, and nothing but a slave to his manor. And while she was in Town, she resolved to accept every invitation she received and enjoy herself thoroughly. Why should she be buried down here in Kent with a bear of a husband who could not even be bothered to converse with her when there were any number of agreeable men who would be delighted to see that the Countess Norwell was well entertained? And perhaps, she thought with a little thrill, if Peter arrived and saw how sought after she was, he might stop behaving in this silly, objectionable way.

She had just resolved to speak to him after dinner of her plans when Tramble, who had been supervising the footmen at the sideboard, went to answer an urgent knock at the dining-room door. Lorna turned her head at this unusual occurrence, and Peter raised his brows and put down his knife and fork. Tramble's quiet words of inquiry were drowned in a burst of excited chatter.

Peter half rose from the table. "Who is it, Tramble?" he asked, and at the sound of his deep, inquiring voice, all conversation ceased, and the butler turned and held the door wide. Lorna could see one of the farmhands there, his rough hands twisting his cap, his jacket askew and his eyes wild.

"Milord, it's me cottage," he cried, trying to step past the butler, whose arm still barred the way.

"Sam Rogers, is that you? Come here, man," Peter ordered, and at this, the farmhand pushed past the butler and almost ran the length of the room. He was so distraught that he forgot to bow to Lorna and began to speak in quick, nervous gasps.

"Milord . . . the cottage is on fire. The lads are 'elping with the buckets, but the roof 'as caught, an'—"

He had no time to say more, for Peter threw down his

napkin and, grasping him by the arm, hurried him away, saying over his shoulder, "Excuse me, madam. I must go at once."

Lorna remained seated, her eyes worried. Any fire was a danger, of course, especially here, where so many cottages had thatched roofs. She could not place Sam Rogers immediately, and as Tramble came forward to ask if she wished to continue her dinner, she waved an impatient hand.

"No, thank you. Tell me, Tramble, which cottage is the man referring to?"

"I believe Sam Rogers and his family occupy the one nearest the stables, m'lady," Tramble told her, and she pushed back her chair before he could help her.

"Send a footman for my cloak, and tell him to run! The stables . . . good heavens!"

Her cloak was soon brought down to the hall, and Mr. Tramble insisted on sending a footman with her, with a flambeau to light the way, a precaution Lorna thought ridiculous, for as soon as she came out onto the steps, the flames showed her the way. She could smell the smoke and hear the excited cries of the farmhands and servants and, over their voices, Peter's loud orders. She also heard the frightened whinnies of the horses trapped in the big stables, and it was in this direction she ran. She would only be very much in the way trying to help fight the fire, but at least she could help with the horses.

She found Macintosh, the dour Scot who was the head groom, instructing the two stablehands who had remained, for most of the boys had run to see the excitement and had been pressed into service in the bucket brigade. Macintosh did not look best pleased to see the Countess, but when she told him the roof of the cottage was aflame and insisted she could help him move the horses to safety, he nodded and set to work with a will. The horses were nervous and uneasy and not at all eager to leave the false security of their stalls. One boy was almost trambled by the Earl's big gelding, who reared to prevent his bridle being caught, his eyes rolling in his head with fright.

"Tie a scarf around their heads," Lorna ordered. "If they cannot see the flames, they will be more docile."

Macintosh nodded, already busy with a scrap of cloth,

and a short time later, he and the stablehands began to lead the horses out in ones and twos, to turn them loose in a pasture just down the lane that was out of sight of the crackling flames.

Lorna herself led two old carriage horses to safety, praying all the time that their precautions were unnecessary and that the fire would not spread to the stable roof. She looked up at the clock tower over the main arch and sobbed a little. The stable was so old, so beautiful, and then there was a nearby barn crammed with hay to worry about as well. She almost ran down the lane, tugging the bridles, in her hurry to get back for another horse. After she had the carriage horses in the pasture and had removed their blindfolds, she slapped each one on the rump to start it moving away, and closing the gate, turned back. She hoped it was not just her imagination that the flames seemed lower now, although the men continued to call out and she could hear Peter roaring, "No, not there! Wet down the end wall of the barn. Hurry now, lads, hurry!"

Two more trips and the stables were almost empty. As Lorna yanked a skittish bay who seemed determined to run straight into disaster out of the yard, she felt some drops of rain and almost cried out in relief. If only the heavens would open, she thought, they might yet be saved further conflagration. As she coaxed the bay down the lane, talking calmly and steadily to it, she felt the rain increasing and laughed out loud. The two stablehands had returned to the fire now that the horses were out of danger, and she stopped hurrying. She was tired and her arms ached. She closed the gate behind the bay at last with a thankful sigh and turned to walk back up the suddenly dark lane, and then she stumbled into a rut. Losing her balance, she slipped and fell, barely managing to throw her hands out before her to break her fall.

Slowly, she rose to her knees. Now that the flickering light from the fire was gone, it was pitch-dark, but she did not need a light to know how she must look, her silk evening gown covered with mud, her hair wet and streaming loose down her back, and her hands smarting and filthy. She made a face at the picture she was sure she must present, and then she saw a lantern bobbing toward her.

"Macintosh, is that you?" she called, and a moment later found herself looking up into the harsh face of her husband. Peter set the lantern on the ground beside her and knelt to pull her into his arms in one quick, fluid motion.

"Love, are you hurt?" he asked, his deep voice a husky growl. She was so amazed at his words and the concerned tone of his voice, that she could not reply immediately. Suddenly she felt his hands move to her arms, and he gave her a little shake.

"Answer me! Where are you injured?"

The old arrogant tone of command was back and she stiffened, but then she was pulled against that large muscled chest, her back caressed by two urgent hands as Peter put his face against her hair.

"You should not have come out, my dear," he murmured, his warm breath in her ear making her temble. "Macintosh and the lads could have managed, and I would not have had you hurt for the world."

Lorna took a deep breath. "I am not hurt, Peter," she whispered. "Perhaps my dignity is wounded a little. How could I stumble in such a clumsy way? And now I am covered with mud, my gown is ruined, and I am sopping wet. But no matter, of course I had to come help get the horses to safety. Tell me, is the fire out? Did it spread?"

The Earl shook his head and then he put her away from him for a moment so he could look into her face. "We lost the cottage, but the stable and barn still stand, and with this rain there should be no further danger from a lingering spark." He chuckled and added, "In honesty, I must agree you are a little damp and dirty. So unlike you, love."

Lorna wondered if he were going to kneel there holding her in his arms in the muddy lane indefinitely, but since this was the first time he had spoken to her freely for such a long time, she did not bring their situation to his attention. Besides, it felt so wonderful to be held close to him that she did not notice the rain or the cold night air. The Earl reached up one hand and smoothed her hair away from her face, and in the lantern light the two of them stared deep into each other's eyes. "My love," he whispered, "Lorna . . ."

He groaned a little and then he bent his head and kissed

her, gently but thoroughly. It was not the kind of kiss that Lorna associated with Peter, for it held no anger or wish for revenge, only a warm, loving concern for her that any man might show toward a woman he loved. She responded at once, without considering that her actions were contradictory and might be misunderstood. Her arms went up around his neck and she buried her hands in the dark hair at the back of his head. Still Peter continued to kiss her, and she sighed and opened her lips, moving them softly against his in complete surrender. At once, his arms tightened cruelly, but she could not have cried out if she wanted to, not with that suddenly demanding and passionate mouth on hers.

Was it a moment or an hour later that he lifted his head? She could not tell, for she felt so weak and limp it was as if she had been suffering from a long bout of fever, and if he let her go, she was sure she would collapse onto the muddy ground again. She panted, trying to catch her breath, while her pounding heart overflowed with joy.

She looked up into the dark, rugged face that she had come to find so attractive and so dear, searching for an answering expression of happiness, and then she heard voices calling and saw lanterns bobbing as they came closer down the lane.

The Earl muttered something under his breath, but he was quick to rise and help her to her feet. "Yes? What is it?" he called as Macintosh and a groom appeared.

"M'lord, 'tis Mrs. Rogers! In trying to save the baby, she burned her hands something fierce, and the oldest boy has broken his arm as well. Shall I have one of the lads fetch the doctor?"

Lorna looked at her husband and saw that his face was wearing its old familiar frown. "No, I'll take them to him myself, it will be quicker," he said sharply. "Harness the grays to the phaeton while I see to the rest of the family. They'll have to sleep in the house tonight, now the cottage is gone."

Then he turned to his wife and said in a harsh whisper that only she could hear, "I beg your pardon, madam. What I just did was inexcusable, but it will not happen again.

Please, allow me to see you safely back to the house before I leave."

As he spoke, he put Lorna away from him, the hands that had just caressed her so urgently now as impersonal as a stranger's. Lorna was dumb with shock. She could not know that he was ashamed that he had lost control of himself and broken his word to her, that he was embarrassed that her own passionate nature had overcome her dislike for him and forced her to return, against her will, a kiss that she had never wanted.

The head groom accompanied them back to the house, deep in conversation with the Earl about his plan to leave the rest of the horses in the pasture until morning when the smoke from the stable area would have cleared. Lorna wanted to scream in frustration and chagrin, but none of this showed in her cool, controlled face as Tramble admitted them to the house and the head groom bowed and left them. Then Peter removed the arm he had placed about her waist to support her, and she almost cried out and begged him not to leave her.

"Tramble, have someone escort the Countess to her rooms and summon her maid. I am off to the doctor and do not know when I will return. Sleep well, madam, and again, my thanks for your assistance." He bowed and put on the great-coat his valet was holding ready, and then he was gone.

Lorna did not hear the butler's exclamations, nor Mrs. Lowety's stream of orders as she went up the stairs on one of the footmen's arm. Her head was reeling, and her thoughts were in the greatest disorder. All the while her maid helped her out of the dirty gown and prepared a hot bath, she pondered Peter's inexplicable behavior. Why had he put her away from him like that? Why had he tried to return to their cold, formal relationship, especially after that passionate kiss, those loving words? Was he disgusted with her because she had shown her passion for him so plainly? Did he consider her wanton, throwing herself at him after all her previous avowals of distaste for him? Or—terrible thought—did he think she was teasing him, trying to get him to lose control of himself so she could taunt him with it before she withdrew once more?

She shook her head as she sank into the scented bathwater and leaned back and closed her eyes. She did not understand, but she would find out tomorrow if she had to go to him and admit her love and beg for his.

It was disappointing that Peter had had to leave tonight, but his concern for his tenants was one of the things she most admired about him. He had shown in countless ways that he was kind and fair under that gruff, scowling demeanor, arranging time off for a footman so he could go to his sick mother and seeing that a tweeny with a bad sprain was taken to the doctor, and she knew the Rogers would be provided for as well. And as she further considered what she had learned of her husband since their marriage, she admitted she admired his intelligence, his quick wit, and his firm control and acceptance of his responsibilities. He was autocratic and demanding, it was true, but here he was Earl Norwell and, as such, like the captain of a ship, whom everyone on board looked to for orders and guidance.

He had not returned by the time she was comfortably installed in her warm bed, sipping the drink the housekeeper sent up, and she resigned herself to a further wait. She fell asleep thinking about him and what she would say to him on the morrow, and a small smile curled her lips as she fell into a deep slumber.

The next morning when she came down to breakfast, she discovered Peter was already in conference with his agent, and to pass time she tried to work on her needlepoint after her daily interview with the staff. She was so anxious to speak to Peter that she had difficulty concentrating on the design, and after a few moments, she threw down her canvas and went to the window. The blustery April weather caused the clouds to race across the sky and blew the dead leaves in the garden along the wall where some early tulips braved the chill. She felt as restless as the leaves, and rang for a footman to have her horse saddled. Perhaps a brisk gallop would help to pass the time before her interview with Peter.

When she came out the front door, dressed now in her favorite sky-blue habit, she discovered that Macintosh was holding the bridle of the Earl's young gelding. She checked for a moment in surprise and then continued down the steps, calling a greeting as she came.

Macintosh did not look at all pleased to see her this morning.

"Beggin' your pardon, milady," he said as he touched his cap. "I thought it was milord who wished to ride. It will not take me a minute to fetch Chessie for you."

Lorna put up her chin. "Nonsense, Macintosh! Since you have saddled Rasputin, of course I will ride him. There is no need for any delay, for to tell the truth I have been anxious to try out his paces. Give me a leg up at once."

Thus directly ordered, the groom shrugged. Milady knew what she was about, for he had seen her ride, and mayhaps the Earl had given her permission. The groom shook his head. He knew that bridegrooms were often foolish, besotted men, and he wouldn't be at all surprised if that was the case, especially since he had seen them in each other's arms last night in the lane.

Rasputin sidled and snorted as Lorna settled herself in the saddle, but her hands on the reins were sure and strong. Nodding, she signaled the groom to release the bridle, and in a moment Countess Norwell and the huge gelding were cantering away down the drive.

The Earl walked down to the stables an hour later. Tramble had told him that Lorna had ordered a horse saddled, and he thought to ride out and meet her. He was anxious to see her and try to discover a clue to her feelings for him, wondering how she would react to his presence after his lovemaking in the dark lane. God, how he wanted her! But it was more than that, he knew. He had come to love her for her courage in difficult situations, her calm efficiency in dealing with problems, and even for the way she stood up to him and fought him for her rights. She was beautiful and intelligent and full of fire, and he found himself wondering what their children would look like, if ever he could get her to release him from this shackle of abstinence. He grinned realizing it was the first time in his life that he had ever thought of a woman as the future mother of his children. Lorna and he would make a noisy, passionate brood between them, of that he was sure.

But when he discovered that she had taken Rasputin out, his harsh face grew grim again. For several minutes Macintosh, two grooms, and three stableboys were treated to a review of their deficient mental capabilities and what the result of their insolence in disobeying his orders would be in allowing the Countess to be so rash. For, he was quick to add, if any harm came to her, they would all be turned over to the impressment gangs of the Royal Navy, but only after he had horsewhipped the lot of them.

During this tirade, Macintosh had been busy saddling the second fastest horse in the stable, and the Earl was able to conclude his speech and swing into the saddle without breaking stride. He thundered out of the stable yard in desperate haste, cursing aloud at the servants' stupidity and Lorna's impetuous, careless ways.

When he found her, she was stopped before the cottage of one of his pensioners, leaning down over the horse's neck so she could chat with the old woman at the gate. Lord Peter ran his eyes over his wife and his prize gelding, and was relieved to see that no harm seemed to have come to either of them. Rasputin was behaving very well, only now and then tossing his head or taking a nervous little step as if to remind his rider that this was not what he was used to, to be hanging about the village street in the company of cart horses and donkeys.

Lord Peter joined them and after only a few brief words, bade the old servant good day. Lorna's tremulous welcoming smile faded and she raised her brows at his abruptness, but she obediently turned Rasputin's head for home. She could not fail to notice Peter's thin, white-lipped mouth and ferocious frown, and guessing the reason, she prepared to defend herself, even though she was disappointed their meeting must begin this way. But when she tried to speak to him as they rode abreast, he turned angry eyes to her and ordered, "Be quiet. We will discuss this when we reach the house. Until that time, I do not care to converse with you, madam."

After that first wonderful feeling of relief that she was safe, Peter found himself growing angry in the way only Lorna seemed able to stir him to. How dare she ride his horse without permission? And how dare she cause him worry and anxiety for her safety again? Fore gad, this time he would teach her a lesson she would not soon forget!

They rode home in a silence as thick as any they had ever

shared, and Lorna felt a few flutters of alarm. It was unlike Peter not to rant and rave immediately, and although she had been relieved to be spared the indignity of a public chastisement in the village, now his stern, silent attitude could not but frighten her a little. When they reached the house, two grooms came rushing to take the bridles, and she slid without help to the ground, patting Rasputin before she turned to climb the steps.

The Earl had still not spoken, and now he grasped her arm so tightly she almost cried out as she was marched quickly into the house and across the front hall. As he forced her up the stairs at a breathless pace, she asked, "Where are you taking me, m'lord? I must protest such treatment."

"You will keep silent," he ordered in a tight, strained voice. "We are going to your room, madam. I find I have an urgent need of privacy for the next several minutes. You will soon come to agree that you would not care for the servants to overhear us."

By this time he was hustling her along the corridor, causing an upstairs maid to freeze against the wall to allow them passage, her eyes wide with fright. Lord Peter flung open the door to Lorna's rooms and thrust her inside. She collapsed on the nearest chair, trying to catch her breath, while he went through to her bedroom and dressing room to make sure her maid was not within. When he returned, she noticed with an uneasy eye that he still held his riding crop and was swinging it back and forth in one big hand. Surely not even he would dare . . .? She forced her eyes to his face and sat up straighter.

"Now, madam," he said, coming over to her and pulling her to her feet, "perhaps you will be good enough to explain what possessed you to take Rasputin out this morning, especially since he was bound to be touchy after the fire? I have told you how dangerous he is even in ordinary situations, and you have seen the trouble I have controlling him on occasion. You knew you were never to ride him by my express orders. Well? I am waiting to hear your explanation."

Lorna began to remove her gloves, her eyes lowered to the tiny buttons at her wrist to gain time, but the Earl took her chin in one big hand and forced it up until she had no choice but to look at him. His gray eyes seemed almost opaque with anger and the planes of his face carved from stone.

She took a deep breath to steady herself before she said, "It was all just an innocent mistake. Macintosh thought you had sent the order to the stables and saddled Rasputin for you. When I saw the gelding, I decided on the spur of the moment to try him, instead of waiting for Chessie to be saddled." She paused, and when the Earl had no comment, she added a little nervously, "I fail to see why it was so bad of me, or why you are so angry. I will apologize, of course, for I know it was wrong of me to take your horse without permission, but since I came to no harm—nor, might I add, did your precious mount—there is no need for these fire-breathing dramatics." She tried for a light laugh and a shrug and found herself being shaken hard.

"So, you dislike my dramatics, do you, madam? You might have been killed, you little fool. Rasputin is not a good-natured beast, and you are not strong enough to hold him if he should have decided to bolt. It was just your good fortune that he did not. Why is it that you must thwart me at every turn? Why must you disobey my orders and flaunt your own will? I will not have it, *I-will-not-have-it*, do you hear me?"

Lorna was sure everyone in the house could hear him as she pulled free and backed away from him. The Earl followed her until a table stopped her progress.

"But we have a contract, sir, as you were quick to remind me last night," she replied in a bitter tone. "And even though we are married, you know you promised me you would not interfere with me, that I could go my own way—"

But she was not allowed time to say more. The Earl picked her up under one arm as if she were a rag doll and marched over to a straight chair. Sitting down, he turned her over his knee and threw her habit and petticoats over her head.

After the first stunned moment of disbelief, Lorna began to kick and pummel him as hard as she could, screaming at him to release her this instant. The next thing she knew, his large hand was smacking her lace-trimmed drawers hard, over and over again. Tears of fury at her helplessness ran down her face, for it was not so much that he was hurting her as it was the humiliation of being spanked like a small, naughty child. Indeed, she knew he must be restraining himself, for his blows smarted only a very little.

It seemed a long time before he stopped and stood her on her feet again, to glare down at her angry, tear-streaked face, her tumbled curls, and disheveled habit. She swung her arm back to strike him and he caught her hand.

"Stop that! I must remind you that I have the authority over you by law, wife, and I hope that spanking will teach you a much-needed lesson. I have wanted to school you as you deserve since the day we met, for it is obvious that that part of your education has been sadly neglected. You may be grateful that I refrained from using my riding crop on your backside to do so. Know that I am master here, and learn that lesson well. I will not tolerate another instance of your willfulness."

Lorna's breath was coming in little sobbing gasps and she dashed her free arm across her face to brush away the tears. It was true that, as an only child, she had been petted and spoiled, and no one in her entire life had so much as lightly slapped her hand. But now, this brute not only dared to tell her he was her master, he had actually beaten her as well, and all because she had taken a horse out without permission. Her blue eyes flashing her defiance, she glared at him, for once in her life speechless with rage, and all thought of confessing her love for him gone from her mind as if it had never been.

The Earl dropped her hand, but he did not retreat. Instead, his gray eyes grew intent as they studied her face, and if Lorna had not been so blinded by tears and fury, she would have noticed the sadness and regret that was written in them.

"My dear," he said in a softer voice that was full of emotion, "I am sure we can do better than this. In fact, we had better set about learning how immediately, if we are not to end up murdering each other. Come! I forgive you for riding Rasputin. Will you forgive me for losing my temper and beating you? Let us pledge anew to try and live together more serenely. I promise I will try with all my will, and here's my hand on it."

He held out his large hand in supplication, the same one that had just spanked her, Lorna noticed. She stiffened and backed away.

"Forgive you? I hate you!" she gasped. "I will never forgive you for what you have just done to me, never, as long as I live. Leave me at once, sir."

The Earl's hand dropped to his side and his expression changed, the harsh planes of his face hardening in disappointment at the dashing of his hopes, hurt at her recalcitrance, and not a little bit, in anger at his own stupid loss of temper.

"Very well, madam, it shall be as you say. No peace, no truce, no new beginning. But I beg you to remember what happened today and learn to control yourself. I will not stand for any further defiance from you, and if you force me to it, I will take steps in the future to ensure your cooperation. I trust I make myself clear?"

He paused, but Lorna had no comment. Picking up his crop and gloves, he went to the door. "I will be leaving Norwell House tomorrow, m'lady, and will be gone for several days. I think some time apart will be beneficial to both of us. You may continue to reside here or go to London and join my great-aunt. Suddenly I find I do not care very much what you do or where you go, only that you remember that you are Countess Norwell and conduct yourself accordingly. Good-bye."

Lorna heard the door close softly behind him and burst into tears again. She went into her dressing room and washed her face, and as she was drying it, she remembered his last words. He was leaving Norwell House and he had told her he did not care where she went or what she did. Even in her misery, she told herself she was delighted to hear it. She removed her habit and put on a soft robe to brush her hair, not wanting to call her maid, and her eyes were troubled as she stared at her face in the glass. I will not stay here alone, she told herself. No, I will go up to London as soon as possible, and when Peter returns, he will find me gone, with only a cold note to tell him of my destination. He will have no cause to complain of incivility, but neither will he find me here, meekly waiting for my lord.

Lorna did not go down to luncheon, and telling her maid

she was a little indisposed, she had a tray brought to her room for dinner as well. She heard Peter and his valet talking next door, and stared at the connecting door in fearful anticipation, but Peter did not knock or ask to see her again, and when her maid brought up her chocolate in the morning, she also brought the news that the Earl had left very early, driving his phaeton with his baggage strapped on behind. Lorna set her to packing her trunks and went to the library. It took her a long time to compose her letter to Peter, but she was satisfied when she had finished it. It was meticulous and correct, and as cold and formal as she could make it.

She spent the rest of the day making arrangements for the running of the household in her absence with Tramble and Mrs. Lowety, and after she had ordered the carriage for nine in the morning, she went to bed.

She told herself she was doing the only thing that was possible after Peter's inexcusable behavior, but she did not have to wonder why she felt so sad and depressed. It was all she could do not to weep every time she thought about him and remembered his kiss and his warm embrace. To think I was going to confess my love for him, she cried to herself, pummeling her pillows into a more comfortable position. No, after daring to beat me, he can make the first move, for I never shall attempt it again.

Finally she dropped off to sleep, and her last coherent thought was to wonder how long it would be before he came to join her in London.

12

The Dowager Duchess was delighted to welcome her to Berkeley Square the following afternoon and fortunately did not remark on the promptness of her arrival, only one day after she herself had returned to Town. Lorna told herself only a few days later that she had completely recovered her spirits, for she did not think of Peter more than ten or eleven

times a day, and she was so busy searching for a suitable
house, shopping, and renewing acquaintances that she did
not have time to brood.

But Peter did not come to Town, nor did he send her any
word. This surprised her, for she was sure he would not be
able to resist answering her letter. She wondered, a little
uneasily, if she had angered him past redeeming. Could it
be that her behavior since their wedding had given him such
a disgust of her that he never intended to spend another
minute by her side? There were marriages like that, she
knew. Why, it was common knowledge that when Lord
Stevens came to Town, his wife left for the country that
same day, and on his return she was so quick to take her
leave that sometimes, it was whispered, both carriages were
drawn up before the house at once, the trunks and boxes
being loaded and unloaded passing each other on the steps.
She had never expected that kind of marriage, but it seemed
that that was the sort Peter now intended to have. She tossed
her head and told herself she did not care. If she did not
have to see him, it would be easier to hide the ache in her
heart, and now at least she was free of his autocratic, unreasonable demands at last.

Melanie was quick to call on her, and Lorna heard in
great detail all about her beaux. She noticed that although
Melly claimed she could not decide which gentleman to
favor, she spoke most often of Sir Digby, the roses coming
into her cheeks as she did so. Lord Landford, wearying of
her continued reluctance to accept his suit, had left London
in despair, although Melly claimed she could call him back
to her side at any time. Lorna was able to observe her with
Sir Digby herself shortly after her arrival in Town when the
Dowager gave a small reception, but she soon lost interest in
Melly's concerns. It seemed that Lorna too would have an
admirer for the Season.

She was introduced to a Lord Geoffrey Allendon by her
Grace, who warned her right to his face not to believe a
word he told her, for he was a terrible rake, a womanizer,
and a heartbreaker as well. Lord Geoffrey only laughed at
this condemnation of his character as he bowed over Lorna's
hand.

"Now you have been warned, we may be comfortable,

m'lady," he told her, taking her hand in his arm and leading her to a nearby sofa.

Lorna smiled up at him. He had a handsome face and light-brown wavy hair, and his tall, graceful physique was clothed in the latest of fashionable attire. His blue eyes glowed with such an air of appreciation for her face and figure in its lavender silk gown that she had to laugh at him in return.

"I shall be on my guard, sir, never fear," she answered him lightly, the deep dimple in her cheek in full display. "But surely you are not as bad as the Dowager has pictured you?"

"Worse! Infinitely worse," he said firmly, taking the seat beside her. "There are some things even dear Aunt Aggie doesn't know—at least I hope she does not."

"It would be most unwise of me to inquire what those might be, would it not? I shall change the subject and ask when you arrived in London."

Lord Geoffrey leaned closer and took her hand. "Alas, I was far, far too late! If only I had come last fall . . . But I did not know that you were here then, or that my cousin Peter would marry you in such haste. Of course, now I have met you, I understand completely." He sighed and looked so sorrowful that Lorna had to smile again. "M'lady, life is indeed unfair. You are so beautiful and desirable, yet you are lost to me before I even had a chance with you. It is more than mortal man can bear."

Lorna removed the hand he had captured and was pressing so intimately, and she said, "Lord Geoffrey, I begin to think the Dowager did not do you justice. Surely her assessment of your character was much too tepid and restrained."

He nodded and smiled as he said, "Yes, you are quite right to be on your guard. But at least you will grant me the honor of being your sole escort since Peter is not here . . . And why is that, m'lady, and so soon after your wedding, too? I am sure I could never leave your, er, your side."

Lorna looked a little startled, and he was quick to add with an innocent grin, "My escort is not only perfectly proper, it is a clear obligation. After all, I am a relative of yours now and, as such, it is my duty to protect you from the unwanted attentions and eager suitors and dissolute rakes, and knowing the type as well as I do, I am sure to be successful in the performance of my duty."

Lorna had to laugh in spite of herself, and in the days that followed, she came to find Lord Geoffrey's attentions very welcome. His admiration for her soothed her wounded spirits. He was quick to compliment her on a bonnet or a gown, and openly admire her face and figure with the eye of a connoisseur, and it reassured her to know that at least there was one handsome man who was not cold and indifferent to her. She could not imagine Lord Geoffrey agreeing to a marriage of convenience for a moment. No, he would laugh away her protests, woo her with all his considerable ardor and polished address, and refuse to take no for an answer.

She had expected the Duchess to object to Lord Geoffrey's almost constant attendance, but outside of warning Lorna several times that he was a complete scamp and not to be trusted, she seemed to accept the situation with an ease Lorna might have questioned, if she had not been so busy.

The Season was in full swing now, and there was seldom an evening that Lorna was not invited out. Similarly, her days were filled with all the activities with which the Haut Ton amused itself from April to July. She rode and walked in the park, she played cards and listened to the concerts and opera, she attended the theater and the various receptions, tea parties, breakfasts and soirees, and although she sometimes refused Lord Geoffrey's escort from a vague sense of propriety, he was more often at her side than not. London began to whisper, but she did not hear.

Then Miss Jane came to her early one morning to tell her that a friend had mentioned that the Kingsley-Jones were leaving for the country in a week, due to a death in the family, and that their house in Charles Street would be vacant. She insisted on taking Lorna around that very day to inspect it, and although Lorna was sorry to have to gain possession of a house under such sad circumstances, she was delighted with it, for its furnishings were just what she liked and it was just around the corner from Berkeley Square and in easy walking distance of Hyde Park, Bond Street, Burlington Arcade, and St. James's Place.

She decided to have Peter's man of business take over the lease without delay. If she waited to hear from Peter, she would miss this wonderful opportunity, and all the other suitable houses had been taken. Of course, she knew she must write to him at once, for she would need to hire servants in London if he did not care to give up Tramble and Mrs. Lowety to her and had no plans to come to Town himself. She was distracted that afternoon as she strolled in the park with Lord Geoffrey and his friends, Captain and Mrs. Belfors, for she was composing a formal letter to her long absent husband in her mind, and in doing so was remembering him more vividly than she had for days. The letter was written finally to her satisfaction and posted to Kent, and a few days later, the Kingsley-Jones left Town.

Soon after their departure for the country, she took Lord Geoffrey for a tour of inspection of her new house. She was as excited as a child with a new plaything as she showed him the drawing rooms, the library, the pretty dining room that overlooked a small garden, and the elegance of the front hall.

Lord Geoffrey leaned against the newel post at the bottom of the stairs. "Am I allowed to see the bedrooms, Lorna?" he teased, looking up in a suggestive way, and she shook her finger at him.

"No, you are not. Geoffrey, why do you try so hard to be such a rake? It would be so much more restful if I was not constantly parrying some outrageous remark or rebuffing some eager advance of yours."

"But as a rake, my company is not supposed to be restful and you must consider my reputation, my poppet," he murmured, coming over to stand close before her and taking her face between his hands. "If it is seen that I am not pursuing you with all the ardor I can muster, if you cease to smile at me or let it be known that my presence does not please you, why, then, my reputation will be ruined. And since I live on my reputation, I beg you to have a care."

"Now you are being ridiculous, sir," Lorna said, removing his hands and backing away. Lord Geoffrey was much too close for comfort. "I beg you to have a care for my reputation too, for I am a married woman, after all."

"How good of you to remember it, madam," a deep voice

grated from behind her, and she whirled, one hand going to her heart.

"Peter!" she cried, but Lord Geoffrey noted with a raised eyebrow that she did not run to where he stood in the doorway glaring at them. "Why are you here? I did not expect you at all . . . I mean, how wonderful to see you in Town at last! I trust all is well at Norwell House?"

Lord Peter nodded curtly as he came forward to shake his cousin's hand. "I see you are back from foreign climes, Geoffrey. I am forced to say I am glad to see you, for at least we should begin on a pleasant note, don't you agree?"

"Who would ever suspect it from that black look of yours, cuz? And what a cold reception from one who should be all smiles and gratitude that my attendance on his wife has spared her from being annoyed by many a lustful beau and Corinthian on the strut," Lord Geoffrey replied, smiling easily.

"It rather puts one in mind of a fox set to protect the hen run, does it not?" Lord Peter remarked to no one in particular.

As Geoffrey laughed, Lorna steeled herself and went and took Peter's arm. She felt the hard muscles tense, and she made her hand rest lightly there as she said, "You must go away at once, Geoffrey, for I want to show Peter the house. But I do thank you for your escort, and I shall look forward to our waltz at this evening's ball."

"With that to look forward to, I shall strive to be content. But stay! Perhaps Peter is only here for a few days? I am sure some duty must call in Kent, does it not, dear boy, and now that you see how very well taken care of Lorna is, you need have no qualms about leaving her again."

A small smile appeared on Peter's well-cut mouth. "How sorry I am to disappoint you, Geoff! No, I am here for the Season. Until this evening, I shall look forward to renewing our acquaintance then."

He bowed, and Geoffrey took his leave. As soon as the door closed behind him, Peter turned and stared down into his wife's face as if he were searching for something, and his own face grew harsh when he did not seem to find it there.

"Of course I might have expected you to fall prey to someone unsuitable, but once again I beg you to remember that you are Countess Norwell, wife," he said in a stiff voice. "Lord Geoffrey is a premier rake without a single moral to his credit. He will not be content for long with only the privilege of flirting with you, but will soon demand much, much more."

He paused, as if considering adding to this statement, and Lorna interrupted, "How can you say so, Peter? He is a relative, and in spite of his wild ways and profligate past, I find him very amusing."

"I see," Lord Peter said in slow tones, and then he shrugged. His face was still cold and no smile lit those icy-gray eyes. "Of course I know from experience that you will do exactly as you wish without regard for my feelings. I quite understand. But my indifference to your activities, madam, will be swift to disappear if I find your name being bandied about in every drawing room in Town. I do not care to have my wife the subject of cheap gossip. I trust I made myself plain?"

Lorna nodded, her rising anger telling her it would be unwise for her to reply.

"I suppose it would be useless to suggest that now that I am here to take you about, there is no need for Lord Geoffrey's services anymore?" he asked next, his cold eyes still intent on hers.

"But it is not at all the thing to be continually in your husband's company, as you know. Do you wish me to be called a dowd?" Lorna asked, wishing that he would change the subject and that her heart were not behaving in such a disturbing way, and wishing above all that he had not bothered to come up to Town, for here he was again, telling her what to do and whom to beware, and acting as if she did not have a brain in her head. He had not changed his ways at all.

"I cannot conceive of that ever happening. You are too much in the mode. Is that a new gown? It is most becoming," Lord Peter said, changing the subject at last. "Now, shall we go over the house? The staff will be arriving later today, but I suggest you remain with Aunt Agatha until they have all in order."

"Will you stay in Berkeley Square too, Peter?" Lorna asked, her voice hesitant and soft.

"I think not. That might be too difficult a role to maintain before the Duchess and those two sharp-eyed bosom bows of hers. We shall say that the business of getting us settled keeps me here, but I will come to dine and to escort you to the ball. I have made all the arrangements, for I stopped there on my arrival and it was from Miss Eliza that I learned that you and my cousin were here, and all alone."

At that, Lorna went and opened the drawing-room door, beckoning him to come and inspect it. She had no intention of discussing Lord Geoffrey with her husband again.

That evening she dressed very carefully and was the last to appear in the drawing room, several minutes after Peter arrived, for she had spent a long time pondering wearing the ivory silk that he had found so distasteful in Kent. At last she decided on another gown of cloth of silver, and with it she wore the sapphires and diamonds that had been her wedding gift.

The Earl seemed in a pleasanter mood this evening, and he spoke with animation of Norwell House and the improvements that had been set in train there before he asked for the latest *on-dits* and *crim.-cons.* of the fledgling Season. The Duchess was delighted to oblige, and Lorna did not have to exert herself by joining the gay conversation and was able to remain in the background and watch her husband, who was seated across the table from her as he chatted with his great-aunt.

All the *beau monde* were treated to the sight of a very attentive husband that evening, one who remained firmly by his wife's side for the most part, and one whose warm smiles and general air of happiness with his lot managed to quell some of the worst rumors that their separation was only a matter of time. Lorna tried to play her part as well, but when Lord Geoffrey took her aside for a moment and questioned her, he noted her eyes were troubled.

"Here now, love, what's amiss? Can it be that you and Peter are not such a happy couple after all?" he asked, watching her closely.

Lorna tried a light laugh. "How can you say so when you see how delighted we are to be together again?"

"I do not believe it," he contradicted her. "Shall I tell you why, sweeting? If you were happy with your husband, then

surely this afternoon you would have run into his arms as
soon as you saw him, and I would have been forgotten in a
blissful embrace of reunion. Instead, you stammered and
ruffled up like a peahen, and I can tell you, dearest Lorna,
nothing could have revived my spirits more."

"I beg you not to refine in our meeting too much, m'lord,
for it was only that I was startled. Besides, I cannot discuss
Peter with you, not now or ever. It would not be the act of a
. . . a gentleman."

"And you must ever be the 'gentleman,' eh, my dear? I
myself do not labor under that handicap as you shall see,"
he added, a small smile playing over his lips. Then there was
no time for any more, for the Earl was beside them, demanding his dance.

Lorna moved into the house in Charles Street the next
day, glad that Tramble and Mrs. Lowety had made all
ready for her, and soon the household settled down into a
placid routine.

Lord Peter grew accustomed to finding his cousin Geoffrey on the doorstep every day, and while it certainly did not
please him, he knew he must endure it. Rake though he was,
he was a relative and at the moment had done nothing to
enable the Earl to banish him. Lord Geoffrey was aware of
his frustration and was being very careful.

Melanie too was a frequent caller, for as in the days when
she was growing up, she still sought out her cousin for advice
and took great pains to tell her everything Sir Digby had
said, how he had looked as he said it, and how she had
replied. She also brought all of Lord Landford's impassioned letters that he sent from his exile in the country.

Lorna tried to appear interested, but many times her
mind wandered, especially when she saw Peter leave the
house for his club or on an expedition of pleasure with his
friends.

Although they were forced into each other's company
more and more, there was no change in their attitude to
each other. Peter treated her with meticulous but distant
politeness, and she responded in kind. Only in public did
they smile at each other and touch, and Lorna found she
was looking forward to soirees and balls especially, for then
she could go into his arms for a few minutes at least.

She pondered this longing of hers over and over again. Surely she had not forgiven him for his cruelty and the way he insisted on dominating her, she told herself. And yet there were nights when she wished she were brave enough to go across the upstairs hall and knock on his door and beg him to take her in his arms again. She daydreamed of what the results of such boldness might be, but then fate intervened in the comely shape of a lovely little blond.

Mrs. Starwell had on many previous occasions through the years enjoyed a flirtation with Lord Peter, although she had never been his mistress. Her husband was a serious, scholarly man who was not often in Town, but under the protection of his name, the lady enjoyed herself very much without him. As a married woman, her reputation was safe, and she was free to take a lover or flirt as much as she cared to. She was a dainty little thing, not much taller than Melanie, but with a much more voluptuous figure, and she was quick to see with her sharp little brown eyes that all was not well with the Earl and his new bride, and she had no compunction about exploiting such a situation to her own advantage. Accordingly, she made herself available at every party for a dance or a quiet *tête-à-tête* in a secluded alcove, her conversation full of hints and *double entendres* that were impossible to misunderstand. Her obvious admiration for him soothed Peter's wounded spirits as much as Lord Geoffrey's constant attendance smoothed Lorna's ruffled feathers, and he was not at all loathe to encourage the lady. At least Harriet appears to want me for her latest flirt, so why should I not oblige her? he asked himself as he watched his cousin's handsome head bent close over his wife's and saw her gay smile and the way she put out her hand in pretended reproof, only to have Geoffrey capture it and hold it close to his heart for a moment before he kissed it. In a rage, he pulled Mrs. Starwell even closer into his arms as they danced, and she gave a little scream of alarm.

"Dear Peter, be careful. You would be amazed at how easily I bruise," she reprimanded him, and then pressed even closer, completely destroying the credibility of her scolding words. "I think you have grown used to holding a somewhat more robust lady in your arms," she added, pouting in Lorna's direction.

Peter followed her gaze and saw Lorna rising from a curtsy as she made ready to join the dance with his cousin. He thought she looked magnificent, so stately and graceful, her white shoulders rising above her gown of violet *peau-de-soie*, and her beautiful breasts swelling in such an alluring way. He admired her slim waist and round hips and wished he had her close to him, her auburn curls tickling his chin as they danced, but he tore his eyes away and smiled down at the lady who was there instead. He promised to always take the greatest care of such fragile loveliness, and Mrs. Starwell smiled in triumph.

From a distance, Miss Eliza and Miss Jane kept up a running commentary for the benefit of the Dowager Duchess, who waved her fan in disgust.

"Now why did that promiscuous Harriet Starwell have to interfere," she mourned. "And just when things were going so well and Geoffrey's pursuit of Lorna was annoying Peter so! Dear me! I thought we were on the verge of making him lose his temper once and for all and sweep her off to bed in a fit of jealousy."

"Shall we draw Mrs. Starwell off the scent, your Grace?" Miss Eliza asked.

"Not yet. Perhaps we can turn her flirting to our advantage, after all," the Dowager pronounced.

"Dear Lorna does not look at all pleased to see her snuggling so close to Lord Peter," Miss Jane informed them. "She has frowned twice now and seems as jealous of Mrs. Starwell as Lord Peter is of Lord Geoffrey."

"Patience, my dears, patience! I shall call on Lorna tomorrow morning and see if there is any way we can exploit this situation. Otherwise, I am afraid I will have to turn Geoffrey's eyes to Mrs. Starwell, and I hope it will not be too difficult and expensive to do so. He appears quite mad for Lorna, and it was never my plan to have the man falling in love with her, as you know."

But the following morning when she called at Charles Street, to beg Lorna to join her on a shopping expedition, she found the girl subdued. No amount of gentle teasing could discover the reason, for she would not confide in the Duchess in any way. This lady's lips were set tightly as she took her leave to step alone into her carriage. She had no idea that Lorna, returning from the ladies' withdrawing room the previous evening, had seen Peter and Mrs. Starwell standing close together in a small salon, and she had not been able to turn her head away and so did not miss seeing the lady reach up to draw her husband's dark face down to her own with such eagerness and abandon.

It was all she could do not to fly in at them and tear the lady away, creating a noisy scene. How dare she kiss Peter? she asked herself in seething rage. She has a perfectly good husband of her own, why doesn't she kiss him? And then she told herself she was being childish. The Mrs. Starwells of this world were never content with only one man at their beck and call. She wondered if Peter had enjoyed kissing her, and for the remainder of the evening she was so quiet and thoughtful that Lord Geoffrey was alarmed. His much-vaunted charm did not appear to be winning fair lady, and he resolved to expend even greater efforts in the future.

Lorna studied Peter carefully on the drive home after the ball, but she could read nothing from his cold, expressionless face. He inquired if she had enjoyed herself, and then proceeded to stare out the window of the carriage as if she were not even there. Lorna went up to bed completely miserable, for as Peter had handed her down, he had announced he was going to Brooks for a while, for the evening was still young.

As she climbed the stairs to her room, she was sure he was going to Mrs. Starwell instead, and by the time she had been undressed and put to bed, she had a vivid picture in her mind of him taking the lady in his arms and making love to her, and she proceeded to lie awake in her misery until she heard him come home at last.

It would have been better for the peace of everyone at Number 14 Charles Street, if the Earl had not gone to Brooks that particular night, for as he was striding along the hall to one of the card rooms, he heard the plummy, elderly voice of Sir Reginald Pierce. Ordinarily, he would not have bothered to listen, for Sir Reginald was a bore and only his advanced age prevented many a gentleman from calling him out for his comments on the morals and manners of what he considered a decadent Regency. Sir Reginald did not hesitate to name names.

It had not been so in his day, he was wont to say, sighing as he remembered the golden age of his youth when George III had come to the throne, and courtly behavior and gentle chivalry were the order of the day, and promiscuity was frowned on and condemned.

Now, Peter heard his wife's name on the old gentleman's lips and paused in astonishment to listen.

"It's a disgrace, that's what it is," Sir Reginald was informing his unwilling audience. "Young woman barely married two months, and already carryin' on with that disgustin' rake, Geoffrey Allendon."

"I say, m'lord," Roger Banners tried to interrupt, "easy over the ground there, I beg you. Lord Geoffrey is a cousin of the Earl's. Can't forbid a relative the run of the house." Mr. Banners sounded almost regretful, as if there were several of his he would like to banish, and the sooner the better.

The old gentleman snorted, "Relative, my foot! Saw him myself this evenin' at the Hanleys' ball, kissin' her hand and leerin' at her, and I never knew that scoundrel to waste many leers on *innocent* damsels. It's a shame and a scandal, and if Lord Peter had any sense at all, he'd take his wife in hand. If he can't bring himself to forbid the man the house, at least he can forbid him his wife's bedchamber! What's the matter with the man to allow it? Are all you young jackanapes without an ounce of starch these days?"

"None of our business," Lord Banners broke in, and was loudly seconded by two other gentlemen.

Peter felt his temper rising and for a moment wanted nothing more than to burst into the room and demand an apology from the old peer. Knowing how futile this would be, and how embarrassing for them all to know he had heard the conversation, he turned on his heel and left the club, to spend the next hour and a half striding through the dark streets in a cold rage.

When he had dressed and had his breakfast the next morning, he sent a message to Lorna ordering her to curtail her morning activities, for there was something he wished to speak to her about in the library at once.

Lorna, who had been writing some letters in the morning room after the Dowager Duchess left the house, was mysti-

fied, but she nodded to Tramble and said she would come
immediately.

As the butler left the room, she rose and smoothed down
her simple white morning robe, wishing that she had put on
a more formal gown and that she had had her maid do
something more to her hair than just thread a blue ribbon
through it. I look like a milkmaid, she thought as she pushed
back a dangling curl, and then she remembered Mrs. Starwell's elaborate coiffures and toilettes, and she put up her
chin, her eyes glinting dangerously as she went to join her
husband.

When she entered the library, she found Peter studying
some papers on his desk, his eyebrows drawn together in a
deep frown and his expression difficult to read. Was he
angry and annoyed at her or the papers he was perusing? she
wondered.

Motioning her to a seat near the fire, he gathered the
papers together, put them away, and rose to face her. They
stared at each other, Lorna beginning to feel a little
alarmed, while Peter's heart grew bleak. How lovely she is
he thought, so fresh and innocent in that white gown, and
then the frown returned to his harsh face.

"There was something you wished to see me about,
m'lord?" Lorna asked, mystified by the silence, which was so
unlike him, and wishing he would sit down so she did not
have to look so far up that tall frame of muscles and masculinity.

"There is something, indeed. You will remember,
madam, that when I first arrived in Town, I warned you of
the inadvisability of becoming my cousin Geoffrey's latest
flirt. You may also recall that I warned you as well that I
would take steps if I found you the object of gossip, with our
name being dragged into all the titillating conversations of
the Ton. Do you remember, Lorna?"

"Of course I do, Peter," she replied, cautioning herself
not to volunteer any information until she found out what
this was all about.

"You will be distressed to learn, I am sure, that that time
has arrived. I found your name being discussed in Brooks
last evening, in a most derogatory way."

Lorna's eyes flashed. "I wonder you did not speak to the gentleman who dared malign me, sir," she said quickly, all good resolutions gone.

"I found it impossible to call him to account since all he spoke was the truth. If anyone told lies about you, I would be quick to come to your defense, but in this case I was forced to eavesdrop and then take my leave unseen. You can imagine how that made me feel."

Lorna rose to her feet. "And now you insult me, too! How dare you assume that what they were saying was the truth, when you should know me better? And what were they saying? I demand to know!"

"Know you? I do not know you at all," he was quick to answer. "As for your conversation, they were speculating on whether you had admitted Geoffrey to your bed yet and why I was so cowardly as to allow it."

Lorna gasped, one hand going to her mouth to still its trembling. Peter had made her angry before, but it was nothing compared to what she felt at this moment. Before she could speak and revile him, he continued, "I tell you this, madam, that unless you give me your solemn word that you will have no more to do with Geoffrey, I will be forced to take those steps I promised you to remedy the situation."

"Of course calling Geoff out will certainly still the wagging tongues, won't it?" Lorna asked sarcastically.

Peter's belief that she had allowed Geoffrey to become her lover angered her so she made no move to deny it, a fact her husband noted with a bleak feeling of despair.

"I have no intention of calling my cousin out. That will not be necessary. No, wife, I shall simply take you back to Kent and keep you there. There will be no more trips to London, nor will you be allowed to have any visitors, and as for driving or riding out, the stables and carriages will be forbidden to you. How long this situation will continue will be up to you, but until you give me your word to comport yourself as Countess Norwell should, you will remain secluded."

"You would not dare to keep me a prisoner," Lorna exclaimed, her voice rising. "I will *walk* to London if I have to, to escape you."

"And I will bring you back and beat you every time you try it," his answer came as quickly back. "Must I remind you again that I am your husband?"

"No. How could I ever forget it, miserable as I am?" she panted. "But you yourself seem to have forgotten you are a married man."

His eyebrows rose. "Whatever can you mean?" he asked, sounding genuinely puzzled.

"How dare you accuse me of indiscretion with Geoffrey when you are dallying with that insipid little blonde? I notice you do not think you must be reminded of how Earl Norwell should behave, or punished for your liaison with Mrs. Starwell."

His sudden grin infuriated her, and it was all she could do not to fly at him and try to hurt him.

"Why, Lorna, one would almost think you jealous of the lady, how can that be?" he asked in an amused voice, and she took a hasty step toward him before he held up a detaining hand and added, "And if you do not want me yourself, you can hardly object when other women do."

"I might say the same to you, sir. Since you have no desire to make love to me, why should I not have sought consolation elsewhere?"

Peter's grin vanished at once, and he grasped her arms so tightly that a moan escaped her lips. "Be very careful, Lorna," he threatened in a deep growl. "You are in a more precarious position right this minute than you have ever been in all your life."

He stared down at her defiant blue eyes, and then with an effort, he put her away from him and said stiffly, "The cases are not at all similar, for no one in the Ton has been talking about me. I know how to be discreet; I do not flaunt the lady as you flaunt your paramour."

So he was admitting the affair. Lorna lowered her eyes so he would not see the tears there.

"And now, wife, I will have your promise to give up this adventure, or I will order your trunks packed and the carriage called."

Lorna would have liked to scream her defiance, but she controlled herself, for she knew he meant every word. "You must allow me some time to think about it, m'lord, and permit me to speak to Geoffrey before I decide."

And how surprised he will be, she thought drearily, to hear me giving him up when I have never had him, but she could not proclaim her innocence, not when Peter had just admitted his affair.

"You are not to see him again. I shall speak to him myself, thus sparing you what could only be a distressing, emotional scene," he replied coldly. "Go and remain in your room. I will expect you here in the library at two with your answer."

He bowed and went to hold the door, and Lorna put up her chin and marched past him to the stairs. She noticed he remained standing there until she reached her room, and as she quietly closed the door, she felt as much a prisoner as any felon in a Newgate cell.

13

For an hour, Lorna paced up and down her room, first in anger and then, as all the ramifications of the situation occurred to her, in hopelessness. She had no appetite for the tray of luncheon that Peter had sent up, for she had happened to glance from her window, to see him striding away down Charles Street in the direction of Berkeley Square. She wondered if he were going to call on his cousin, and what Geoffrey would say to defend himself in a situation where he was being falsely accused for what must be the first time in his entire rakish life.

She wished she did not feel so miserable and sad. She did not even want to revile Peter for the unfairness with which he had treated her. He had showed her that while he could do what he liked, she could not, and that he had no intention of allowing her to make her own decisions or live her own life. Why, the only part of their bargain that he had kept since their marriage was his promise not to touch her, and now she was honest enough to admit that she wished he had broken that particular promise as well.

Perhaps the best thing to do would be to continue to defy him, she thought. At least to do so would remove him from Mrs. Starwell's orbit, for he would have to take her down to Kent and watch her until either she gave in to his demands or he himself relented. And then she realized he would not even have to do that. He was perfectly capable of hiring someone to guard her while he returned to the capital and that horrible woman's eager arms.

At one-thirty a knock came on her door and Tramble entered at her call to present a visiting card. Lorna was surprised, for she had thought all the servants knew she was confined here. As she read it, her brows rose. Lord Geoffrey here? Whatever was she to do? And then, suddenly, she knew she must see him.

"Tell m'lord I will be with him presently, Tramble, and send my maid to me at once."

The butler bowed and departed, and Lorna began to undress. It was several minutes later before she had been hooked into a smart afternoon dress of deep-blue muslin, had had her hair dressed, and had washed all trace of tears away.

She found Geoffrey pacing the small drawing room, ignoring the wine that Tramble had poured for him to help pass the time. His generally elegant bow to her was sketchy, and he began to speak at once.

"Now perhaps, my good girl, you will be so kind as to explain why you told Peter those thundering lies about us this morning?" he asked, his good-looking face pale and grim. "It had better be something quite out of the common way, my dear, or it will be difficult for me to forgive you for placing me in such an awkward situation. Whew!" he added, wiping his brow with his handkerchief. "I have never spent such an uncomfortable half-hour in my life."

"Did you tell him it was all a hoax?" Lorna asked.

"My first reaction was to deny it at once, of course, but then it occurred to me that you must have had a good reason for saying what you did, and I had better keep silent until I found it out, so I let him rant and rave at me while I remained as mum as the most guilty adulterer. But why on earth did you do it, Lorna? For what reason?"

"He heard some gossip about us and believed it to be true before he even asked me, and I was so angry. I let him continue to think so. Besides, he admitted that he and Mrs. Starwell are lovers."

"Even if they are, what has that to say to anything?" Geoffrey asked, completely bewildered. "You do not repay a husband's infidelity by claiming a perfectly innocent man as your own lover, you know. And although I have often had to bear being reviled by the husband in the case, my poppet, at least at those times I had the memory of the lady to console me. I find I resent being rebuked and abused and threatened with nothing to show for it. In fact, I was lucky that he did not call me out, and Peter's a devilish fine shot."

Lorna looked at him with troubled eyes. "I am sorry, Geoffrey. I never meant to get you in a scrape with Peter, but there is no way I can explain why I did what I did. I must ask you to forgive me without asking any questions."

Just then the door to the drawing room was thrown open and Lord Peter came in. Searching his face, Lorna thought he looked most unwell, the severe planes and angles of his strong face taut and his lips set in a tight, uncompromising line. His arrogant jaw thrust out when he saw them together, and he said, "So, madam, in spite of my clearly expressed orders, you continue to defy me. Did you send for him as soon as I left the house? You must love him very much."

Lorna put out her hand to him, shaking her head a little in denial, and he sent her a look of complete contempt.

"Since you desire it so much, you may have a half-hour with Geoffrey. At the end of that time the carriage will be at the door and we will start out for Kent. As for you, cousin, I shall see to it that after today you are never alone with the Countess again."

He made to leave them and then he turned and said in a colorless voice, "Surely I was cursed in my cradle if it was predestined that I wed you, madam. You have made my life such a misery I cannot believe that I am not being punished for some great sin, although what it could be I have no idea.

But miserable or not, we are married now, and I will never consent to a divorce, even though I will regret the day I first met you to the end of my life."

Lord Geoffrey watched Peter stride away and slam the drawing-room door behind him, and then he sighed when he saw the tears streaming down Lorna's face.

"Come now, my dear, do not despair. You are very bad for me, you know. I find I have a burning desire to help you when by all rights I should be helping myself, now your husband has cleared the way. It is most unlike me."

Lorna buried her face in her handkerchief and sobbed.

"You love him so much, then?" Geoffrey asked, dropping his tone of raillery, and if Lorna had been listening more closely, she would have heard the quiet note of regret there, and amazement, and, yes, even envy.

She nodded and blew her nose, and Geoffrey smiled. "Then wipe your eyes and attend to me, my child. There is nothing I cannot tell you about how to regain Peter's regard, and out of the goodness of my heart and a sense of family feeling I did not realize I even possessed, I am prepared to do so. No doubt you would prefer to pour out your troubles to another woman—in fact, I am sure the Dowager Duchess would be delighted to oblige if she were here—but you must make do with me. First, sit down and then tell me everything: how you met Peter, how he courted you, and what your life has been like since the wedding, and leave nothing out, no matter how insignificant. It will be easier if you think of me as some elderly mentor who, at the age of eighty and gout-ridden and world-weary, has seen everything time without number, and whom it is impossible to shock."

Lorna had to smile a little at ever being able to consider the handsome and elegant Lord Geoffrey that way, but she took a deep breath and began her story, starting with their meeting in Dorset and proceeding right up to this same morning, and although sometimes her voice faltered a bit and grew soft and embarrassed, she did not omit a single thing.

At times Lord Geoffrey chuckled, at other times he frowned, and more than once one mobile eyebrow rose alarmingly, but he did not look at her or comment, and somehow that made it easier for her to be honest with him.

When her voice died away at last, he whistled and then he

said, "What a tangle! Who would ever have thought that Peter could restrain himself? Well, let that go."

He pondered for a moment, caressing his chin with one shapely hand while a now-silent Lorna watched him, and then he asked, "Why do you think he beat you that day?"

"Why, because I disobeyed him when I took his horse," Lorna replied, a little surprised at that particular question.

"You are an idiot. He beat you because he had been so worried for your safety. Do you understand what I mean? He wanted to protect you, to show you how he adored you. But he had few opportunities to do so. You fought and defied him at every turn."

Lorna shook her head. "That cannot be true, Geoff, for he has said he does not love me or want me time without number. He married me only because he had to, and since that time I have seldom seen him without a black frown or in a furious temper, and after our wedding there was only that one kiss in the lane, and he regretted it at once."

Geoffrey sighed. "How else could he act after you scorned his suit, told him in the cottage that you would never marry him, and only agreed at last because it was to be a marriage of convenience? Peter is far from a handsome beau and he knows it, so he would accept your distaste for him without question. Then, too, consider the jewels and sable cloak, Lorna. He could have given you some token to satisfy convention, but, no, he decked you out in unbelievable splendor. And just now, even though he thought us mad for each other, he refused to consider a divorce. If that is not the act of a man in love, I'll turn respectable."

Lorna stared at him, her eyes glowing with hope as he continued, "Have you any conception, sweeting, what it meant to Peter to be married to you, especially after that one searing kiss in London that showed him what he was never to have? Think! He has to sleep right next door and he has not been able to go to you and make love to you. And to have to admire you in that revealing ivory gown you told me about, so near and yet so far, no wonder he ripped up at you. Have you any idea of the agony he has endured? No wonder the man looks black and has an uncertain temper."

"Yes," Lorna whispered, "in a small way, I do understand."

"Well, then, what are you going to do about it, my dear?"

For a long moment there was silence in the room, and then Lorna nodded and, looking straight at him, said, "What I should have done a long time ago, Geoff, even though I am afraid it is far too late."

Lord Geoffrey chuckled. "And I am sure it is not. Peter was thirty-five when he married you, and if he had not wanted you more than any other woman he had ever seen in all those years, nothing the Dowager could have done to force him to it would have prevailed. He married you because he loved you, because he had to, for he could not live without you even if it had to be a bleak marriage of convenience, and even if it meant a running battle for the next fifty years. My dear Lorna, I am not suggesting you will ever stop fighting with Peter. Knowing the two of you, that would be most unlikely, and I am sure you will find him in great need of a set-down every now and then for his arrogance, but I am sure you will also find that the battle begun and ended in love will be easier for both of you."

He leaned back and sipped his wine, and then he said, "Run along now and find him before he stops being so noble and restrained and decides to come back and run me through. I can find my own way out."

"I have been so stupid, Geoff, but I promise I will be so no longer. Thank you, dear friend, for all your help."

As she jumped to her feet and held out her hand in farewell, anxious now to be gone, Lord Geoffrey rose and said, "May I say how much I envy Peter, my dear, and how very much I regret that what you told him this morning is not true?"

Lorna reached up and patted his cheek. "Flirting still, Geoff?"

He put his arms lightly around her waist, and she saw his serious face and wondered at it. "I am not flirting now, Lorna, for I love you, too," he said, and then, when he saw his words had upset her, he added in a lighter tone, "The delicious irony of my help paving the way to your marital bliss, my poppet, will no doubt restore my spirits eventually."

Lorna put her hands on his shoulders and reached up to kiss his cheek, wondering even now if he were in earnest, and just as his arms tightened around her in a farewell embrace, the drawing-room doors were flung open.

As if she were frozen in some impossible tableau, Lorna watched Peter stride across the room and tear her out of Geoffrey's arms. His face was harsh with a rage so thunderous that she cried out in terror, sure he meant to murder the pair of them. He thrust her none too gently aside, and she stumbled onto the sofa in a heap, her hands outflung as he turned to his cousin again and in one mighty, lightning-fast blow knocked him to the floor.

"How dare you touch her, you scoundrel? She's mine, she will always be mine," he shouted, his deep grating voice barely under control as he stood over Lord Geoffrey, hands on hips and legs spread wide as if daring him to get up and fight back.

Geoffrey lay back massaging a jaw that was rapidly changing color, wincing as he did so, and making no move to regain his feet.

"I see that from family consideration I have been too lenient altogether. You will choose your weapon and name your seconds, Geoffrey, for I find this insult impossible to forgive."

At that Lorna struggled to her feet and ran to her husband, putting an urgent hand on his arm and crying, "No, no, I cannot bear it. You must not."

Lord Peter's gray eyes were bleak as he stared at her. "I know he means a great deal to you, madam. How unfortunate for you that he will not be in the world much longer."

Lorna shook her head impatiently. "I don't care about Geoff," she panted, causing both men's eyebrows to rise. "I only meant that I could not bear it if you were to be hurt. Suppose he shoots you first and wounds you. Suppose . . . suppose he kills you? How could I bear to live without you?"

Lord Peter turned his back on his recumbent cousin. "What nonsense is this? Could not bear to live without me, did you say? Why, madam, are you trying to save your lover by pretending you will be a proper Countess Norwell at last? That I should live to see the day! No, madam, this subterfuge is useless, for I do not believe you."

At these words, Lorna forgot all her good intentions. She went to him and grasped his arms angrily. "No more! And do not call me madam ever again," she ordered. Before the astounded Earl could comment, she rushed on. "Peter, I must talk to you. I hardly know where to begin, but let me confess, first, that what I told you this morning was a lie. Geoffrey has never been my lover; instead, he has been a good friend to both of us."

Behind them, the gentleman under discussion was rising cautiously to his feet, still holding his aching jaw and grasping a chair back for support. "What she says is true, Peter. I could not deny it this morning when you accused me, not until I had discovered what Lorna was about."

The Earl turned from his intent perusal of his wife's face and his eyes grew harder. "And you expect me to believe this fairy story? Then why were you kissing and embracing her just now? You must think me a blind fool if you expect me to forget that."

Geoffrey managed to straighten up, and when he answered, his voice was cool and dignified. "I was kissing her good-bye and wishing her good fortune, but she will explain everything to you, I am sure. M'lady," he bowed, before he went to the door.

The pressure of Lorna's hand kept the Earl still.

Just before he left the room, Geoffrey turned. "I will not deny that I love Lorna, cousin, because I do, more than I thought it possible to love any woman, but she has made it very plain to me that there is only one man in the world for her, and that man is you. You had better treat her well or I will be asking *you* to name your seconds."

He bowed again and left the drawing room, closing the doors behind him. The Earl turned once more to his wife, his gray eyes going to where her hands still grasped his arms, and in some confusion, she dropped them and moved back a little.

"Geoffrey said you would explain everything. I am most anxious to hear what you have to say. Perhaps you could start by telling me why you allowed me to think Geoffrey was your lover?" he suggested in a quiet but determined voice.

Lorna bowed her head in a little prayer, and then she looked at him. "That was wrong of me, but I only let you think so because I was so angry you could believe that vicious gossip you heard about me, and because I saw you kissing Harriet Starwell last evening."

"Shall we say she was kissing me?" Peter asked, not a muscle moving in his rugged face. "Do go on, I find you interest me very much, madam—I beg your pardon, Lorna."

Lorna looked down at her clasped hands, and then she raised her eyes resolutely to his face again. She would not be a coward, not now. "It is true that I disliked you at our first meeting, but that was because you angered me, you were so overbearing. And my refusal of your suit, as if I were in truth Melanie, was simply because I knew you were not the husband for her, nor she the wife for you. I know that was wrong of me, Peter, but I am glad I did it."

She paused, but he did not make any comment and so she hurried on, "And then you were so furious with me when you discovered the deception, and you treated me so badly all the while you courted my cousin. I tried to be friends, but you would not let me. Why was that, Peter?"

"I wanted to repay you for your dislike of me. In other words, I wanted revenge. That was not well done of me and I apologize, but I did not want you as a friend," he said, emphasizing the last word.

Lorna wondered why he did not take her in his arms now, but the Earl stood very still, not moving a muscle, and so she was forced to continue.

"On the day of the Frost Fair, when we went to save Melly and you had to propose after we were stranded in the cottage overnight, I could not let you know that my feelings toward you had changed, for it was obvious to me that you were proposing only because you had to, as a gentleman. You do see how I had to continue to pretend that I did not care either, don't you, Peter?"

Her blue eyes begged for his understanding, and Peter had to clench his fists to keep from sweeping her into his arms.

"It seems to me that we have both been remarkably foolish," he commented, his voice not quite steady.

"I did not realize the depth of my feelings until the night of the Dowager's party, when I kissed you at parting. That was not playacting, my dear, not at all. But then you went away, leaving only that cold note, and so I had to pretend I still did not care."

Lord Peter put his hands gently on her arms and began to caress them, still making no move to draw her closer. Lorna felt her knees begin to tremble at his touch as he said, "And when we were married at last, what I should have done was to confess my feelings for you, but you had hurt me so many times I was afraid you would laugh and refuse me, and I did not think I could bear that. No, it seemed better to go on as we had agreed, but, Lorna, that was the reason we had so many arguments. You seemed so content with your lot and happy with the situation, and you were so busy setting your new home in order, there seemed to be nothing I could do to get you to want me and come to me."

Lorna smiled, and he lifted one strong hand and touched the dimple in her cheek.

"Shall we start again, husband?" she asked in a whisper.

"There is one more thing," Peter said in his deep voice, and he moved away from her for a moment to pace the drawing room.

Lorna watched him, wishing he had not left her. She could still feel the pressure of his hands on her arms, and she felt chilled now that he had removed them.

"I must ask you straight out how you feel about me, Lorna. You have not said, you know," he said as he came to stand before her once again.

"Why, my dearest, is it so difficult to understand? I love you, of course. I have loved you for a very long time."

The Earl's gray eyes glowed with a sudden urgent light, but he reached out for her slowly, as if he were afraid a sudden movement might cause her to disappear. He drew her into his arms with infinite tenderness, and she reached up to put her arms around his neck and draw that dear, dark head down to her own. When his mouth was only a few inches away, he paused to whisper, "And I love and adore you. I always have."

He saw her eyes light up with joy as she held up her lips, and he bent his head still farther so his mouth could possess hers at last.

It seemed he could not get enough of her kisses, nor could

he stop caressing her, but every so often she would whisper to him and he would reply, and in that way they told each other of their forgiveness and their love.

He chuckled a little when he recalled the way he had lashed out at Lord Geoffrey that morning, and how confused the man must have been, as innocent as he was, for once. "A salutory lesson for him, my dear," he said, his lips just brushing her cheek and the tendrils of hair at her brow. "It will do him no harm, you know, and perhaps might even make up for some occasion when he escaped censure."

Lorna smoothed back a lock of black hair that had fallen over his forehead, and he turned his head to place a kiss in her palm, and Geoffrey was forgotten.

There was suddenly so much to say, so much to explain. Peter told her how he had tried to make her fly out at him when he was supposedly courting Melanie so he could give her a set-down she would never forget, and how his intentions gradually changed until he wanted to make her care for him and know what it felt to be dismissed, and how eventually he just wanted her to love him as he loved her.

Lorna smiled and shook her head at such folly. When she asked why he had turned so cold after their embrace in the lane the night of the cottage fire, and learned he thought he had distressed her by breaking his promise, she called him an idiot, an epithet that made him grin and meekly agree to. Then Lorna confessed how many times she had wanted to come across the hall to him in London and ask him to take her in his arms. At this he kissed the hand he held and pulled her closer to him.

"If I had only known," he said, his deep voice unsteady. "Or if only you had known how often I could not sleep for wanting you."

They went over all the arguments they had had and laughed uproariously about the well-traveled Adam commode and her indecent ivory silk gown, which Peter claimed he was most anxious to see her wear again.

"I think it was when you called me madam in that cold, formal voice that I felt the lowest," she confessed next.

"I promise I shall never do so again, for I intend to address you only as my love, or dearest, or wife," he said. "I shall never do anything you dislike, ever again."

At this sweeping statement, Lorna burst out laughing again, and when he asked the reason, she told him he was making a promise he could never keep. "We are sure to come to dagger points, and probably more often than not, my darling," she said, the sweet name she called him taking the sting from her words. "We are still the same people, strong-minded, independent, and used to getting our own way. I will still be careless and impetuous, you autocratic and demanding. But perhaps it will be different now—when we quarrel, I mean."

Peter thought she sounded a little doubtful, and he told her that if it were possible to argue while deep in love, he was sure their fights would be splendid. "And think how glorious it will be when we make up," he added with a grin.

"And of course you will never, ever beat me again, will you, m'lord?" she asked. "You notice I mean to extract your promise now, when you are in such an amiable state of mind."

"I shall only beat you if you need it," Peter replied in a deep growl, trying to sound stern and ferocious.

"Heavens! I see I must be very, very good and try my best to please you, then," she said, glancing at him to see his gray eyes fervent on her face, and such naked longing written there that she felt the heat rising all over her body and she turned in his arms and raised her face for his kiss.

They were still lost in their embrace when a discreet knock came at the door. Lorna jumped up in alarm, to straighten her gown and smooth her tousled hair, but Lord Peter lounged back at his ease, a wicked grin for her embarrassment on his face.

"Come in," he called even as she waved at him to give her more time, and Tramble entered the drawing room with two cards on his salver, to bow as he informed them m'lord Allendon had taken his leave, but new guests had arrived.

"We are not receiving, Tramble," the Earl said firmly as Lorna read the cards.

"But we must, Peter," she contradicted him. "It is Melly and Sir Digby come to call, and, oh, dear, I had quite forgot today is my at-home day." She turned away from Lord Peter's frown and said, "Ask them to come in, Tramble, and advise the cook a tea tray will be needed, but for how many I have no idea."

The butler bowed himself out, and the Earl caught her around the waist from behind and pulled her close. "Do you mean to say we are going to have throngs of people marching in and out of here for the rest of the afternoon while you preside over a tea party? No, I absolutely forbid it. After waiting for you so long, I find I can wait no longer."

He turned her around and pulled her back into his arms. "Tell 'em you are indisposed, or I am, tell 'em the house has been quarantined because of infectious fever—that at least bears a semblance of the truth, love, for I find I do have a fever, a throbbing, burning fever."

Lorna put her hand over his mouth. "Behave yourself, Peter. It will not be for long, but you must see I cannot turn my cousin and Sir Digby away."

"If you had not just shown me otherwise, my sweet, I could almost suspect you still have a yen for that 'parfit gentil knight,' " he remarked, reluctantly releasing her from his arms. "Very well, I shall summon my last ounce of self-control, but do not let Miss Melly draw you aside for some long, girlish chat, I beg you. A crisp twenty minutes or I will be showing them the door."

Lorna went to the looking glass to fasten back some curls that had come undone, and then she went and took his hand, and the Earl quite meekly allowed her to lead him to a chair.

Melanie was all smiles and blushes and Sir Digby proud as they came in, so they did not notice that their hostess was not her impeccable self and their host wore a somewhat fatuous grin, for they had become formally engaged only that morning. After kisses all around and congratulations, Melanie said, "We came to see you first, dear Lorna, for, of course, you must be my attendant now."

"I hope you are planning a long engagement, Melly," Peter remarked, still watching Lorna's face. "We may not be here. In fact, I can say with some truth that you should not look for us in Town before August or maybe even September."

Melanie looked surprised and would have questioned her

cousin, but just then Tramble entered, followed closely by a very distraught Lord Landford.

"Say it is not true, Melanie, not after I came back up to Town last week especially to see you," he explained, pushing past the butler and rushing to her side. "You could not have meant what you wrote in that cold, formal note. How could you do this to me, you cruel, heartless creature?"

"Here now, I say," Sir Digby interrupted while Melanie looked a little frightened. "I cannot allow you to speak to my fiancée that way, m'lord."

Lord Landford smote his breast. "So it is true, after all, and you have chosen wealth and position over love, have you?" he sneered.

Lord Peter rose to his full six feet, three inches, and the young peer whirled as he said, "Now this is too much. Let me advise you, sir, that you have only twenty minutes, so instead of all these lengthy and impassioned periods, I pray you speak your speech trippingly and all that, and then take your leave. This is not the Drury Lane."

"Aye, you can make mock, m'lord," Lord Landford replied. "*You* have never been scorned and reviled."

"Haven't I just?" Lord Peter asked no one in particular, and Lorna sent him a burning glance of reproof.

Nothing more was said for a while, for Tramble came back to the drawing room followed by two footmen bearing the tea trays, and Lord Peter drew his butler aside for a few moments of quiet conversation. Lorna noted that Tramble nodded his head several times and left the room in haste as Peter rejoined the group and said, "Take a seat, Percy, and let Lady Truesdale pour you a cup of tea."

"Tea!" Lord Landford exclaimed in a voice of loathing. "I don't want any tea!"

"Of course not," Peter agreed, taking the cup from his wife and avoiding her eye. "But we are not, alas, serving hemlock this afternoon. Cream? Lemon? Make up your mind, you have only fifteen minutes left."

"Whatever is the matter with Lord Peter this afternoon? Has he been drinking?" Melanie asked, leaning close to whisper in her betrothed's ear and causing Lord Landford to cover his eyes with his free hand and groan.

"Come now, my dear Lord Landford," Lorna smiled at

him, trying to lighten the atmosphere of this ridiculous tea party. "As a gentleman, you must wish Melly and Sir Digby happy, you know. You are not trying to imply that my cousin led you on, I am sure, for I know her better than that."

Lord Landford looked sulky as he said that although she had not, in so many words, he knew she returned his regard.

Melanie was looking less frightened all the time, for she enjoyed any drama that centered around her, and now she spoke up. "M'lord, you know very well that when you proposed to me I told you then I felt we would not suit, and it was you, after all, who refused to take my no for an answer."

Lord Landford looked at her with reproach, and Lorna was quick to change the subject. The Earl could be seen to inspect the clock over the mantel at regular intervals throughout the rest of the visit, asking Lord Landford if the time were correct and Sir Digby whom he and Melanie were calling on next.

Sir Digby was feeling vaguely uncomfortable, and as soon as it was possible to do so without causing offense, he suggested to his fiancée that they should take their leave.

"Capital idea, old boy," the Earl applauded, coming quickly to take their half-empty cups and help Melanie to her feet. "Don't suppose you'd care to take Percy along with you, would you? No, no, I quite understand. Awkward business, that."

Lord Landford found himself rising too just as Tramble's voice announced, "The Dowager Duchess of Wynne, Miss Eliza, Miss Jane, m'lord, m'lady."

Lorna sent her husband a warning look as the Dowager surged in, followed by her companions and looking for all the world like a large schooner towing two little gigs in her wake. The party reassembled around the tea tray and everyone sat down again.

"Sir Digby, Miss Melanie, and Lord Landford were just leaving," Lord Peter remarked after the first spate of greetings died down.

"Excellent!" The Dowager nodded, brushing back some wisps of gray hair, peering at her great-nephew, and settling down on the sofa as if she herself meant to make a long stay.

"There is something concerning your marriage that I wish to speak to you and Lorna about, Peter, but I will wait until we can be private. I have been as forbearing as possible, but the time has come when, as matriarch of the family, I must and will speak. I am sure anyone will tell you I have never shirked my duty, and my duty here is plain and must be done, no matter how uncomfortable or embarrassing that might be."

She looked quite fierce, and Melanie rose with alacrity.

"That's the ticket, Melly," Lord Peter encouraged her as he came to shake her hand. "Sir Digby, take Miss Melanie away at once and do not linger for a moment or all might be lost. If she were to hear one of my great-aunt's blunt, earthy discourses on the married state, you might never get her to the altar at all. I assure you, no time to lose."

He turned to the Dowager's companions and bowed. "Miss Eliza and Miss Jane, perhaps being single ladies you had better trot along as well. So upsetting for you! Besides, the tea is very weak today and the cream puffs are going off. I am sure you would not care for them."

"But we just this moment arrived," Miss Eliza said, looking bewildered.

"All the more reason to toddle along, before you have to sample those cream puffs. I shall consign Lord Landford to your care. Having to hear a discussion of marriage can only distress the poor boy at this time, and besides, he is in dire need of your expert assistance. Come along now and do not hesitate on the order of your going and all that. We quite understand."

Everyone looked bewildered as they rose and collected their belongings and murmured to one another, except Lorna, who seemed to be trying not to laugh. Suddenly, Tramble's voice announced from the entrance to the drawing room, "The curricle is at the door, m'lord, and the baggage has been strapped on behind."

"Thank you, Tramble, excellent, excellent," Lord Peter exclaimed, rubbing his hands together. "You must excuse us, Duchess, for urgent, unfinished business calls us away. Lorna and I are for Kent, and even in my racing curricle behind the grays, I am afraid we will arrive at Norwell

House so late there will be nothing for it but to go to bed at once."

The Dowager Duchess opened her mouth and then shut it as Lorna dissolved in helpless laughter and Peter put his arm around her and drew her close. "That is, we will if you agree, love?" he whispered.

Lorna replied when she could stop laughing, "Peter, how could you? You are disgraceful."

The Dowager chuckled as she gathered up her stole and reticule and shooed the others before her from the drawing room. As she disappeared, Peter caught his wife in his arms again and his mouth came down on hers with such passion and urgency that neither one of them noticed the Dowager peering back at them around the door until she remarked, "I am delighted to see that you do not need my lecture after all."

A moment later, Peter and Lorna heard her authoritative voice in the hall saying, "Now come along, Lord Landford, and be so good as to give me your escort. Wasn't your mother a Blenningham before her marriage? Yes? In that case, we are distantly related and there is something I have been wanting to discuss with you . . ."

About the Author

Barbara Hazard was born, raised, and educated in New England, and although she has lived in New York for the past twenty years, she still considers herself a Yankee. She has studied music for many years, in addition to her formal training in art. Recently, she has had two one-man shows and exhibited in many group shows. She added the writing of Regencies to her many talents in 1978, but her other hobbies include listening to classical music, reading, quilting, cross-country skiing, and paddle tennis. Her previous Regencies, THE DISOBEDIENT DAUGHTER and A SURFEIT OF SUITORS, are also available in Signet editions.